RESURRECTION RUNNER

Robert Wood Anderson

Tautly Sharp Publishing

Bellevue, Nebraska

Robert Wood Anderson / Tautly Sharp Publishing
c/o PO Box 1566
Bellevue, NE 68005-1566
www.rwanderson-author.com

Publisher's Note: This is a work of fiction. Names, characters, places, and incidents are a product of the author's imagination. Locales and public names are sometimes used for atmospheric purposes. Any resemblance to actual people, living or dead, or to businesses, companies, events, institutions, or locales is completely coincidental.

Book Layout © 2017 BookDesignTemplates.com

Cover design by Tanja Prokop of BookDesignTemplates.com

Editor, Michele Burford

Resurrection Runner / Robert Wood Anderson. -- 1st ed.
ISBN 978-1-7347698-0-7

J/M/J

Resurrection Runner is dedicated to my dear wife who showed me the way back to my faith; for her love, forgiveness, patience, and belief in me.

I also honor all those who have worked with me or encourage my writing and helped bring this story to print: My father and mother, daughter Michele, son Robert, sister Jean, sisters-in-law Jannette and Jennifer, the Strange family, Harry S., Mike and Mary L., Ken Z., Sean F., Dan W. and schoolmasters Below, Wilhelms, and Kedrovsky; English, Latin, and Russian, respectively.

Also, I praise the many people who read Resurrection Runner and provided their heartfelt thoughts concerning composition, grammar, voice, harmony, and rhythm.

I owe a special debt to the late Scott Meredith, whose irrepressible enthusiasm for *Resurrection Runner* invigorated me so much.

You're a cynic and do no good.
I'm an optimist and do as little.
We are both being led by the nose until dead.

CHAPTER ONE

Steven Popoford's gut told him it would be the darkest of days, but he twisted his premonition as only a great assassin could. He ignored his gut and put on a pleasant face. It would be the lightest of days.

"Good morning, Mrs. Marshall. Mighty nice to have a little sunshine."

"Oh dear, young man, I've never seen the rain go on like this. And Mr. Marshall and I've been living here for almost thirty years. Why I think it must be a message. I think God must be telling us something. You know, it could be that it's the Last Days."

"Yes. I'm sure that must be it. You don't happen to have any mail in there for me, do you?"

The old woman stepped over to the pigeonholes where she'd sorted the daily mail. She was the postmaster for the little town. All the mail came to her. She knew the names of every person who'd lived there since she took the job and since she was also the telephone operator and the nurse who waited for the circuit doctor, her husband, to return to Whimsy, she knew their faces and the stories of their lives. At least it seemed that way to her.

Take this particular young fellow for instance. A pleasant enough person, but he always changed the subject when she mentioned God. She was used to people who didn't believe, but she was sure to let him know what she was thinking by the way she raised her eyebrows.

"Yes, yes, here we are," she said to him. "There are two letters here for you. Two at once. My, that's more mail than you've been getting for a long time, Mr. Popoford. Isn't that nice? Someone wants to tell you something nice. I just know it. Just you see. There's good news in one of these."

"Thank you, Mrs. Marshall," he replied, smiling and changing the subject again. "You should try to get outside for a little while. The weather report says that there's a new front moving in. This spring day won't last for long."

"Oh, I do wish I could do that, Mr. Popoford, but I have my responsibility here. After all, I have a window open. The sun sure can come in that way if it wants to. Mighty welcome, too."

"You're right about that," Popoford said. "Well, I've got to be moving along now. Thanks again. I'll see you tomorrow."

"Someday you'll have to come over in the afternoon, Mr. Popoford. I can fix you a cup of tea, and you can tell me something about yourself before you came to Whimsy."

"That would be nice," Popoford said while backing out of the room. "Thank you again, Mrs. Marshall. See you tomorrow."

Steven Popoford backed onto the sidewalk and out of the post-office-telephone company-hospital-general store. Everyone in town just called the one-room building "Gert's," Mrs. Marshall's given name, but the sign over the door with its weather-beaten framing said, "Dr. Marshall's Emporium." Dr. Marshall was rarely in town. He had set out to travel the circuit nearly twenty years earlier, never to return. But the fact also was that he was still alive. At least that's what the rumors said. Seems he'd been seen on the western side of the mountains. Mrs. Marshall talked like she'd seen him recently. Yet she seemed to be a lonely woman, and Popoford couldn't trust her to be truthful about a departed husband.

"See you tomorrow, Mrs. Marshall," Popoford called while waving at her through the big front window. He saw her wave back, her face framed in the barred hole that was the post office.

Popoford turned and crossed the street. He headed for the corner. He had to read his mail. He would want a drink when he was done.

He entered the bar and sat on a high stool.

"Make it a double whiskey, Sam."

"Right you are, Mr. Popoford," Sam said with his best English accent. "Won't be a minute."

Popoford liked Sam. He was a big laugh most of the time, but he knew when to shut up and back away. Sam poured the whiskey, picked up the newspaper, and went to the back corner of the bar to leave Popoford alone.

Popoford opened the first letter, the one addressed to Steven Popoford. It was a note from his brother back East, dated March 14, 1986, just a few days ago. He read it without much interest. He opened the other envelope, pulled out the note inside, and put it on the bar before reading it. Then he took a long gulp of whiskey, waited a beat while his nerves gathered forces, and slowly unfolded the note.

It didn't make sense at first. It was a sales pitch about insurance for his home appliances: junk mail. Then he saw something odd. He'd seen the same thing in countless "B" movies, here it but was in real life. There was a hidden message within the sales pitch. Every so often a character was underlined with a light blue line. Steven Popoford took a pen from his pocket and copied the underlined characters on a bar napkin. The message was simple then, the true message, and Popoford felt faint when he read it:

"We found you, George Mixer. You're dead."

Popoford's gut clenched. It really was the darkest of days.

"How the hell did this happen?" he muttered.

He'd feared this letter for a long time. He'd waited his lonely nights for it to come. But now that it had arrived, he hated all the time he'd wasted worrying about it. It had come anyway, even with the worrying. Nothing could have stopped it. Nothing except his death. That seemed to be the only, final solution, the only thing that would make them happy. The terminal solution, not this half-baked disappearing act, but real death. And for a moment he considered killing himself to be done with the trouble that had come to him in the mail. Then he slugged down the last of the whiskey. He'd been found, and that was that. Now he had to act.

"Thanks, Sam. Might see you tonight."

"Right, Steven."

Popoford stuffed the letters and the napkin in his pocket and left the bar. As soon as he hit the street again and felt the sun strong on his face, the last of his suicidal thoughts were gone.

He looked up the streets to the west. Clouds were building over the mountains. The rain was coming again, and even then he felt the breeze come up in advance of the storm. The temperature would be dropping soon. He would have to be on his way before the storm arrived.

There wasn't time to waste now. No time for worrying. He had to run, and he figured that Home Office was going to be his best bet. He would have to make contact with Home Office.

Popoford walked rapidly to his little cottage. It was a flagstone afterthought of the original settlers of Whimsy, a place where they'd hoped to keep the bastard son of the mayor captive so as not to offend the eyes of God. It was the source of a strange tale of the middle forties that had been carried along as local color by the residents who cared to brag about such infamy. Popoford had rented the cottage when he first came to Whimsy three years earlier and had been thought a fool for doing so.

The place hadn't been used since the mayor's son died of botulism. The locals thought there was a curse on the place, and Popoford could come to the same conclusion if he wanted to believe the parochial superstitions. Yet the wild imaginations of addled minds couldn't explain his past, nor could they explain what his future would necessarily be.

He walked up the gravel path and opened his front door. He went inside. He turned on the light, and he reacted to what he saw with the direct and decisive action that his training compelled. There was no hesitation, no thought as he reached beneath his shirt and pulled out his pistol. There was only fluid motion, a ballet of death, as he rolled onto the floor, twisting, aiming, squeezing off three rounds, placing them all in an inch-wide pattern, drilling the life out of the great, ugly man seated at his breakfast table. Popoford completed the roll and came up standing on his feet, then crouched, his pistol outstretched, waiting for a response. There was silence in the room and the building wind roared down from the mountain top.

"Damned clod," Popoford muttered. "They could have sent someone a little better."

The man hadn't fallen from his chair in death so sudden. He sat there as if he were waiting for a beer and some polite conversation. But Popoford couldn't afford such pleasures. They had come for him already.

He went to the dead man and collected the identification. The wallet had several hundred dollars in it and several credit cards. According to the cards and the driver's license, the ugly man's name was George Mixer, his own nom de guerre. The identification would do him no good. The money might so he shoved it into his jeans. Then he took the man's pistol out of his hand and stuck it into his belt.

The man was a giant, fat, repulsive hog, and Popoford had a very hard time dragging him from the breakfast table.

"This is the last time I invite you to break bread with me," he muttered. "Damn. Won't you ever learn when to quit?"

He struggled with the body but finally managed to get it out of the back door. It would take a little longer for anyone to find it there, though no one from town ever came out that way. However, if he couldn't get back to bury it, the stink of its rot would drift into Whimsy with the pine-laced breezes and someone would eventually come. He would be gone by then. Gone from the country if he had anything to say about it. Gone as far away as possible and buried as deep as any dead man might be. Home Office would see to that. Only this time he wanted it to stick, to never be discovered. Never. Popoford packed a bag, leaving everything behind that had no use to a man on the run. He burned the letters and the napkin with the deciphered code and left a light shining in the window for the curious. Then he jumped in his car and drove out of Whimsy and out of its valley. By nightfall, he was over the mountain top, driving down the west slope of the mountain range and into the thick of the storm.

CHAPTER TWO

The heavy raindrops began to peel the layers of forgetfulness from Popoford's mind. He drove along the mountain roads searching his thoughts for his mistake. He strained to see the curving road barely revealed by his headlights through the slashing rain. It made ribbons of the cold night air and obscured the road. His thoughts were equally blurred. He could barely find his past clearly remembered. There were moments when it was all plain, long seconds when the precise thought he needed was there in his grasp. Then it was gone, struck out, the thought itself forgotten; the knowledge that the thought was once held the only, melancholy memory.

Damned brainwash was too successful, he thought. Can't keep much of it anymore. Not the details. They're gone.

H.O., the head of Home Office, had personally mandated the Memory-wipe protocol. And that was the way it was. Popoford had consented to the routine himself. He would have never made it with the memories intact. That much was certain. He still recalled the words H.O. had used. "Might melt your resolve." What he meant was "you might decide on retribution or insanity if you could remember." At any rate, he hadn't needed to know details. It had been best to forget. Now, however, he needed those details. Now he had to know what he had been, what he had done. Exactly. There was no other way to survive. Without those details, he could never understand why he was being hunted. It certainly wasn't on general principles. Who would waste their time? No. This was something special. Something that required him to return to Home Office, to come out of forced retirement, to remember the details of his past.

The rain made a layered wall, constantly renewed, repeatedly pierced by his car, yet remaining virginal throughout the night. It was a rain that seemed never to slacken nor even to give hope that it might, yet Popoford plowed his way into it and forced its drops apart, gaining one slow mile after another until he had finally descended to the other side of the mountain.

The rain didn't stop then. There were no prophetic moments. There was no insight on the other side. There were the streetlights that Popoford could see in the distance. They didn't illuminate his thoughts. They didn't illuminate the road. The rain stayed thick. His mind remained forgetful. When he finally arrived at the small town of Elgin Base, he was tired. He needed to take a shower. He drove to the Sanctity Hotel and registered.

"Mr. Popoford? Yes. And what brings you to town on this particular morning?"

"What...? What do you mean? What's so special about today?"

"I'm sorry, Mr. Popoford. I meant nothing special. No need to be irritated. I'm only referring to the weather. You know they say that low pressure can cause irritability?"

"Yes, of course. Forgive me. I thought, perhaps we'd met. Perhaps there was something that you thought odd about my being here."

"Why, no sir. It's only a polite question. None of my business, really. I'm sorry. May I take your bags, please? I'll show you to your room."

"There's only this one. I can manage it. If you'll just give me the room key, I'll find my way."

"Certainly, sir. Here you are."

"Thank you," Popoford said. "By the way, is there a phone in the room?"

"Of course."

"And is it a direct line out?"

"No. It comes through the switchboard. Why?"

"Are you alone here?"

"Why, yes. Why do you ask?"

"I have a call to make. Strictly private."

"But you have no reason to think it should be handled otherwise. All calls from this hotel are private. It's the strictest policy."

"But of course. I'm just making sure."

Popoford took the room key from the desk and smiled briefly at the man. "Room service available?" he asked.

"Yes. Breakfast will be served beginning at seven. That's in ten minutes. There's a menu in your room."

"Good."

"I hope your stay with us is memorable, Mr. Popoford."

Popoford stopped short and looked the man in the eye. He saw only apologetic ignorance there. The man didn't seem dangerous. It had only been a poor choice of words. Popoford turned away and went to his room.

It was on the second floor. The door looked like any of the other five doors on the white-carpeted hall. They were all extra-wide, freshly painted olive green, brass handled, and peepholed. Popoford's room number was 240. The room faced the street. That was good. He wanted to see the street. He might see trouble before it announced itself.

He inspected the door before he opened it. He wasn't going to make the same mistake again. He was wanted, a marked man, and his would-be killers were several steps ahead of him. The second installment might have already arrived. He drew his pistol and eyed the door for the scratches of an amateur. He was almost sorry that he didn't find any. Circumstances pointed at pros, everything did, but he had a strong need for the impossible to rear its beautiful head and save him from the consequences of his forgotten past. It didn't happen like that.

Popoford slipped the key into the tumbler and slowly turned it. The latch clicked, the door cracked, the faint odor of Lysol drifted into the hall, and Popoford kicked the door open to silence.

It was his Colt .45 officer's pistol that led the way into the room. Its deep bluing reflected the simple, warm room. Popoford strained his eyes, gathering every corner of the room into his peripheral vision, and he squatted slightly, following the pistol, letting it speak for him.

But it had no one to talk to.

The bedroom was without a welcoming party. The bathroom was empty. Only the white-tiled floor and quarter-paneled walls met Popoford. He relaxed.

He came out of the bathroom and took off his jacket. He threw it on the bed and did the same with himself. He laid there for a minute. His thoughts were of weary hours spent running. He seemed to have a past like that. Perhaps he would have a future like that as well with both past and future promising to be similar. He had run and would run for reasons he couldn't now remember. Not unless he could get to Home Office headquarters without trouble. And only if they clued him in about the crimes he had perpetrated in the name of his country.

Popoford rolled over and picked up the phone. The line remained dead for an extra beat then it rang with an extra-long interval and it was an aggravation to Popoford.

"Damnit, answer!" he said under his breath.

"I'm sorry, Mr. Popoford, I didn't catch that. Will you repeat?"

"I would like some breakfast," he said, recovering rapidly.

"Oh, but of course. And what may we prepare for you today?" the clerk said in his most solicitous voice.

"Well, I'm not sure. I had a feeling that you might come up here and take my order. That way you can bring me a morning paper."

"Well, that's not our usual way, but for you, Mr. Popoford, we'll do the unusual."

"Why?" Popoford snapped.

"But sir . . . I'm sorry . . . Have I said something wrong? I don't mean to offend you. It's only that you're as special as any of our guests to us. We would do unusual things for any of our guests."

"Yes . . . yes of course. I'm the one who must apologize. I just thought that we might have met before. But we haven't, have we."

"Yes, Mr. Popoford. That is correct. We've never met."

"And you don't know what I do for a living?"

"No, Mr. Popoford."

"I see. My apologies. I'm quite tired. Please forgive me."

"Mr. Popoford. There's no reason for an apology. I'll have the paper at your door in fifteen seconds."

"Hold up!" Popoford's said. "Before you come up here, will you please get me an outside line?"

"Certainly. Right away, Mr. Popoford. Just hold the phone."

The dial tone, the tone of the first electronic age, as Popoford called it, came. He dialed the operator.

"Yes," the voice said sharply and left him wondering whom he had reached.

"Hello?" he asked.

"Operator. Yes."

"Operator?"

"Yes, this is the operator. May I have your room number, please?"

"Two forty."

"Thank you. And your call?"

Popoford spoke the numbers one by one, crisply, distinctly, lifting each one from the part of his memory left intact. It was a lifeline, that number, his only thread to Home Office, to safety in the arms of government service.

"One moment please."

Clicks, whirs, crosstalk, and fuzzy interference mingled on the line. A ringing sound was added to the auditory confusion. Then the phone was picked up at the other end, and all extraneous noise was gone.

"Speaking," the voice of an old woman said. "Why do you bother me today? Call when George is home."

"But George is home," Popoford said.

"Hold," she said, and Steven was cut off.

He waited. There was a knock on his door. He got up, grabbed his jacket, and put the pistol in his pocket.

"Come in," he called and put the phone to his ear again.

"Yes, Sir." A man's voice spoke on the phone. "Time and date of service. Speak plainly."

Popoford knew that Home Office was running his voice for a match. He responded without hesitation, fearing disconnection.

"Time of service: thirteen years active. Operational but inactive: six years. Service date: 1967."

"Accepted. Please hold."

The clerk was in the room. "Your paper, Mr. Popoford. What may I bring you for breakfast?"

"Just bring me some scrambled eggs and a rasher of crisp bacon. Grapefruit and rye toast. Tell whoever brings it to leave it outside the door. Understand?"

"Certainly, Mr. Popoford. I will see to the meal myself."

Popoford hoped the clerk's special thoughtfulness wouldn't make for a poor meal. He slipped five bucks into the clerk's shirt pocket and waved him from the room. He thought how awkward it was to hold a gun on someone while fiddling around in that person's pocket.

Popoford often had little insights into the amusing details of his life. They seemed to occur most often when he was under stress. He had never gotten used to them, but he had trained himself to collect them for a lighter time. Always, he remembered the axiom of the perpetually hopeful: Someday, he would look back on his life and laugh. But he had reflected on his past before and couldn't remember most of it nor could he find a reason to laugh. He didn't want to have more memories of absurd twists of the mind. But it seemed he had little choice. His identity had been discovered. Until he stopped those who wished to kill him, there would be peculiarities in his thinking. Some part of his brain would never catch on to the danger and fear with which the other parts were dealing. Some parts would always be hopeful, while all of him prayed that he wouldn't die without a chance to find something worthy of laughter.

The clerk left the room, and a voice on the phone spoke.

"The line is clear. Talk. Questions will be answered for thirty seconds. Go."

Popoford was caught off guard in his thoughts. He had forgotten the routine.

"I ... Ah, I want the name of the man I killed in my house. Who is after me?"

"One question at a time." The voice was curt but not disrespectful. "Describe the man."

Popoford told the voice about the fat man. There was silence on the line.

"What's the matter? Who is he?" Popoford sensed trouble. "Hurry. Tell me who he was."

"No time for other questions. The man was ours. Advise you to stay where you are until we contact you."

The voice hung up.

"Dammit!" Popoford whispered. Then he yelled. "Dammit! Who the hell is after me? What do you mean he was ours? Why didn't you bloody well tell me you were sending someone? What kind of game do you think this is? It's my damned life, you bastards!"

Popoford slammed the phone down as he ranted, and then he jumped from the bed and began to strip off his clothes. "You bastards never learn. You never do learn a damned thing. Damn!" He slammed his hand into the wall. He had been in similar messes before, and they'd always been at the hands of Home Office. Popoford wished that he didn't have to use Home Office. Not now. Not after he'd made such a stupid mistake. It wasn't killing the fat man that was the mistake. The mistake was that he'd thought that he could go to Home Office at all. He'd been discovered by his enemies. Discovered in Whimsy. Hadn't that been enough error on the part of Home Office? Popoford knew he should have stayed away from them. "'Advise you to stay put,' my ass. I'm on my own from now on." He marched into the bathroom and turned on the shower, hot. He stepped in and tried to relax.

CHAPTER THREE

Popoford shut off the water. He was still angry, but he was beginning to think.

He was on his own. But so what? He was always on his own. Even when he was on active duty with Home Office. What the hell did he expect from them now? They'd sent their own man to him. They'd tried to warn him. The identification that the fat man had on him meant that Home Office wanted him to return to the field. That they had not told him that their man was on the way didn't matter. The effect was the same. He still would have to solve the problem by himself. But the good news was he wouldn't have to put up with Home Office's picky regulations. It was better this way. Better to be on his own. Free to move. Free to hunt. If only Home Office had told him who was after him. It would have helped.

Popoford dried himself as best as possible with the skimpy towel. It was an ill-fitting world for the tall man. The phone rang before he could feel sorry for himself.

"Yes?" he answered. There was a loud knock on the door. "Just leave it outside," he called.

"Popoford? Is that you?" the voice said on the phone.

"Identify yourself," Popoford said. The knock came again. "I'm on the phone. Leave it outside."

"This is Hendricks, Steven. Don't you recognize my voice?"

"Perhaps I do. What's your I.D. code?"

"Damn, Steven. That's going a little far, don't you think?"

"What's your I.D.?" The knock came a third time, but still, it was loud enough to startle Popoford. "Hold the line a minute. Don't hang up."

Popoford went to the door and threw it open. He found himself staring into the twin barrels of a twelve-gauge shotgun sawed-off on both ends till it was the size of a pistol. It was held in the hand of a rather plain girl. He quickly judged her to be about twenty-five, and her wild eyes told him that she was unpredictable. He froze.

"Do not speak. I have little time. I know you, George Mixer. You're a dead man if you see H.O. Tell Hendricks good-bye."

With that, she pushed the breakfast cart toward Popoford and backed away to the stairwell. She kept her weapon on him all the time. He didn't move. He let her go. She would be easy to find. She would probably return on her own.

Popoford went back to the telephone and picked up the receiver from the bed. He looked at it for a second.

"I'm back. What is your I.D.?"

"4477-9."

"Hendricks? What's happening?"

"There's a contract out on your life. We sent our man to contact you. I guess he crossed you, huh? You said you had to kill him?"

"I killed a fat man in my house."

"Careful with what you say. You're getting rusty out there."

"Not rusty, just impatient. What's happening? Tell me," Popoford said. He looked up and saw that he had left the room door open. The breakfast cart was inside his room. A maid was looking at him like he was some kind of a nut. Popoford realized that he was standing there with only a towel partially wrapped around himself. "Sorry," he mouthed to the maid, then he went over to the door and closed it.

"Anyone there with you, Steven?" Hendricks asked.

"No. Not now. Go on. You were about to explain yourself."

"There isn't much I can explain on the phone. We knew you were compromised. We intercepted a radio signal directed at your little village. You were called by your operation name. Whoever received that signal was instructed to go forward with your death. Contact was made, and you were to be eliminated. Why? We don't know."

"Why was Home Office monitoring signals near me?"

"It's only routine. You know that."

Popoford heard the change in Hendricks' voice. It was no longer the voice of a friend. It was his boss.

"No, I don't know. It seems a practice that is far from ordinary."

"Well, it's ordinary. Believe me."

"What do you know about little girls running around with shotguns?"

"Someone tried to take you out?"

"I'm not sure. I doubt it. But I was warned. I was told to dump you for my own good."

"Interesting. I wonder what it means."

"So do I. You tell me, Hendricks."

"What are you talking about? How the hell should I know? What is this crap? You're the one who called us. You need protection. And you know we can give it to you, don't you? You also know what you have to do for it."

"No damn way. I'm not coming back into service. Forget it. There's no way."

"There was a body found on the back porch of your little cottage. It was found by us. Come back, or others will find it, too."

"You bastard!" Popoford hissed. "You set me up. Who was the fat man? Some bad boy? He wasn't very good."

"No, he wasn't, but then he wasn't expecting you to be irritable or edgy."

"He wasn't expecting me to be warned."

"Steven, come on. We need you here. If we wanted you dead ourselves, we would just kill you. It's that simple."

Popoford knew that was a lie. He was too damned good for the lot of them, and where he was a little rusty, he had developed a hard skepticism that made him act before he thought. Home Office couldn't trust him. That was why they'd sent a loser. They had a feeling that he might kill the fat man. If he hadn't, things would be a lot easier now.

"There's nothing simple about it at all," he answered. "Why do you need me?"

"I can't talk on the phone. Use your head, Popoford. It's got to do with the people who are after you. You must come back."

"Horseshit. I'll do some checking on my own. I'll get back to you."

"The fat man will be found tomorrow morning. You'll be forced to come back."

Popoford hung up the phone. He wasn't sure what to do first, so he got dressed and ate his cold breakfast while he decided. He could go back to Home Office without a fight, but that was just stupid. He couldn't give in that easily. By the time he had finished the last crumb of bacon, he had decided to return to Whimsy. On the way, he might run into the girl with the shotgun. The least that he could do would be to try to thwart Home Office. That in itself would be a pleasure, and it would give him a little breathing time. He wiped his mouth and left the room.

As he walked into the lobby from the elevator, the clerk looked up from his work.

"Mr. Popoford! Ah, did you find the breakfast to your liking?"

"It was satisfactory. You should do something about the waitress, however."

"Were you not treated with respect?"

"It was only a smart remark on my part. Please think nothing of it," he said.

Popoford walked through the lobby as he talked. He wanted as little contact with the clerk as possible. It was something in the clerk's manner that bothered him, something that told him that the clerk was untrustworthy, something that connected the clerk and the girl with the shotgun.

"I'm going out. Please have the dishes removed from my room. I'll be back later."

"Very well, Mr. Popoford. I hope you find the day to your liking."

"Yes, thank you. I expect I will."

Popoford left the lobby the way that he left many places: backward, pulling away from an unwanted conversation. He would return to Whimsy that night. Between now and then he would have to get some sleep, but first, he wanted to walk along the streets at a leisurely pace and troll for plain women with sawed-off shotguns.

He walked east into the sunup into the foothills that gave the town precious frailty nestled against sublime granite walls. The spinning earth had worked the sun high in the morning sky. Popoford judged it to be about 8:30. He would stay for an hour. If nothing had happened by then, he would return to the hotel and some sleep.

The street ended at the top of the hill where there was a small café. There were a few tables in front, but he went in and ordered a cup of coffee. Then he took a seat outside that gave him a view down the hill, where he could look into the mountain town spreading downslope into the upper valley. It was a splendid scene as the rustic, cobbled street gave way to the regularity of the gold-town architecture including the hotel, then flowed out to the vast panoramic folds of ancient hills rolling to the river below. He took a great lung full of air. He held its sweet taste a moment and then let it out. He sipped his coffee and watched the people walking up the street. The waiter came to his table.

"May I warm your coffee, sir?"

"Yes, please," he said. "Seen the last of the snow?"

"Perhaps. Winters haven't been very predictable."

"No. I suppose not," Popoford replied as he counted the men walking up the street. He counted the women. It was a habit born of training. He looked especially hard at the women. Three of them had large handbags. One was a modern beauty, one was quite old, one was a child. None of them was his girl. The men were all the same. Each had a briefcase and was wearing a three-piece suit. These were the businessmen of the town, the regulars as it were. They were the ones who had built the town. They were its civic leaders. There were five of these men walking up the hill. There were three walking down. Popoford counted them all and judged the odds of one of them being an assassin. He decided that the odds were too good, so he gulped the warmed-up coffee down and scalded his tongue in the process. He set the cup on the table and stood to go. As he reached into his pocket for his billfold, the table blasted away from him.

Popoford dove to the ground, away from the flying splinters. He pulled his gun, but he held his fire. There had only been one shot. He judged that it had come from about thirty feet away, but the shot pattern was very tight for a distance that great. The aim was incredible. It had been a dramatic warning, for she hadn't wanted to kill him. With the ability to shoot that shotgun pistol so accurately, she could have killed him anytime.

He looked down the street. He saw the women looking back over their shoulders as they scurried to the safety of doorways. Only three men remained, and they were doing the same, finding hiding places. The other five had disappeared. Maybe they'd just gone about their business.

Popoford had been away from this kind of activity for too long a time for him not to have developed a certain softness, a kind of warm-heartedness that didn't fit the work of a professional. He shook his head. No. None of them could be trusted. There was nothing to warrant trust.

He crawled under the tables at the entrance to the cafe. There were no other shotgun blasts, and he scrambled inside without further trouble.

He drew his pistol as he entered the café. The waiter was standing against a wall, his arms in the air. The cook had come out of the backroom and was hiding behind the cash register. Popoford looked around and saw only the two of them.

"Put your hands down," he said harshly. "Is there a way out of here through the back?"

"Through there," the waiter pointed to the kitchen door. He was scared.

Popoford waved the pistol at the waiter. The man backed off, sliding along the wall. The cook fell to his knees to pray. Popoford was startled by his sudden move. Somewhere in the professional's mind, he saw the cook going for a gun. He fired without thought. The slug drove through the counter just under the cash register, finally stopping in the plaster wall. It was only the bowed head of the cook that saved his life. Popoford's aim was flawless, but he had failed to consider the cook's devout fear.

Popoford jumped through the swinging doors.

The kitchen was a filthy mess, a contrast to the quaint cleanliness of the dining room. Popoford slipped on a piece of browning lettuce. He nearly lost his balance but caught himself with a hand on the corner of a greasy cutting board. He stood still for a moment to recover some control. Then he saw her standing on the other side of a torn screen door. The flies were crawling on the mesh trying to get out of the kitchen. Her sawed-off riot gun, was aimed at Popoford's head. He froze.

"You must begin to pay more attention, Mixer. The men coming up the hill were trying to kill you."

"And I suppose your damned shotgun blast was some kind of warning," Popoford said, trying his best to be calm. He hoped she didn't see his fear.

"More of a joke than a warning. You have a better reputation than you deserve, Mixer. You need our protection. I find that amusing. Now try to be more observant. I have better things to do with myself."

"Then go do them," he said.

"Later. There's something more to be said. I told you to say good-bye to Hendricks. You didn't. That was a mistake. Your line was traced and they are back on your trail again. Better look out for your ass, or we'll give up on you."

"You'll hurt my feelings if you go," Popoford said, warming sarcastically to the absurd conversation. But the girl spat on the slick concrete that ran with the liquid draining from the kitchen, and she ducked away.

"Wait, dammit!"

She didn't answer, but Popoford could hear her feet softly grazing the hillside that rose sharply to one side of the walk. He ran outside and looked up the hill.

"What the hell...?"

There she was, the shotgun hanging from a sling. She scaled the sheer granite wall without ropes, her friction-soled shoes, and her bare fingers gripping the little cracks. She made a brisk ascent, and before Popoford could recover, she'd rolled over the top edge of the rock. He listened for a second but couldn't hear voices. Perhaps she was working alone or her team had already walked up the path that swung around the back of the cafe and then ran alongside the adjoining building, emptying onto the street in front of the cafe.

Popoford cautiously peeked at the street as it descended toward the hotel. There was no one in sight. The sun was slightly higher in the sky, and the shadows of midday were growing deeper. The doorways could conceal anything. Someone could be waiting there or in the windowed rooms and roofs that looked over the street.

Popoford was trapped. He looked once again at the granite wall and considered it as a way out. Impossible for him without the right equipment. He turned back to the street, but he heard the distinct sound of a horse's whinny from the ridge above. Then he could hear it galloping away. The girl. He stepped onto the street.

CHAPTER FOUR

Popoford walked casually down the hill. His face was calm, but it was only a mask. He was tense within. His every sense stretched to its limits. His sight expanding to see the total field of view from the distant river valley to the peripheral shadows that draped the shops lining the street. His skin felt the nearly painful touch of the slightest breeze. His ears heard the faint quiver of warming air rising past him. He was returned to the precision instrument that he had once been.

He was no superhuman, but he had a disciplined ability to transform his body into the tool that it could be. He had trained himself to force his body to life, to exceed the human mind's normal concentration, and to spring his senses to their full survival potential.

There was a time when he had kept this intense pressure on his system, always. He had been forced to be that way. The job required it. Those who allowed themselves a moment of relaxation were dead. The strain of constant high-tensioned performance had taken its toll on Popoford, and there had come a time when he had to quit, to find another identity, to disappear. He had survived, but he had to slow down. Home Office had fulfilled their contract, his mind had been cleared, and he had been set up in Whimsy, there to relax and reap the rewards of exceptional service to his country; there to outlast his colleagues. There to die slowly, alone, left to himself as he had been left most of his life. There to finally be able to let down his guard without fear.

That had all changed. That was certain. The thing that Popoford had to figure out was *why* it had changed. He had to know who the girl was and why she had spared him twice. He had to know who was trying to kill him. Was it someone connected with the information that Home Office had purged from his head? Was it the girl? Was it Home Office? He even questioned if *anyone* was trying to kill him.

There was the possibility that someone was playing a cruel trick, though he didn't understand what the hell good it would do. He had gotten the warning in the mail, so someone knew his old code name, and that someone was the girl. But she wasn't the only one. Home Office knew too. Was the girl really from Home Office? It could be, but she wasn't trained by them. She's from the outside if she's hired by Home Office. She could be telling the truth. Home Office might be after him. He'd seen it before. Old operators are always dangerous. He might be considered especially dangerous. After all, they saw fit to make him forget his last job. Perhaps they were afraid that he might remember. Or maybe they were afraid someone might make him remember. The girl could be that someone.

These thoughts raced through his head in a split second. He was at full potential then, his senses gathering points of interest, his thoughts working through the puzzle. But the immediate problems were far more urgent: he had to get down the hill alive, and he had to get the hell back to Whimsy and try to diffuse the murder rap that Home Office was about to lay on him.

He continued walking down the hill; a quiet hill, a hill that might have known he was coming and had ducked within itself to hide. There were no people on the street. Not even one curious head peered around a corner wondering about the shotgun blast up the road. No customers of the shops walked there; no tradesmen showed their faces. The street was deserted. It was an odd feeling. To walk in the morning heat down a normally busy street and find himself alone, filled him with foreboding. But the foreboding was a false apprehension. No one bothered him, there was no one there. No killers jumped from the blackened doorways, no mad assassins squeezed off magazines of high power rounds, no devilish young thugs darted across his path to stick him with poisoned darts. No romantic play unfolded for his senses to gather, for his mind to react to, for his body to crush. There was just no one on the street.

Had the Home Office boys been scared off? Would they be waiting for him somewhere else? Perhaps at the hotel? Or was this part of the game; a masquerade, a falsehood, just a deception, the girl's deception? Home office might not be the one to fear. It might be that he truly had to fear the girl and whoever was behind her. Home Office had disgusting ways of forcing its old operatives into re-entering the service, but perhaps they only wanted him to return, not to die. Maybe he'd better find out.

Popoford walked into the hotel lobby having come down the hill without incident. His nerves were still exposed. They would be that way for a while.

"Hello, Mr. Popoford." It was the clerk again.

"I'm going to be checking out about four," Popoford said. Will you please call my room at three-thirty? And I don't want to be disturbed until then."

"Yes, sir. There will be no disturbances. You can be sure of that."

"Good," Popoford said and went up to his room.

He held his gun in his hand while he slept and when the phone rang at three-thirty, he was thankful that his trigger finger was up against the trigger guard. He jerked at the sudden interruption to his dreams but didn't pull the trigger. He set the gun down and answered the phone.

"Yes, I'm awake."

"Once again, you're wrong." It was the girl. "Wise up. Get out of town. Home Office has your number. You're a dead man if you just lie there and let them pick you off. Wake up and get out." She hung up.

Popoford looked at the receiver and put it back in the cradle. The phone immediately rang again. "Wake up call, sir. Three-thirty."

"You're three minutes late. Get my bill ready."

Popoford hung up first. The damned girl certainly has balls. She must have pretty good resources, too. Then he got out of the bed and threw his clothes in his bag and went downstairs to the front desk. He wasn't truly rested, but somewhere within him, he was thankful for the several hours of sleep that he'd managed to have. It was because of this thankfulness that he was half civil to the clerk.

"I appreciate being able to sleep for a while. Thank you for screening any call I might have received."

"Well certainly, Mr. Popoford, but there were no calls."

"No calls? That's odd. Are you certain of that?" Popoford had a devilish smile on his mouth. "Are you quite certain?"

"Yes. Without doubt."

"Not even just before you called my room yourself?"

"No, sir. Certainly not."

"Could someone have called my room from another room here in this hotel?"

"No, Mr. Popoford. Like I told you before, all calls come through my switchboard."

"Ah, yes. You did say that. How forgetful of me." Popoford had his fingers on his gun, just in case he needed it. "Do you have my bill ready?"

"Yes sir, right here."

Popoford paid for the room with his bank card. He almost gave the clerk the card that had "George Mixer" stamped into it, but he saw his error and used his own instead. He didn't want to ever become Mixer again if he could help it. H.O. wanted him to, but he needn't give them a helping hand. He thought about throwing the card and the rest of the Mixer identification away, but he didn't. He had a lousy feeling that he was going to be needing it before this mess was all over.

He went to his car and paused a moment before he opened his door to gaze at the lowlands stretching hazily down to the river. The building glare of the descending sun only caused his sense of loneliness to heighten. The local atmosphere seemed to isolate him, to set him off by himself to serve natural law. He had the awkward feeling that he had been handpicked, that somehow the argument between H.O. and the girl concerned only him. He had a fleeting moment of thinking that what he would do could be of some importance. As usual amid his grand thoughts, Popoford cut himself off.

"What kind of high falutin' garbage are you hauling today, my fine Mr. Popoford?" He shook his head violently. "Leave it be, man. There's nothing of importance in your line of work. It's so much dreaming."

He got in the car and drove away. He ascended the gentle slope of the foothills and passed through the rubbled piles of talus sifted along the roadside. By the time he'd reached the first curving roads of the young mountain, the sun had fallen too low to filter through the coastal pines. The air-cooled rapidly. Popoford closed his window and turned on the heater.

He drove through the twilight at a fast speed. He took each curve like he imagined a Grand Prix driver might. Somewhere in the forgetting part of his brain, the skill of how a driver should best approach a particular curve had faded, but still, he drove with an imagined skill that allowed abandon. For his efforts, he only just managed to gain the mountaintop without losing everything else.

Over the top, he slowed down. He didn't like driving down mountains. There was too much skill involved in doing it right. Too much braking and shifting. So he drove carefully and watched the mirrors for other cars, and thereby reached the outskirts of Whimsy just before dawn, later than he might have been, but better off for it.

He parked the car on the outskirt road that circled back around Whimsy and walked the rest of the way through the autumn fields of swollen wheat. The larks were already perching on fence posts and singing to the day. In the distance, a dove nestled hidden from sight calling a wistful, hollow dirge that died a vacant death in the beginnings of a glorious morning. The deep blues of humid atmosphere rose with a thick effort from the damp earth.

Popoford came to the cliff that walled his backyard. He walked along the upper plateau rim until he had come to the farthest edge. From there he could look directly down on top of his house and see everything. He lay flat on his belly and watched. Something had happened: the fat man's body wasn't where he had left it.

Suddenly his ears perked to the sound of a cracking twig. He tensed his body but tried to keep as still as possible. He didn't want the intruder to know he had been warned. He waited, breathing naturally, peering over the cliff edge, but turning his senses behind him, straining to hear another mistake. He wanted too much. The next second a body fell upon him without the slightest further warning. A sharp blade was pressed to his throat. He twitched slightly and the blade cut a thin line beneath his Adam's Apple. He was frozen then with prudence, and the long black hair that fell over his cheeks didn't move him. Nor did the scent of a sweating woman pressed close to him make him twitch again. He was stone. Professional stone.

"Home Office wants more than your services. They want your life," the woman said. "We want you, too, and we will have you."

"Pull back on your knife. I can't talk," Popoford hissed through his clenched teeth. The blade was withdrawn from his throat and pressed instead against his ribs.

"You'd better have something important to say. You've wasted enough of my time . . . Say you'll join us or say nothing and die right here."

"But I don't even know . . ."

Popoford's words were cut short by the blade pushing deeper into his side and breaking the skin.

"With us or not?"

"With you," Popoford said, thinking that he had never heard such a stupid demand. What the hell did this woman expect from a man who would die if he didn't comply?

"Good. I had a feeling that you could be persuaded with a little force. You scorned my daughter's warnings, but then I knew you would. I also know that you're a practical man. Put your gun on the ground."

"But I'm with you. I'll need it." The knife stuck again.

"The pistol. As far away as you can reach. Now!"

Popoford rolled slightly to his left and pulled the pistol from his belt. He felt her blade's constant pressure between his ribs. A sharp thrust and his heart would be filled with steel. He took that chance. No damned woman, no matter how good she was, could make him join her without an explanation. He suddenly rolled back to his right while withdrawing his pistol. He rolled completely over and leveled the weapon at his assailant. It was a mistake. Her blade had already sliced across his wrist, and his grip on the revolver had released. The woman had meanwhile shoved her gun, a sawed-off Remington 870 sixteen gauge shotgun, against his temple. Popoford froze again. He had been defeated two out of two.

"What's this world coming to?" he asked, keeping a light tone in his defeated voice.

"It came already. You just missed it."

CHAPTER FIVE

Popoford had grabbed his wrist to clamp the trickle of blood. It was a scratch. The blade had been handled expertly. He looked up at the woman and saw in her eyes the expected emptiness, the gray, cold steel inhabiting the rationalized minds of every professional.

"What is your agency? Home Office?" he asked. She looked back at him without a smile. "Won't say? Well, tell me, what's your name? What do you want of me?"

"Be quiet. We'll talk in a moment. First, we must get away from here. You can't be seen here. Come on. Move."

"No way," Popoford said. "I'm going down there. There are a few things that I need. There are a few answers that I want."

"I have the answers for you. I have your clothes and papers in the car. There's no need to go into the house."

"My dear," Popoford said. "There's something fishy about your operation. How do I know the fat man's body is gone? Maybe it's just inside my back door. I want to take a look. Wouldn't it be foolish of me to just walk away without looking?"

"It would be foolish of you to go down there."

"I'll look." Popoford glared at her but he didn't move against her shotgun. "I'm of no use to you if I can't trust you. I'll look. It's to your benefit."

"Shut up. You're wasting my time. You would never trust me anyway. You can't trust anyone. That's how we both live. We'd be dead any other way. I know that. You know that. So shut up and move."

She waved her sawed-off in his face. She'd beaten him again. Three out of three. The world *had* changed.

She poked Popoford into the woods. They followed an old path that wandered from the cliff up to the dusty road and through the light-shafted woods that skirted the meadow. They didn't talk. No question couldn't wait. Popoford had finally taken the correct estimate of this woman and knew her to be a thoroughly professional agent. He had then fallen into step and had returned wholly to his former compartmentalized self, living in each of his intellectual rooms, deftly maneuvering imaginatively against his country's enemies, pushing his brilliance to the extreme but never so far as to allow philosophy to intrude and ask why. He would wait until everything revealed itself to him. For now, he would play a waiting game, a game of survival.

They came out of the woods and walked for a while along the road. They passed Popoford's car and walked a little further. Then he heard another car coming. The woman had heard it, too. Together they dove into the tall grass. The car sped past. It was the police racing down the road toward his house. Popoford and the woman hadn't been seen.

They stood up and dusted off their clothes. Their looks at each other weren't of fondness nor of caring. They were only the glances of professionals compelled to be together.

Popoford smiled a little to himself. Somewhere in his mind, even when he was in the trance of survival, a bit of heart couldn't be silenced. He had always considered it a failing, this little, needling voice that constantly told him that what he did was the biggest lie of all. But after his retirement, he had discovered that the pesky thoughts were the only things that kept him sane. His survival had always been because some of the dreaded philosophy didn't creep into his head. There was nothing he could do about it now but to smile a little and hope that he could get back to that more placid life soon.

The woman pushed him on the ground, knocking him flat out of his humanist's dream. Then Popoford heard it. It was a third car following slowly behind the police car.

Popoford tried to raise his head, but the woman kept him pinned against the earth. "Don't move. No matter what. Don't move," she said and released her grip on his neck. Popoford stayed still. She lay quietly pressed against him, not breathing. Popoford held his breath. Their bodies were warmed by the morning sun. Then they heard the car stop. They'd been seen.

The woman spoke rapidly.

"My daughter will help you. She's one of us. Stop Home Office."

With that, she stood up and walked toward the car. Popoford didn't move. There was a shout from the car. She walked toward it. Then he heard a door open, a sawed-off shotgun exploding, a pistol snap, the heavy thud of the woman's body on the dusty shoulder of the road. He heard voices whispering sharp orders. The woman's body was pulled into the car. The door was closed, and the car was driven off. Popoford lay still for a second.

When he was certain that the men in the car wouldn't be returning, when he was through wondering why the woman had intentionally died to save him in some insanely idiotic, altruistic game for an unknown and fleeting taskmaster, he had tired of thoughts of any kind and cautiously got to his feet.

The dust from the car hung in the still air and blurred the road leading to his house. His car was in that direction. If they'd been expecting to find the woman but not him, then they must have seen her car up the road. They would see his car in a second and they would be coming back for him. He ran away from the dust. He hoped the woman's car was close. He hoped that it hadn't been tampered with. He hoped that it was unlocked. He ran and hoped a new hope with every step. Then he saw her car, and he forgot to hope.

Its windshield had been smashed. The door on the driver's side was open. The chances that it would run were remote. Still, he had to give it a try.

Popoford got in. The car was facing down the road towards his house. He glanced further down the road. No one was coming. He ducked under the dash and pulled out a few wires. He touched two of them together and felt great relief when the car started. There was fuel in the tank. That was a very comfortable feeling. Things were going better than they might. He got out of the car and walked around it. There were no flat tires. Another good sign. He found a heavy stick and finished knocking out the windshield. He pulled the larger sheets of glass and film from the car. He brushed the shards from the seat. He got in and revved the engine. It was a hot motor. The woman had been a driver of some skill to have driven this thing. Hopefully, the suspension under the great American machine could hold it to the mountain road without wallowing. He looked up through the empty frame and saw the other car just as it rounded the bend. "Damn!" he yelled and slammed the floor shift into first and gunned the car into a power spin.

What a race, what a pulse filled his head. It was the surge that adrenaline pours into the heart when a man runs for his life. Popoford had felt it before. It drove his thoughts from every little compartment and tunneled them into concentrated awareness. There was nothing but the road ahead, the car behind, and the wind blowing on his unprotected face. He didn't know where he was going. He didn't need to know such things. Accelerate, brake, punch the pedals, whip the gears till the engine screamed, brake, accelerate. Drive. Drive. Drive until you're dead or free. Or both. But don't think.

And Popoford did drive and couldn't think. His hopes about the car's suspension were fulfilled. It was a stiff unit able to respond to his slightest touch on the wheel and pedals. Instinct and training allowed Popoford to slip into a beating wave with the machine. Together they joined and churned the roadbed up into great clouds behind. Together they drove the winding road back out of the valley, away from Whimsy, back to the other side of the mountain.

There was but one road, and, once on it, there was no way to get off until the other side. There were no villages on the way, no gas stations or telephones. The builders hadn't seen fit to design even one turnout. Thankfully for everyone, it was three lanes with two ascending so that a slow driver wouldn't necessarily back up traffic. It was a thoughtful gesture in the construction of one of the world's most dangerous roads. It wound through the mountain, squeezed against sheer-faced granite walls as if it was forever recoiling from the precipice, forever afraid to look over its edge at the valley floor. The drop was an ever-present danger on the way up the road, for a car that was coming down the mountain would dodge toward the inside curve, and fear alone took its toll on every driver that had dared to chance the road.

For Popoford, however, the road was a breeze as if he had driven it at speed many times. He drove the car through the curves like he knew the road by heart. He drove it as if there was no danger, no cliff, no shoulder to offer slim forgiveness for his errors. He made no errors, and the machine was driven without care.

Popoford didn't know if he wasn't being followed, so he raced over the mountain as if by himself and came off on the other side so smoothly, so gracefully, so self-confidently, that he failed to see the car that waited for him there, shaded by a thicket of weeping willows. He failed to notice the clouds building across the valley, billowing over the hills, promising another rain. The sunny hours had been but a counterfeit promise of hope to come, a respite, and nothing more.

CHAPTER SIX

Popoford drove past Elgin Base though he did so with some misgiving. He had already had enough of the place and of the dangers that lurked there, but the girl might also still be around. She might be waiting there for him. However, she seemed to know every move that he had made so far. She hadn't made a mistake yet. Why should he expect her to make one now? She would be waiting for him where he was going. She would know where that was even though he hadn't taken the time to figure it out himself. Somehow, Popoford understood this, that she would be waiting for him, and he looked at the receding skyline of the town and felt an odd warmth in knowing that he would see her again. No reason other than that. If asked, he would say that he didn't give a damn about her, but he had the feeling that he would see her again. If she was still alive. She was in danger. She would need help. But she could take care of herself better than he could. Time to stop underestimating her.

When he was past the town completely, when it was gone from his sight, he realized that he hadn't taken the time to check his rearview mirror for any car that was following him. He pulled off the road, to wait a few minutes, and watch for it. Several cars passed, none of them the car he remembered. But he knew far better than to think that the only possibility. They could have switched cars. They could have called ahead to have another car take up the chase. The cars that passed Popoford could each one be the car that was following him. If it was Home Office on his tail, they probably changed cars three times before they came off the mountain. That would be like them. Tediously fastidious, punctilious to every fault imaginable. Home Office: transparent, boring, and demanding. Their agents had always been the best, but Popoford had suspected that a good counter-agent could have easily used their precision against them. "Of course," he thought, "That's what just happened to me!"

He slumped in his car seat, confused, and shocked by his sudden glimpse of memory. His mind was only partly on the men following him. They were probably in front of him now and would soon pull over and wait for him to pass.

The little flash of memory gnawed at him. Where had it originated, that memory? Had it come from the start of his last job? Had it come from the end? Did he have to remember what happened next or what had happened before? His style had marked him and could have destroyed him. Logic told him that he needed to figure out what had led up to the little bit that he had remembered. There was probably a long story behind it: his "Mission," as Home Office liked to call their special thuggeries, their marvelous assassinations that did little more than add a sentence to some extremely narrow and forgettable history of a government's inhumanity.

So much seemed to be coming back to Popoford. But all these thoughts were things that he already knew; that he had never forgotten: Vague ideas that bordered on moral questions, the questions that assassins never considered.

Popoford knew that even thinking there was a possibility for morality made him unacceptable to Home Office. That must be why they'd retired him. It had to be. What other reason could there have been? What better reason than that he was too much of a thinker about things that got in the way. He had to search his deadened mind for the answers to why he had failed, and why he was so desperately needed now. Then he realized that no matter what it was that Home Office had wanted him to forget, it certainly couldn't have been because he was a bad agent. Who the hell would want to bring a worthless agent back into the fold? No, Popoford had been good. He could remember everything that had happened before his last official effort. He had been extremely good. He had been so good, so precise, and ultimately so predictable, that he had worked himself out of a job. Maybe that was the thread that had to be followed.

Popoford hoped that his reasoning showed some semblance of intelligence, but he was off balance and trapped by his memory and conscience. He suddenly understood that he was trapped. He had to go to Home Office if he expected to find any answers. They alone would have the whole story, though they alone would never tell him. It was an impossible situation, but Popoford drove, undaunted by logic, with a mind inspired with a new determination, even passion. They had the fat man, and now the woman they'd killed. He had been easily blackmailed. He had become soft in his new life, and the false hope that he could live a life that approached sanity. He would have to play into their hands if he wanted to have any chance of knowing what had happened.

The road took a sharp left turn as it entered the woods. Popoford drove fast through the rich yet narrow band of foliage that drew life from the stream. He had to cross the next wave of mountains to the west before he came to the Bay Area and on to Home Office. It would be an easy drive now that he knew where he was going. The car that was probably following him was of no concern. They were going to the same town, to the same building. Home Office was providing an escort. It was expected of them. In a way they were welcome. Popoford was good at accepting the inevitable. He would change things when he could. Until then he would wait and listen and pray. He had to if he was to have another chance at a quiet, if not peaceful, life. Someone would make a mistake, and he would take advantage of it.

And so he drove around Sacramento and past the Napa exit. He wished, as all natives do, that he had seen certain attractions of his backyard which he had always intended to see. He believed that New Yorkers rarely visit the Statue of Liberty, that Los Angelenos hardly ever go to Disneyland, and that the working stiffs of San Francisco and the surrounding cities seldom get up to taste the wine. For Popoford it was true. He had never been to the wine country, and he had never visited the Winchester Mystery House in Campbell. Someday he might. Someday after he got Home Office off his back.

For now, he headed south on I-80 West over the Carquinez Straits, down into Richmond past the spreading of the Sacramento River Delta. He drove beyond the Bay Bridge and continued south along the uneven surfaces of I-280, south through Oakland, past the airport, past the burned-out structure of Carpet Circus, past the Levitz Furniture sign that was the most memorable San Leandro landmark that could be seen from the road. He took the "A" Street off-ramp in Hayward and came to a stop at the bottom of the ramp.

Several cars had followed him off the freeway, but it was the third one back that interested Popoford. There were two men in the front seat. They were dressed in moderately priced suits and wore dull looks on their faces. They were all too obvious even in Popoford's rearview mirror and through all the glass of the other cars. They were so obvious that Popoford had to laugh to himself. It was as if they were trying to emulate the popular stereotype of the secret agent.

Home Office had slipped quite a bit, or maybe they thought that he had slipped. That idea was slightly worrisome. Popoford wasn't sure that he hadn't.

The light changed to green. The car behind blared its horn, and Popoford lurched into the intersection. He turned left toward the hills but slowed as he drove the long block to Castro Street.

The only car that had turned left with him was the one with the two men in it. Popoford waved to them. They ignored him. He turned left again on Castro and drove past the glass container factory. He pulled into the gravel lot in front of the dilapidated frame house across the street from the factory. The other car pulled in beside him, crunching the gravel as it stopped.

Popoford looked at the men. They didn't return his glance, but stared straight ahead, their eyes blank, little smirks on their mouths. Popoford gave them a brusque gesture to get their attention but they still didn't respond. When he got out, they did the same.

"Welcome home," Popoford said as if he had never left. "You boys had better brush up on your fundamentals. I knew you were there all the time."

The two men didn't answer. They waited for Popoford to approach the old house, and they followed.

Popoford knocked on the door. It was as ill-kept as the rest of the house. Its paint had peeled in great patches exposing bare wood that had bleached gray in the weather. Once it had been a fresh new door, but now it was hung on this old tract house and was painted a common California pink that Popoford found revolting. Little swatches of the original color tenaciously stuck to the door, but there was less paint than Popoford remembered, and the general decline of the old building had advanced to such a degree that he felt a sudden twinge of nostalgia for the particular crumpled state that he had known. The old building might soon collapse on its own. Home Office would have to relocate. He knocked again, and the two men waited behind him.

Popoford heard approaching footsteps. He knew the routine. The haggard voice would ask questions from behind the door.

"Who is it?"

"It's Pop . . . no, it's George Mixer," Popoford's throat choked out the nom de guerre.

"Never heard of ya. What you want?"

"Hendricks wants me. I've been sent for."

"Don't know no Hendricks. Get out of here."

"Check your files. I'm old school. George Mixer."

"You trying to collect? Forget it. Nothin' here."

Popoford grabbed the doorknob and rattled it. "Get Hendricks. He wants me."

"If you're trying to serve papers, I'm not about to take them. Get out of here before I call my old man."

Popoford was getting tired of the stubborn exchange. "Open this door!"

"Go to hell!"

Popoford was surprised when one of the men spoke up.

"The pattern is wrong, Mixer. Things change. Passwords change."

"Well, what the hell are you waiting for. Get over here and make her open the door."

The man smiled with insolent pleasure. "Anything for an old boy."

Popoford remained cool. "For some reason, you don't seem to like me. At least we feel the same about each other. Now please get me inside."

"At your command," he said and approached the door. "Open Up!"

"Who is it?"

"Sometimes I wonder."

"As have I."

"We are alone in our wisdom."

"And joined on account of it."

"If you wish."

The door was opened.

"How preposterous," Popoford said.

The man looked at him with a distaste that surprised Popoford. He couldn't understand the reason for such hatred from a man he had never met. At least, he couldn't remember having met him. "After you," he said to the man and his companion. They stepped aside, however, and indicated that he must enter the house first.

Popoford recognized the threat and walked across the threshold. A wave of warm air thick with the stink of poverty and death grabbed him as if it were a pair of thick fingers pinching up his nostrils. He was repulsed and wanted to turn back, but he was compelled by the same stink to step deep into the dank house and find out what had become of his old mother agency, Home Office. The place had always smelled the same. It had become a familiar odor to Popoford, one which he sometimes had remembered in Whimsy, one that had brought back some of his most exciting memories, memories of deeds that time had filtered of ugliness and truth. Now he had entered the unlikely house and was overcome by the full horror of the secrets it masked.

"Welcome back, Mr. Mixer."

"Thank you, Sarah. You had me worried for a while."

"We must be sure of our visitors. You know that."

"Of course," he said. "You haven't changed, Sarah."

"You have."

She had always come to the point, and Popoford had always responded as he did then. "Be clever, Sarah. You're playing life too sternly. Not so blunt. Learn to play with your prey."

As always Sarah didn't respond. As always she walked over to a ripped, overstuffed chair and sat down. As always her excess weight puffed a tuft of kapok into the room. As always Popoford wondered at the endless supply of kapok.

"Go back," she said and adjusted the dirty print dress around her sweaty body. She motioned to a door behind her and then wiped her nose with her forearm.

No, she hadn't changed. She was still a minor actor whose talent had exceeded itself in a role that she was employed to maintain, always. She had become the lowlife, lonely, crotchety old woman she was meant to be. She had become afraid of the outside world. She had become the best front that Home Office could have had. But she was still a Home Office agent: dangerous and skilled in deadly ways.

"Go back. You're expected."

"Now you tell me."

"We had to be sure it was you."

"So you said, but how do you know that it's me? You have yet to gather proof of who I am. You haven't even looked at my identification. You don't know for sure."

"Don't count on it," she said and sneezed a great burst of spray into the room. Popoford moved hurriedly through the door. The men went with him.

CHAPTER SEVEN

The other side of the door startled Popoford, even though he had seen it so many times. The stark, bright light that hit him made him close his eyes. He finally squinted a peek, and gradually became used to the coldness and the brilliance of the bare halls. Behind the dilapidated facade, Home Office shone like a "Man from U.N.C.L.E." set. The white walls were lit by solid banks of fluorescent tubes, and they were interrupted regularly by plain, white doors with black handles. The floor was white tile. It seemed to Popoford that the very air was white, and as always, the dazzling purity struck him with fear. He didn't expect that kindness would long survive in such sterility.

He walked directly to the very end of the hall. The door opened into the reception room. It was also the public interrogation "cleansing boy" room. Hendricks would be waiting for him in the room beyond.

He opened the door and went in. The other men stayed out in the hall and closed the door behind him. He waited, standing still for the sensors that lined the walls of the small inner room to complete their scan; covering his eyes against the strong spotlights that illuminated him for the scanners. When the machine had completed its task, the wall in front of him slid open, and Popoford was exposed to the office within.

"George Mixer. My God. It truly is you. Thank God. I'm so relieved. Do come in."

Popoford lowered his hand from his eyes. "Hendricks," he said coldly.

"Why so stuffy, George? At least I'm not a hypocrite. Home Office will be served. Come on, George. Relax. Treat an old buddy with a little kindness. Please stop calling me Hendricks. Call me Alex. Like old times. Right? You remember. Huh, George?"

"My name is Steven."

"Please, George. We have our security. Try to maintain discipline. You're been recalled, George. Start off on the right foot. Toe the line right away. There's no place for the likes of you outside of Home Office. You know that. We know that. Now let's talk about your assignment."

"Not so fast. I'm not here because I want to be."

"So what? How could that possibly matter?"

"I'm not a zealot. I'm not a mercenary. I've come to you so that I might avoid an inconvenience. I expect to be *asked* to perform my assignments. I expect to be on an equal footing with you, Hendricks. I'll have a say in things."

"I suppose," Hendricks snapped, coming out from behind his desk and sitting on it, "that stupidity makes you so pompous."

"Go to hell, Hendricks! And stuff your assignment. I want to talk to the old man. Now."

"That is not possible. He does not want to see you."

"Does he know I'm here?"

"Of course. You're here because he wants you here. The assignment which you'll undertake is for the old man."

"Let him tell me."

"I'm telling you that it's impossible."

"So is my working for you."

"Look, Mixer, let me set you straight. You killed a man. Your "fat man" was an agent of the United States Government. You also killed the woman. You're a wanted man. Cooperate or you'll be turned over to the police. You wouldn't want that, now would you?"

"It wouldn't happen like that. You know that" Popoford said. He remained standing even though there were several chairs available. "I would never be held by the police. Even with the trumped-up evidence that you must have, they would never hold me. Professional courtesy alone would get me out. Then I would come after you. Understand Hendricks? I'd come after you. It would be better for you to let me have a say in things right from the beginning. If you don't, it means your ultimate death."

"George, George, don't waste your breath. The world is different than you remember it."

"I've been out in the world. I know what's out there."

"I don't think so. Don't forget, George, our information is much more reliable than whatever you saw out in the world. The atmosphere has changed, George. The people are in no mood to praise the likes of you. Good times have made hypocrites of them all. If you want hypocrisy, just go back out to the people and you'll find it."

"What are you talking about? Aren't you confusing a lack of information with hypocrisy? Damn, you know there's nothing new about folks being ignorant. Especially about what we do. Hell, it wouldn't work any other way."

"Let's not get too fundamental. Just face the facts. The mood of the people has changed. They'd hang you. You're the enemy. Don't think you aren't. What you've done, you did in their name. I know that. But the problem is they know it too. And they don't want to be reminded of it. An assassin like you will be squashed if you're exposed. You interfere with the status quo, and they'd string you up."

"There's nothing new about that. It's always been the same. The people easily make enemies of their soldiers. So what? The police wouldn't hold a government agent."

"With my help, you could be lynched."

Popoford took a seat. He wasn't startled by Hendricks. He sat down calmly and kept his voice calm. "The truth will out."

"Don't be theatrical. The point is we have a lot of shit on you. you'll do what we want. Anyway, we've taken over your private accounts. You have no money."

"Brilliant," Popoford said, thinking of the several secret accounts that he had opened with money he had deferred from Home Office funds. They were in other names. No one knew about them. He even had a hard time recalling the names he used, and one of his greatest fears had been that he would forget the pseudonyms and lose the only security Home Office had ever provided him.

"Don't think that I'm missing something, George. We know about all of the money, all of the accounts."

"What are you talking about?"

"No more cat and mouse. You bore me. You're too good an agent to waste so much time."

"I'm getting soft. I'm no good to you."

"Perhaps, but you'll work for us, and you'll work well."

Popoford took a long moment before he replied.

"Yes," he sighed. "I can see your point."

"It's about time. Now, let's stop screwing around. I have a job for you. Actually, I want you to finish the last job you were assigned. The one you didn't complete."

"The one you made me forget."

"The one you'll remember."

"I see," Popoford said and closed his eyes. There was a weariness in him that longed to be recognized. It would have to be forestalled. "When do we begin?"

"Now."

"I'm hungry."

"Later. We'll feed you later." Hendricks turned away from Popoford, but then turned back and looked him in the eyes. There was no warmth in his face. "If you still have the stomach for food."

Popoford didn't blink. Such dire words of foreboding were mandatory from Home Office. They were especially appropriate from Hendricks. He was the old man's lieutenant. He could be expected to be the old man's parrot. H.O.'s parrot.

"Are those H.O.'s exact words?"

Hendricks scowled at the slight and went behind his desk, where he picked up a phone and asked for the escorts to come in.

Outside in the other world, the real world, the world which agencies like Home Office were meant to protect, lightning struck close to a power transformer and flickered the current. Faint rumblings of a rolling thunderclap filtered into the room. The rains had returned, and Popoford felt a distinct pit in his belly.

He was beginning to think that he wasn't the marvelously superior agent that he had thought himself to be. The threat of being too upset to eat had gotten to him. Maybe he was getting soft in his old age. He never had been perfect. He had always had certain flaws. He was like every other man that way, but now there was a slowly growing doubt in his belly, and it would want to thrive and have a life of its own. He would have to fight it. The very nature of doubt would weaken his resolve to fight. He had to fight it now. And Popoford did fight it as best he could, in the way that he had always fought doubt. He tried to ignore it. It might not go away, but it would hold in remission long enough for him to get through whatever disgusting revelation Hendricks had for him.

The two men, the escorts, were at his side.

"Take Mr. Mixer to the table," Hendricks quietly ordered.

"Wait a damned minute," Popoford shouted.

"Relax, George," Hendricks said, as the two men grabbed Popoford's arms. "I'm only going to ask you a few questions. There will be no pain involved. The fact is, I think you'll like the drugs. They're necessary. You know the routine."

"The hell I do! What are you going to do to me? I don't want any drugs."

"Gentlemen. The table," Hendricks said, and the men pulled Popoford over to one of the white walls where a thinly padded bed was elevated on a stainless steel pedestal. They roughly pushed Popoford onto the table and strapped him down. "The straps are necessary, George. We must protect ourselves."

"From what, damn you?"

"You're a very violent man, George."

"Bullshit." Popoford was scared. "What are you going to do?"

"I told you, George. We'll be administering a drug and then asking you a few questions. It's all quite simple. We want you to remember, George. You must remember everything. You must be given a reason to work for us, George. We aren't stupid men. We know that you would never willingly work for us again under these circumstances. Blackmail and abduction are not exactly the way to a man's heart and loyalty. We know these things, George, but we had to get you here. We had to defeat a certain distaste for your old work that we had planted in your mind. Part of making you forget was to make you not want to remember. We couldn't have you trying too hard to remember. That would never have done. That's why we planted a nagging feeling in you that what you'd done had taken its toll on you. We led you to believe that you were over the hill. A useless old agent on a pension, soon forgotten."

Popoford looked up at Hendricks, and then he closed his eyes for a second. He couldn't believe what he was hearing. He felt like a character in several books he'd read. He felt like the man who discovers that in fact, he is no man at all, but instead is a robot of man's making. He had been programmed to think in certain ways. He had been programmed to forget, and he had forgotten.

As the needle was jabbed into his arm and the drug took him completely, Popoford understood how his whole life was just a continuation of programming, from the first days of adolescent life when he was encouraged to go into the Army, through boot camp, through one training session after another, through battles that were so numerous that they seemed to be only one, protracted day of service to his country. His whole life had been nothing more than a programmed response to the needs of the people. He truly had been a robot: the mind he had always thought was his own was theirs.

Popoford drifted and rolled into a semiconscious state, and for a moment he thought that he was one with the thunder, one with nature, one with the world. But these details of dreaming were to be driven from his head; to be replaced with other thoughts that would take the place of dreams and were required for the fulfillment of Home Office's needs.

CHAPTER EIGHT

Popoford felt his body strapped to the drifting bed. He'd been stripped and washed all over with warm water. Then again he was washed, this time with cool water and dried with a soft towel. He felt his body lying naked on the bed and recognized that he felt no shame in his nakedness. Hendricks was standing off to one side, waiting. The two men had prepared him for the interrogation. Hendricks would be the interrogator, the two men his assistants.

"First of all, George," Hendricks began in a calm and reassuring voice. "This is not an interrogation. And secondly, you needn't mumble. Just come right out and say what you want to say. No one here wants you to be afraid of saying what you want. We're all on your side. We're your friends, George. You can trust us."

Popoford was startled to find that he'd been talking out loud. He would have to be careful about that. No matter what Hendricks said to him, the fear remained in Popoford's mind. He had no one to trust. No longer. Not since she'd died. Not since she'd been killed. Gretchen had been killed.

"I'll tell you right from the start, George, we want you to remember Gretchen. We must have you remember Gretchen. You must remember how she died. You must remember who killed her. Can you start me out, George? Will you help me tell the story? George?"

"I...I'll try," Popoford mumbled, his washed mind flashing an instant of total fear.

"Good. Why don't you tell me how it was between you two. Tell me what it was that made Gretchen important to you."

Gretchen had been killed, Popoford thought, the memory of her racing around in his thoughts, she'd been killed. God how it hurt to even think of her name. "She was my friend . . ."

"Yes, George. She was your friend. She was your very good friend, George. She was the woman you loved. Remember? Can't you see right now her beautiful face before you? Can't you smell her skin, George? Yes, you can remember her touch. Her voice. Her fragrance in bed. George, in bed. Remember? George? Can you see?"

Popoford nodded. He could see. He was having thoroughly realistic memories of an afternoon just after they'd met. What Popoford didn't know, what the drug didn't let him see, was that Hendricks was projecting a film on the ceiling. It was a prod to push Popoford to the desired conclusions. Popoford watched his own memories and accepted the subtle alterations of the truth as if things had happened just as Hendricks presented them. The drug gave him little choice.

"She was more than your friend, George. She was your friend and your lover, and she was everything that you wanted a woman to be. George, she was everything to you. George. Your friend, your lover, George, your equal, your better, everything."

Popoford was smiling at the memory. A tear hung on his face.

"Good, George, you do remember the full beauty of her. But, George, one thing bothers me. There's one thing that I want you to tell me. Something that you alone can remember, George. Why did you kill her, George?"

The film abruptly cut to an execution of a blindfolded woman, and Popoford stiffened against the straps. His head exploded and he wanted to cover his face against the horror within and without. He gagged and choked, and squeezed his eyes as tightly closed as he could. Somehow he would crush his thoughts. Somehow he would fight them. Somehow he would keep them from developing in his head. He would make his thoughts stay away because he couldn't live with them.

"Yes, George, you do remember. You killed Gretchen, and brutally, too. I've just never been able to understand what came over you, George. It must have been something especially important. Was it, George? Was it something that she did? Was it something that Gretchen did, George?"

Popoford shook his head. He strained at the straps and forced his mind to the thunder and sound of falling rain. He wouldn't think about her. He couldn't have killed her. She was everything to him. "NO...!" His voice forced his thought away again and left a fog behind in his mind. Hendricks answered as if Popoford's words were for him.

"Yes, George. There's no doubt. We have proof. You sent it to us yourself. But let's not go through all this again. We haven't got the time. You understood that last night."

"What?" Popoford asked.

"Gretchen. George, you killed Gretchen. Remember?"

"When?" Popoford's mind was suddenly sharp.

"Ten months ago."

"No. Not that. When did you say that I understood all of this?"

"Last night, George. Last night. Remember?"

"No," Popoford said, confused again. "No. I don't think so."

"Yes, George, you do remember. You remember the conversation we had last night. You remember that you finally understood what you'd done. After four days of effort, we finally got you to remember the act. We've done that already. Now we have to understand why you did it. Are you helping, George? Please help. It will go so much faster if you help."

"Yes, I remember. Gretchen. Dead, but why did I do it?" He shook his head and put his hands to his eyes. The straps had been loosened. "Why did I kill her?"

"Right, George, that's right. We must know why you killed Gretchen. But, George, please do hurry. We've been asking that question of you for four days straight. My patience is running out. These men are getting tired. I'm getting tired. George. Damn, you must be worn out too. George?"

"Yes?" he mumbled, trying to remember the cadence of time. When had they started this? When had he driven to Home Office? Days ago? Or was it now, just now? Days ago? Yes. That was it. Hendricks had said it. Four days of questions. Yes, he was tired. "We're all tired, George. Give us a hand, won't you? Tell us why you killed her."

"I don't know."

"Well, George, we have ideas. Maybe we can help you remember."

Popoford's mind raced around his head. He was looking for a way out. He needed a savior to take responsibility. 'Christ,' he thought, "help me."

"Christ can't help you, George."

Popoford squeezed his lips together to keep his words to himself.

"George? Are you thinking out loud?"

Popoford shook his head violently. He wasn't certain what he was doing. One second his mind was clear, his thoughts sharp, logical. The next second and he was wandering aimlessly with them, all his cares gathered into a unit of confusion lashed up and tugged by the drugs and the films.

"That's good, George. We want you to stick to the subject, O.K.?" Hendricks hovered over Popoford. His face filled

Popoford's eyes. "Now, George, I want you to consider how devoted you've been to the service of your country. I want you to consider the people for whom we struggle. I want you to realize that you're the greatest champion that the people of this country have ever had. George, you're God's gift to all of us. Our enemies all fail when Home Office sends you against them. Remember, George, you've killed many people who have threatened our way of life. You've killed with great passion. You're not a cold man, George. Not like the others. you've killed for a reason. Always for your country. Always for the people. George, tell me. That was why you killed Gretchen, wasn't it? You must tell me, George. Gretchen was a spy, wasn't she? She was an agent."

"What? Gretchen?"

"Good God, George. Pay attention."

"I am. Gretchen was an agent?"

"You tell me, George. That's what we think. H.O. wants you to confirm. Can you do that?"

Popoford was confused again. "Gretchen was an agent," he said matter of factly.

"That's right, George. Good. Yes. That's just the confirmation that we needed." Hendricks looked at one of the guards. "Report to H.O. directly. Tell him that we have confirmation concerning Gretchen Stricklin. She was one of them." Hendricks turned back to Popoford. "Thank you, George. You've given us the necessary piece to our puzzle. We thought that was why you killed her. Now we know."

"You must have known before," Popoford mumbled. "You made me forget. You made me forget all about it."

"We made you forget nothing, George. You made yourself forget. When you killed her you were through as an agent. You were through. You weren't of any use to us then. Times have changed, though. We need you now, George. We must have you back. You're the only one good enough to help us now. That's why we have you here. That's why we've put so much effort into making you remember. We need your mind clear. We need you to operate without the killing of Gretchen hanging over your head. Now that you've helped us know why you did it, we can get on with cleaning this whole mess up."

Popoford was having a hard time piecing together what was happening. "You made me forget," he said, not knowing what to believe.

"No, George. That's not true. We let you believe that. It was a lot easier that way. We told you what would make you more comfortable. You'd been our best man. We hated to lose you, but we had to issue your pension. I'm sorry that we couldn't leave you in Whimsy to enjoy it. We need you again, George Mixer."

"What for?"

"I'll let H.O. tell you that himself. Later. After the drugs wear off completely. We'll take you back to your room now. Sleep awhile. Rest. You've suffered a great deal for your country. Rest a little before we ask you to suffer a little more."

Popoford stayed lying on the bed as the remaining guard pushed him out from under Hendricks' face, out of the interrogation room, out into the white corridor, down to a small, empty, white room where he was left alone behind a locked door.

He was so confused by what he'd heard. It seemed like only a few hours had passed since he'd driven up to the dilapidated house that fronted the offices of his old agency. Hendricks said that he'd been there several days. And Gretchen. How could he have forgotten her? How could he have forgotten that she died? How could he have forgotten that he had killed her? How could he have forgotten that he had loved her, had been living with her before his last assignment. How could he have lived such a placid life in Whimsy if all that had happened? It was impossible.

Another tear came to his eye, and when he began to realize the truth, that she really was dead when he started to remember everything, he doubled up into a ball and sobbed himself into a raging sleep. He dreamed of anger and hatred. He killed himself over and over again. He cursed Gretchen for her deceit. He strangled her for her treason. He dreamed hard in the little room until he'd dreamed himself into believing all that Hendricks had told him, wondering only what sort of assignment H.O. had for him, wondering only how he could atone for having been Gretchen's sucker and for having broken down under fire. Popoford didn't dream about the woman who had been gunned down outside of Whimsy. He didn't dream about the girl who had warned him.

CHAPTER NINE

When Popoford awoke he felt exhausted. He felt that he'd been working through the night, and he had. His dreaming had kept his muscles contracted and mind tense. He opened his eyes and let out a deep sigh. He knew at once where he was. He knew that he had a mission. He knew that he had allowed Home Office to be betrayed. He knew that he had killed Gretchen. He knew all the things that Hendricks had wanted him to know. He knew everything that would prepare him for Home Office. Still, he felt that something was missing

Popoford pushed himself halfway up on one elbow. "Somebody get me a cup of coffee." When there was no answer, Popoford sat up. He realized that he was naked. "Get me my clothes. Hey, Hendricks! Get my clothes."

Again there was no response, and Popoford got out of the bed and walked to the door. The white tile was cold under his feet.

He tried the door and found it unlocked. When he opened it there wasn't a guard, and the sterile emptiness that presented itself along the abandoned hall surprised him. He was alone in Home Office.

"Hey! Are you planning to leave me alone without any clothes? Hendricks? Hey! How about a cup of coffee?"

There was no answer. He started down the hall ignoring his nakedness. However, the idea that Home Office had been abandoned caused him a second thought. A vague fear tried to catch him, but he let it pass because he was certain he wasn't being watched. He was reasonably certain that he wasn't in any danger.

Then he heard a voice. "Just keep coming this way, George. The door at the end of the hall is the one you're looking for."

Popoford noticed the loudspeaker grill, white and nearly hidden, mounted flush against the white wall.

"Hendricks!" Popoford called. "What are you trying to prove? Where is everyone?"

Hendricks didn't reply. Popoford shrugged and walked to the door at the end of the hall. He opened it and stepped into a richly colored room that was the antithesis of the sterility in the rest of Home Office.

"To answer your question, George," Hendricks said as he closed the door behind Popoford, "Most of our agents are in the field right now. They are already involved in the operation for which you were recalled."

"Interesting. Where is the backup? Where is the support? There's no one here."

"There are three of us. That's all we need. H.O. is personally directing this operation. It's that important."

"I see," Popoford said.

"You will soon. Here. Put on this robe and have a seat. H.O. will be here shortly."

Popoford put on the rough, gray robe and sat near the fireplace. There had been a fire burning for several hours. Ashes were piled on the brick firebox, and hot embers glowed just under the dusty, suffocating surface. The room smelled of smoking oak. "How about a cup of coffee? I'm a little fuzzy."

"Certainly," Hendricks said and pushed a button on the side of the great desk that dominated the room. "It will be here soon. I had coffee prepared as soon as you started to wake up. I figured that sleeping for two days would leave you a little weary."

"Two days?" Popoford said. "How can that be?"

"You were tired George, and the drugs we gave you to make you remember were a little brutal. You can't expect to feel great for a while."

There was a knock on a side door. "Here's the coffee. Have some. It'll help you wake up a bit. I'll go get H.O."

Hendricks left through a side door and let a little balding man in. The few strings of hair that had lingered on his skull were plastered to it with heavy grease. He was carrying a silver tray with a silver coffee service and delicate china cups. He was a gross creature next to the precious objects that he carried, and Popoford, having once caught his eye, didn't want to look at him again. The man was evil if the glint that flashed behind his scarred and folded lids could be believed. He was evil if such proclivity could be read in the crumpled posture of an old man shrinking with age. But this wasn't just any old man. This was a man who showed signs of rot. He was revolting not because he was old, but because he made Popoford feel like life itself was a disgrace. The little old man shuffled over to Popoford and placed the tray on the side table.

"Thank you," Popoford said. "That will be all."

The man didn't say anything. Instead of going, he merely stepped back a few paces and waited. Popoford refused to look over his shoulder at the little man. "I said that would be all. You're dismissed."

The man didn't move. He didn't speak, and Popoford was forced to pour coffee and drink it while the little man waited silently just behind him, out of sight, but distinct in Popoford's mind.

Popoford was uncomfortable and self-conscious of his slurping. He tried to force his thoughts away from the wretched old man and on to H.O. himself.

He had never met H.O. As far as he knew, Hendricks was the only man directly connected to the agency who had ever seen its director. He was an enigma to his operatives, and as such his appearance was left up to the individual's imagination. Popoford had always fancied the director to be some kind of middle-aged, slightly graying, aristocratic gentleman of breeding. He might look like an ambassador, or perhaps he was more like a leading man who was growing old with mellowing grace. At any rate, he was a special man in whom the president had every confidence. The head of Home Office was in charge of the greatest information gathering agency in the world. He was also in charge of, and privy to, all its clandestine plans and actions. He was a man of power that extended beyond the term of one elected official, beyond the narrow concerns of one fashionable political absurdity or another. He was a man who stayed in the background so effectively that few even knew his name. Everyone referred to him as H.O. He was the agency personified. Yet only Hendricks knew who he was. Popoford surely didn't.

Popoford fought an urge to turn around and look at the ugly creature waiting with him. He poured himself another cup of coffee and wished that Hendricks would hurry up.

Five minutes passed. Hendricks didn't come. H.O. didn't come. Five minutes is nothing, Popoford thought, though he was beginning to get nervous.

Ten minutes passed. Then twenty. Then thirty-five. Popoford stood up and started for the door.

"Where do you think you're going, Mixer? Sit down."

Popoford had forgotten about the ugly little butler. Slowly he turned to scowl at the man's audacity.

"What did you say?"

"You heard me. Sit down."

"Go to hell!" Popoford lashed out at the man. "I'm fed up with the stalling. I'm getting out of here right now. See you around, little man."

"Mixer! There's only one thing I don't understand. How you stayed alive all these years. You're the most incompetent, stupid agent that I've ever seen. Sit down before you harm yourself."

Popoford couldn't believe his ears. This runt was talking back to the best agent Home Office had ever had. "I don't believe this. You've got to be kidding. Do you know who you're talking to? Do you know who I am?"

"Better than you do. God, but you're an arrogant ass. Hell, if you were half as good as you thought you were, we wouldn't be in the fix we're in now. Yes, I know you, Steven Popoford, alias George Mixer. You're one of the hundreds of blowhards I've hired over the years but more incompetent, and conceited as any of them. I'm H.O., Mixer. You catching on?"

Indeed Popoford was catching on. He felt like a foolish little boy who had been discovered perpetrating some embarrassing little sin by a minister in civvies or by a policeman in plain clothes. He was embarrassed, and the shame made him hate the ugly man even more.

"Don't go on about how you didn't recognize me. You've never seen me before. And no bullshit about how you should have known. That goes without saying. It's my place to put your conceit in perspective. Now, sit down."

"Yes, sir," Popoford said, with a slight edge to his voice. He hated the little man even as he felt overwhelming respect for the deeds, real or rumored, of the Director. The little Director of Home Office. "I'm happy to finally meet you, Sir," Popoford said, trying to recover some of his dignity.

"Knock off the crap. We have too much to do. Now sit up and listen." H.O. sat down at a little desk. He opened a leather attaché case that was on the table, and he removed a folder. "Take a look at this," he said and wiped a greasy, errant strand of hair from his low forehead. He didn't give the folder to Popoford, who had leaned forward to take it, but instead, he only raised it off the desk so Popoford could read the title page.

Again Popoford found himself off balance. "Yes? What does it mean?" he said, sitting back again.

"Operation 'No Tell.' It's the reason you killed Gretchen Stricklin. It's the reason that this country is threatened by the worst catastrophe it has ever faced. It's the reason that you were originally assigned to California. Now it's the reason that you've been taken out of retirement. I'm giving you another chance to take care of this matter. You screwed it up once, maybe you can do it right this time."

"I'm sorry . . ."

"That won't help you now."

"No. I mean I don't know anything about 'No Tell.' I've never heard of it." Popoford felt his anger building, and he forced himself to calm down.

"I know you've never heard of it. You weren't supposed to hear of it. You were supposed to be involved in it without knowing why. I know my strategy. Give me a little credit for that, please." H.O. was sarcastic and contemptuous. Popoford was steaming under a forced calm.

"How about you knock off the drama?" he said. "I don't know what you have against me, but I'd like to get down to business and get it over with."

H.O. glared at Popoford while visibly holding back his temper. Popoford was relieved when the Director sucked in his breath and continued.

"First, you'd better know that your rash decisions have caused us a great deal of trouble. Had you asked before you killed Gretchen, we might have made her talk."

"It was your idea to keep me in the dark."

"As I was saying," the director continued, without acknowledging Popoford's remark, "We could have made her talk. We could have found out exactly what the scheme was. We could have resolved our little problem. Instead, they'd been slowed down, not stopped."

"Who'd been slowed down?"

"I'll get to that. Just be quiet. Try to listen for a change."

Popoford sneered at H.O. and leaned back in his chair. The little man revolted him. Instead of the dashing aristocrat of his imagination, this man was a slug who left a lingering trail wherever he went, a trail of slimy deeds and offensive odors, the horrors, and stenches of a vile man. This was a man who Popoford found difficult to admire, let alone respect and follow, but this was H.O. This was the man who the president trusted with the security of the country.

"Your assignment, Mixer, is to finish the job you screwed up. You are to kill the president."

"What? You're out of your fucking mind!" Popoford was on his feet and leaning over the desk. His face was within inches of H.O's slack, gray skin.

"Sit down, you fool. You don't even know what I'm talking about. You know, this has always been your problem. You're too damned rash. You cause so damned much trouble I should send you back to Whimsy right now."

"Go ahead. Suits me." Popoford sat again, more on account of H.O.'s breath than because of the command.

The director hesitated. "You're the only one left. I suppose you should know. You aren't up to the challenge, but you're the only damned agent of any caliber that I have."

"Where are the others? Surely there are others you could call in from the field." H.O. didn't answer. "Hendricks said there were others. "There *must* be others."

"There are no others. Do you think that I would call a bungling idiot like you in from retirement if I had even a mediocre agent available? Damn! A man would have to be suicidal to willingly choose you to do anything important."

"And what the hell do you think is going to make me work for you? You're one of the biggest assholes I've ever had the displeasure of meeting. Go to hell!"

H.O. sat at the desk. He just watched Popoford as the agent opened the door, turned around, and then came back into the room. The man at the door had a pistol pointed at Popoford's head. When Popoford had once again found his chair, the man closed the door, leaving the agent and his boss alone again.

"I'm prepared for your outbursts. You're very predictable. Now sit still and let me get to the damned point."

Popoford sat still and listened.

"You will kill the president because you'll see that it's what must be done. You will kill the president because he has betrayed us all. He has betrayed the country. That is enough reason. For that reason alone you'll attempt to kill him. For all our sakes, I hope you're successful."

Popoford stared at the little man.

"How has he betrayed us? Give me proof."

"You don't need proof. You need only know that our duly-elected president is a pawn of an international conspiracy. He has been slipped into office by a very impressionable population, and now he is quietly bringing this country to its knees. Within a matter of weeks, he will deliver us up to our enemies. He must be stopped."

"You're serious," Popoford said softly.

H.O. slammed his fist on the desk. His face was flushed red with anger. "Damned right I'm serious, you oaf!" H.O. yelled back.

"Then why don't you use one of the boys out in the hall? I'm not your best choice for this job. Use one of them."

"You're slow, stupid, untrainable, and without the slightest wit of common sense, but next to those two, you're a genius, a veritable James Bond of Home Office. I'm forced to make difficult choices: You're it."

Popoford backed off a bit from a sharp spray of spittle. "President Bjoonic, a traitor? How can that be? He is so loved."

"'He is so loved.'" H.O. mimicked. "How can he be a traitor? He's *not* a traitor. He's the enemy, Mixer. He has never been one of us. He's not a countryman of ours."

"But his childhood. The people who knew him back in Peoria. What about them. What about his mother?"

"His real mother died when he was born. The rest of them, his friends, the people who remember him so well, they are all part of the plot. They are paid off, most of them. Some are enemy agents themselves. The woman who calls herself his 'mother' is an agent. She is, in fact, his lover."

"What?"

"She's his lover. We know all about them. We know all about the whole conspiracy."

"Then tell the press. Tell the public. He'll be impeached. The law will take care of it."

"Oh, wise up, you idiot. You said it yourself: He's so loved. Who the hell would believe us? Who would believe the director of a disbanded agency? Who would believe you, the man who killed the president's agent?"

"Wait a minute. You're going too fast. What do you mean by 'disbanded agency?'"

H.O. hesitated as he rubbed his temples and gazed at Popoford. "I mean Home Office, of course."

"Who disbanded Home Office? When?"

"We were unofficially canceled just after Gretchen was killed. The president himself signed the secret orders."

"Why? What justification did he give?"

"He said that he was reorganizing. He had developed a new intelligence agency. A modern agency that can better serve the nation. The fact is, we were getting too close."

"Then why didn't he just have you all killed?"

"Don't you wish he had. Well, he has tried. Several times, and he's been successful. Hendricks and I, and of course Sarah, are the only ones left in the offices. The two thugs outside are newly hired. You're the closest thing to an agent that we have."

"You mean that the rest of them are dead?"

"You do catch on fast. Yes, they are all dead. Killed in the line of duty. Most of them didn't even know why they were dying."

"Singleton? Masterson? Contlerust? All dead?"

"Yes. We're the only ones left, and we have to stop him before he stops us."

"It should help that he doesn't know that I'm back in service."

"What? Will you ever wise up? He does know. He knows all about you. Who do you think that woman was, the one we shot? She was going to kill you!"

"Really?"

"Yes. With her dead, however, you have a clear road until someone else is assigned to you."

Popoford thought about the mountain-climbing girl. He decided not to mention her to the director. Let him find out about her himself. Let him instead explain something that would tell a lot about the truth. "That woman tried to save my life," he said.

"Bullshit! She was only trying to get you away so they could torture information out of you. She was Gretchen's replacement. You were her target."

"I don't believe it."

"I don't give a damn what you believe. You have an assignment, and you'd better carry it out. If you don't, the country will fall into the hands of the enemy, and we'll all be dead."

Popoford sat in the chair for a few moments. H.O. allowed him to think, and Popoford decided to play along, at least until he could find out if the director was telling the truth.

"Let me have the file."

H.O. reluctantly handed it across the desk to Popoford. The agent took it and noted the oily stains that the director left on the manila.

"You will find all the proof you need in there. I don't think you'll live long enough to sell that information. No one would believe it anyway."

Popoford glared at H.O. "Your confidence is most inspiring. If the job needs to be done, I'll do it. If not, I might just come back here and show you what it's like to die at the hands of a fool like me."

"Get out of here. I expect you to get it done. Make it clean, and there's a big bonus in it for you."

Popoford stood up and went to the door. "Threats mean nothing to a trained agent of Home Office," he said, deadpan, without turning around. He heard H.O.'s derisive snort as he opened the door. He saw Hendricks waiting there for him. Hendricks and the two guards took Popoford to get dressed. Then they went upstairs, through Sarah's front rooms, and out into the fresh air. Popoford felt sick even in the warm afternoon rain.

CHAPTER TEN

The four of them, Popoford, Hendricks, and the two guards got into a waiting car. The guards sat in the front seats, Popoford, and Hendricks in the back.

"What's with H.O.? The man's out of his mind."

"He may be a bit eccentric, true, but he's not insane. The man is the most remarkable man I've ever met."

"Remarkably belligerent."

"He has his reasons. I've seen him quite calm and loving."

"Get off it, Hendricks. Tell me what's next. What's your part in all this crap?"

"I'm to oversee your work. I'm to remind you that two murders are hanging over your head." Hendricks had been looking out the window at the rain. He turned to Popoford. "You know that H.O. thinks you're the best agent he's ever had, don't you?"

Popoford paused. "I had my doubts. Before I finally met him, that is." He looked out his window and tried to understand the reason for such a great lie. Was it meant to soften his resolve? Was it a persuasive technique? It was disgusting, like everything Popoford had learned about the little man. A man who would be God. He was a man trusted by five presidents. He was a protector of the faith, a little man charged with the safekeeping of ideals. He was a murderer protecting national security. Yet H.O. was contemptible, demeaning, and unscrupulous; even willing to demoralize his own agent. Popoford opened the folder and began to read.

It was one of those lengthy bureaucratic jumbles of endless details collected as if by design but arranged in the most haphazard and confusingly random ways imaginable. There were lists and graphs, footnotes and internal references, italics, and boldface, uppercase emphasis, lower-case subtlety, and every manner of dialectic jargon, all intended to justify the existence of unneeded researchers, and all distilled into three paragraphs in the introduction as a theoretical postulation and appearing again, word for word, in the end, as a surety. The words, front and back, ignored and negated the effort between them.

If it were possible to be more confused by anything, Popoford couldn't imagine what it might be. It seemed the point of the report was to detail the various "proofs" that constituted a need to eliminate the president. In the past, Popoford wouldn't have thought twice about whether those proofs were logical, verifiable, or even truthful. In the past, he wouldn't have questioned the need for the killing of any person H.O. said to kill. He would have merely accepted the assignment. Do your job, serve your country: that had been Popoford's motto. That had been his rationale for continuing to play the role of secret agent, of spy, of assassin. Now he was concerned. Of the proofs, Popoford now felt doubt. Of his obedience, Popoford now felt creeping disdain. He looked up from the page, out to the quiet world of trees and soil nurtured by the rain. For once he wanted more reason than H.O.'s report. To kill the president, Popoford needed a better reason than what he'd read.

"There's no reason to do it," he said offhandedly, as if to himself. "No reason at all."

"How can you say that, George?" Hendricks was shaken.

Popoford slowly turned his head to face the man. "There's no real reason here," he said, waving the report in Hendricks' face. He was getting uncomfortable himself.

"Reasons? What the hell do you need reasons for? No one needs reasons in our business. Greed, power, and love of country have always been enough reason. You've got a job. Do it."

"Just because of the balance of trade? Just because the bastard is supposedly compromising us with the enemy? Impeach the son-of-a-bitch! Don't shoot him."

"That's fucking insubordination, Mixer!"

Popoford was stunned at Hendricks' words. "Insubordination? Hendricks, have you lost your mind? I'm not exactly here of my free will. There is a matter of coercion. You're not my commander anymore."

"Yes, Mixer, I am. You've been reactivated." Hendricks was red.

"Go to hell," Popoford said. "You need me. I seem to be the only agent you have. Without me you have nothing. Without me and my talents, you're nothing but a pair of childish traitors plotting the assassination of the president. This is a conspiracy to overthrow the government. Without me, you have no power to fight such allegations, and you'll have no revenge. Now maybe you could stop talking about insubordination and start talking about reasons. I want real reasons."

Hendricks glared at Popoford. It was the same look that H.O. had on his face, but on Hendricks, it had the look of defeat. He said nothing.

"I'm going to ask you some questions," Popoford said, his confidence rising. "Answer them," he demanded and glanced at Hendricks. The man didn't flinch. He had controlled himself. Popoford saw the look of a true professional in Hendricks' eyes. He would play the game by the new rules. He would be confident that control would soon return to him. Manipulate from a weak position, he would tell himself. Eventually, the agent, Mixer, will

be mine again. Popoford was determined to disappoint
Hendricks.

"Why was Home Office cut back so drastically?"

Hendricks didn't hesitate. "We were getting close to the
president's organization."

"The director has already given me that horseshit. I want
details."

"Where should I begin?"

"Come on. You tell me."

"Well, there were some early whispers, during the primary
campaign, about the president's connection with the enemy's
head of security. They went to school together."

"So what? Everybody knows that."

"Of course, but that was the beginning of our suspicions. We
investigated. That's was nothing new. We investigate all the
candidates. We didn't find anything unusual. After all, our country
has educated many of our enemy's best men. What did catch our
attention was something that happened during the president's
second year in office."

Hendricks paused for a moment and directed the driver
through the streets of downtown Hayward. They went up "C"
past the post office and the old courthouse, past the few derelict
buildings, left behind when sudden growth began to spread the
town toward the bay. They went up the hills to concrete plateaus
where roads met as if by mistake. From there they drove past
Castro Valley Village and into rain-greened Crow Canyon. Even
through the car's ventilators, the air smelled wet and fresh.
Popoford breathed deeply as he listened to Hendricks. There was
a certain pitch to his old boss's voice that gave Popoford the
feeling that he was being told the truth. He couldn't pinpoint it,
but it was there.

"So what happened," Popoford said, and Hendricks continued.

"We received a copy of a telegram that had originated from the capitol. It had been addressed to the president and was from a certain senator."

"Which senator?" Popoford asked.

"It doesn't matter."

"Which senator, Hendricks?" Popoford demanded.

"Senator Boscwell."

"Junior Senator from California. One of the president's closest allies . . ."

"Correct. More so than you know. H.O. himself wanted the telegram looked into. I must say that I thought it was a waste of time. It could have been a fake. It would be so easy to fake a telegram."

"So what did it say?"

"That's the point. It was easy to fake, and it was nonsense. It said, 'Has my piggy gone to market?' I figured it for a hoax. I was wrong."

Popoford was fascinated. "That's kind of a silly code."

"I thought so, but H.O. insisted that I personally look into it. I did just that. It took me a long time and effort, but I can distill my findings for you. The message was a direct reference to the enemy's intelligence officer, David Konklin. Senator Boscwell wanted to know if Konklin had sold our country down the drain yet. He wanted to know if the president had completed the secretly-agreed-to sharing of intelligence information with our enemies!"

Hendricks was incredulous. Popoford was stunned. "But that's treason!" Popoford whispered.

"Exactly. It's treason that has been secretly plotted by our own elected president, our worst enemy's Prime Minister, and several minor officials on both sides."

"Damn! Popoford said. "Is big business involved?"

"Not directly. That surprised me, but only government types are involved over here. Over there the whole intelligence community is working for this treaty. God knows they'd give up almost anything to know what we've been up to. We'd be defenseless."

"Of course," Popoford said, "but how do you mean big business is not involved?"

"Hell, they'd lose everything if that treaty is signed. At first, I thought that there was some kind of one-worlder plot to join the two governments together. You know, some kind of plan to rule the world through its money supply. It's not an inconceivable idea. Lord knows it's been tried before. But that wasn't it with this little plan. No, this was an act of treason. This was a plan to put our enemy's president at the head of both countries. And, George," Hendricks reached over and touched Popoford on the arm, "George, it's working. If he isn't stopped, if another man isn't put in his place very soon, he will completely deliver all of us, including big business, into the hands of tyrants. Don't you see, George? The heads of state will share secret documents while the president will direct our agencies to undertake covert operations which will jeopardize our operatives and the very freedom of our people."

Popoford began to see what was happening. He saw most of the picture. He understood the urgency. He understood the need. He could put the pieces together about the telegram, the California connection with Senator Boscwell, the eventual signing of the treaty with the enemy, the dissolution of Home Office. He could understand why Home Office still tried to operate with limited resources and agents to try to stop the completion of the plot. He could understand all that. What he couldn't understand was why the president hadn't eliminated Home Office altogether. Why had he allowed any money to be fed to it? It made no sense. The other thing that bothered Popoford was how snide the Director had been. There was no reason for his behavior. Popoford would have expected the opposite treatment. Instead of respect, Popoford got blackmail and nasty remarks. Hendricks said that he would say nothing further about Home Office, but the funding hadn't been brought up.

"How do you keep going?" he asked.

"We're kept going with limited funds. They are meant to keep the populace from becoming suspicious."

"But it would be so easy to get some hot reporter to get your story printed. Hell! It's the biggest story in years."

"It wouldn't be believed. You mustn't forget that Home Office is not the most popular agency in the land. Most people think we should be eliminated. Our demise would make a lot of people happy."

"So why doesn't the president just cut us off and take the applause for getting rid of a rotting agency?"

"He's saving that for later. He keeps us in his back pocket for future votes. He has cut the agency back so far that H.O. is personally funding your reactivation."

"Out of his own pocket?"

"Yes. It's the only way."

"But how does that explain the other people who are involved in this thing? How does that explain the men who killed the woman? How does that explain the fat man?"

"The fat man was a lie. He wasn't our agent. We think that he was one of the president's men. We think they wanted you for themselves. He fell into our plans very nicely, however. The others we do not know."

"Then President Bjoonic knows about our plot?" Popoford asked.

"No. We've maintained secrecy. The president wasn't stupid enough to help finance his own overthrow, so H.O. had to do it himself."

"But what about other agencies. There must be some agency that could force him to resign quietly. We could avoid a scandal."

"We must not avoid a scandal. We must expose the whole ugly mess. We must not allow another president to do this again."

"But what about getting help from industry? What about the banks? Surely they would want to help expose the traitor."

"Publicly the banks are out of the question. Privately, they've supplemented H.O.'s contributions, making it possible for you to be our private soldier."

Popoford looked at Hendricks. He knew what a private soldier was. It meant that he was completely out of bounds. He would be working alone. There would be only one chance, and it would be his chance alone.

"You're in a great deal of danger, George. The president's men know that you've returned. That's why they sent the woman. They wanted you for themselves. They were prepared to kill you if they couldn't have you. They're prepared to kill you now.

"You think that the woman was the only agent they sent after me?" Popoford asked.

"The woman, the fat man, and Gretchen. Why?"

"I'm just asking. Can't be too careful."

"No, of course not."

Popoford was still uneasy about Home Office not knowing about the girl. They should have known about her. He could question Hendricks. He could tell him about the girl, but he felt that knowledge of her was somehow an ace up his sleeve. Somehow she was protection for him, and he didn't want to give away good cards and protection all at the same time. He kept his silence, not sure why he trusted what he'd heard, yet taking every word straight to his heart. In his heart, Popoford accepted the assignment, but still, he couldn't allow his guard to drop completely. It was his training. Distrust was always a survivor's companion. He did accept the assignment, and he did intend to believe Hendricks, yet his doubt was kept alive by the girl climbing the mountain.

He thought of the girl as he looked out the window. The rain had slowed, and he could clearly see the ridges of the folded hills in the distance, and he saw a woman standing there, far away, standing on the ridge, waiting. He imagined it was the girl, waiting for him.

CHAPTER ELEVEN

"Where are we going?" Popoford asked.

"To a staging area. You'll receive instructions."

"Final instructions, as always," Popoford said.

"That's right," Hendricks responded. "We never assume our agents will return. We can't count on success. Never. There are always contingency plans. You know that, George."

"Yes," Popoford said, as the car was driven off the paved road and onto a soggy, muddy rut that ran through the woods for several miles.

Hendricks glanced at Popoford and shrugged. "If you fail or are about to be captured, you must end it yourself. Kill yourself."

"Yes, of course," Popoford said to Hendricks' shrug, "That's my problem."

"You know we must be on the outside of this one. Completely on the outside. You'll be operating as if in enemy territory. They have most of the cards. They have the law. They have enforcement. You must work freely, without a leash. And without recognition"

"Ah. The great and mandatory disavowal of the agent and his deeds." Popoford wasn't commenting on the ethics of the agency's code of irresponsibility. It just sounded that way to Hendricks.

"It's the same as always," the commander said defensively.

"Of course. It's what I would expect," Popoford said without gravity. He was looking at the large farmhouse that had appeared in a clearing and was more interested in its aging siding than he was in the commander's feelings.

"This is where I get my papers?"

"In a manner of speaking."

"'Certifiably sanctified, he kills without conscience. Later, in his lonely room, he waits without remorse for the call of thanks that will never come.'"

"Please!" Hendricks gasped. "Spare me the melodrama. Nothing has changed. You know that. Nothing in this business will ever change. The rhythm is constant. It doesn't matter who we're working for as long as we're working."

Popoford turned slowly to Hendricks. He wanted his words to have a heavy impact. "Get this straight, Commander, I haven't changed either. I care who hires me. Remember that." Popoford opened the car door and got out. His foot hit the gravel just as the car came to a stop.

Hendricks got out. He acted as if he hadn't heard Popoford. He told the driver to park the car around back. "And stay with it. I don't want anything to go wrong."

"Like what?" Popoford asked.

"Nothing special, George. It's just the usual precaution."

Popoford growled to show his apparent understanding.

"Come on, George, let's get inside. It's starting to pour."

Popoford and Hendricks trotted to the front door of the monstrous farmhouse and went inside to the cold, empty entry hall. There was a dank odor about the place. There was a feeling that no one had ever laughed within the walls of this house. It never had been nor would be a home.

"Where did you find this disappointment?" Popoford asked.

"We built it for our uses."

"Very humble architecture."

"Yes, I see what you mean," Hendricks replied, missing the point.

"I suppose you do."

"Come, George, let's go into the library. We can turn the heater on. We'll be warmed up in no time."

Hendricks led the way through the great atrium where a wide stairway wound up a curving wall past silvery windows. The light at the head of the stairs was a cold, artificial light that barely lit the house.

On the ground floor, there was a hall. It was dark, and it was lined with countless rows and columns of darkly painted and gold-leafed framed oils worth many hundreds of thousands.

"You'd make a bundle if you sold this place," Popoford said. " H.O. wouldn't have to use his own money to finance our work."

"This is his collection. This is his house," Hendricks replied, with an outburst of vicarious pride.

"Well, well. The little man has done quite well for himself."

"Watch it, Mixer. A little respect, please. You don't know what you're talking about."

"No, don't suppose I do. Who does?"

Hendricks didn't reply and Popoford remembered that he tried never to answer rhetorical questions. Popoford noted again this quaintly non-intellectual, non-courageous chink in the commander's character. Truly, nothing had changed. Truly, the repetition of behavior could be played if need be. Hendricks was so predictable and Popoford could manipulate him and maybe even H.O. himself. Popoford kept that thought for later. It might come in handy if he needed to bring H.O. to the ground.

Hendricks opened the library door and let Popoford in.

"You should be able to find some scotch in that cabinet, George. Pour me a strong one, will you, please. I need to warm up."

Popoford found the whiskey and poured one for Hendricks. He poured a bigger one for himself. Hendricks had knelt and had leaned into the large fireplace to light the gas fire. The distinct odor of sulfurous gas leaked into the room, but his smokey scotch covered the acrid odor as the sulfur dissipated and the room began to warm up.

"So let's get on with it, Hendricks. I don't have time to screw around."

"Nor have I," Hendricks said, taking his glass of scotch from Popoford. He gulped at it without care for the excellent draught, then he set the glass on a table and quickly turned around. He pulled a screen down from the ceiling, pushed several buttons, and the lights went out, the curtain closed, and the projector started to roll.

"This is the entrance to the war headquarters of the president. Here, on October 1st, you will approach the president and assassinate him. The job must be done before five o'clock when the president is scheduled to sign the treaties which we've discussed. After five will be too late."

The film continued to roll. The cameraman had dollied through the various corridors of the war bunker. It was a concrete slab building with thick walls and bare-bulbed halls that glared in an unsophisticated imitation of Home Office. It was the usual government building of the day. It was built for defense.

Hendricks continued. "Here you can see the guard desk. There are two men on duty at the desk at all times. Two more are seated just behind that wall. They are watching monitors with cameras aimed at the desk and the front door. Here are the cameras."

"Yes, I see them," Popoford said. "Where are the other monitors located?"

"There's a group of them on the landings of each floor. That makes six more there. Then there are two more sets on each floor.

They are in the main offices on those floors. That makes eighteen altogether."

"Someone is always watching."

"Needless to say."

"Where do you expect the president to be? What room? What floor?"

"I have no idea. All I can do is draw on what I know of him and his habits. He'll want to have the signing be a public event. He'll go on television. The only rooms, except for his private living quarters, that are prepared for such a broadcast are on the thirtieth floor. Thirty floors underground. They adjoin his quarters. I think he'll be there at five."

"Sounds a little risky. Why must he be reached there? Why must I be so close to him? Why must we be so close to the deadline."

"In the first place, he's there now. There will be no other opportunity for the kill. It must come from you."

"Fat chance that I'll get out of there. Even if I can pass for one of them, I'll be detained. Everyone will be. How can I possibly get in touch with you to confirm?"

"There will be a way."

Popoford glanced up at Hendricks. "From the inside?"

"In a manner of speaking."

"What are my odds? I know you've calculated them. What chance do I have of getting out of there alive?"

"You're a patriot, George. Let's not talk about odds."

"That bad." It wasn't a question. Popoford would expect nothing less than impossible odds in a kill such as this.

"No sense lying to you. You haven't got a chance. Worse, you'll die a traitor. Your fellow citizens will never know what a patriot you are. It would be too destructive to the country's stability to let the plot become public knowledge. The president must die a martyr. You must die a traitor."

"Well, don't bury me yet. I just may get back to you. Stranger things have happened." Popoford had to keep hope alive even as he accepted the inevitability of his sudden death. "If I do get out, I'll need your cover. I'll need your help."

"If the need arises. We'll consider the possibilities at that time."

"Yes, I suppose you will." Popoford poured himself another scotch. "What is your preferred method of death?"

"Weapons will be out of the question. You could never get one into the compound. You could use your hands, but that would take too long and we want to give you every chance to escape. Brute force would be suicide, even for you, George, especially since he must die on television."

"What?"

" H.O. wants the president killed during the broadcast."

"That's absurd. You're crazy!"

"It must be public. There must be public empathy and anguish."

Popoford stared at Hendricks. The man was serious. "You're cutting the timing too close."

"It's important that the public see him die. We'll then have time to round up all the enemies of our country while the people run around hysterically. There will be chaos, and we will get a lot of work done. Anyway, George, martyrs like the president shouldn't die alone when they can have a following."

"Fine. I get the point. So how do I do it?"

"Injection. Precisely timed. He'll die while on the air."

"Plastic syringe?"

"Naturally. Disposable, with time-released strychnine."

"What's that? Something new?"

"Sort of. The poison is encased in viscous bubbles. They'll slowly dissolve in his bloodstream. You'll have ten minutes to get away. Not much time, but all we can expect with present technology."

Hendricks reached into his pocket and withdrew the syringe. By the light of the projector, Popoford could see it wrapped in a clear plastic bag. The bag was factory sealed.

"You get that sort of thing packaged like that and ready to go right from the manufacturer?" Popoford asked. "Is there that big a call for such things these days?"

"More than you might expect, George. The world has gotten very complicated lately."

"Don't you believe it, Hendricks. This is simply an expedient murder. Not complicated at all, and not at all a new idea."

Hendricks didn't reply, but instead, he pushed the buttons again, and the projector went off and the lights came on.

"Go over to that closet, George. You'll find the uniform of a Brigadier. Take it with you. There's I.D. in the pants. You'll find it handy."

Popoford did what he was told and Hendricks continued. "The boys will take you to the front door of the bunker. It's up to you to do the rest."

"Will you be watching television at five o'clock?"

"Day after tomorrow. Make it a good show."

Popoford smiled slightly. One way or the other, it would be a good show. Popoford reached out and took the syringe from Hendricks. Just as he put it into the side pocket of his dress jacket, he heard the hollow report of a short-barreled shotgun. It was muffled and came from outside, from behind the house. Instinctively he dove under a nearby desk. He reached for the pistol that he'd left behind at Home Office. When he realized that it wasn't there, he jumped up again and dashed through the door into the hallway.

"Not that way, George. Back there. There's a door behind another curtain."

Popoford darted through the back door. He looked over his shoulder and saw the girl jumping into the room. He slammed the door before she fired again, and ran down a short hall, through a pantry, and then outside onto the gravel driveway.

Popoford paused for a second. The pouring rain had diminished. He listened. There was only silence about him, silence, and the undertones of birds singing distinct but distant songs through the drizzle. There was a warning in the quiet, and Popoford felt a shiver race up his back. There was no time for contemplation. He jumped back into action. He ran along the gravel driveway, around the back of the house. He found two cars there. Both had government plates. The thugs would be in one of the cars ready to drive away. He'd be out of this jam in a minute.

He raced towards the cars but couldn't see the guards in either one. He grabbed the handle on the first car and opened the driver's door. One of the guards fell at his feet. Popoford rolled the body off his shoes. Its head had no face. He looked into the back seat. The other guard was there on the floor. His face had also been blown away.

Both front and back seats were pools of blood. The upholstery was splattered with unidentifiable flesh. Popoford forced back a gag. The scene compelled him to close the door and hurry to the other car in the hope of escape. He opened the door and got in. The keys were in the ignition.

He couldn't allow himself to think of the butchery in the other car. His mind focused on the situation. The window of the first car was open. The girl must have enticed the men to lower it. In the rain, they would have kept it closed otherwise. Her aim had been unimpeded. She'd done her work quickly, without warning. The thugs had died while they still talked to her. She was badass cold, but she sure the hell wasn't going to get Popoford. Not if he could help it.

He started the car and slammed it into gear. Gravel sprayed into the air. The car fishtailed toward the house, and before Popoford could get it straightened out, it had blasted gravel into the blown-out picture window. He didn't bother to look over his shoulder at the window, the view in his mirror told him enough. Hendricks and the girl were standing side by side, together almost like compatriots. However, she had the shotgun at his temple and he wasn't smiling. Gravel still dripped from their heads. He saw all this in a glance. Details that he would normally commit to memory were blown completely away with Hendricks' head as the girl pulled the trigger.

Popoford wrenched the car around the corner of the house and aimed the nose of the hulk at the road. He drove without thinking, as if in a trance. For a short while, his mind lost all consciousness, and it operated without his advice or consent. Popoford was also badass cold.

When his mind finally took over again, he found himself on the road to Reno. He had passed Whimsy an hour earlier. He was making good time. The drizzling rain had stopped for a while. Heavy clouds lurked on the peaks of the Sierras, but the air was so clean that Popoford could see them clearly. He could see many things clearly.

It was always the same after a scene of great violence-the shift into autopilot, the ensuing clarity. They were just defense mechanisms against the revulsion that he felt when he saw violence. He was a man very ill-suited for his profession, at least it sometimes seemed that way to him. But at times like this, when he could see everything with perfect clarity, Popoford knew that it was men like him, men with sensibilities, with fear and loathing for their work, that were the best assassins. They were men of passion, men of patriotism, men who wouldn't allow the corruption of the country to succeed. He was one of those men. He was a man of duty, a man of intensely-felt pride, and yet a sad and humble man who cried at his life's melancholy. But the greater good was of most importance and one thing was clear to Popoford: the duly elected president aspired to deliver them handily up to their mortal enemies. Popoford would do his job.

A mist developed as Popoford drove into the foothills west of Tahoe. He would be able to kill the president. He would be able to do it with ease. By killing one, misguided man, many lives could be saved, because if the president did sign the treaty, the people would resist. Many would die before the enemy was driven out. Popoford could stop that bloodshed.

He drove on and thought of other possibilities. There were many, but they all were too extreme, all required that he fail. He wouldn't fail. He wouldn't allow the plot to succeed.

A black rain broke into the afternoon. He slowed on the curves leading down the mountain. In the distance, he knew that the lake spread out toward distant forests and peaks but he couldn't see that far. Still, his mind focused as he considered that the people would never rise up. Enemy infiltration had been quietly going on for years. If the treaty were signed, the people probably wouldn't notice. It might not speed up, but it would continue as it had; the enemy merely walking in one by one, to take their seats within the nation's government agencies and corporate desks. They would come and be welcomed as soldiers against inequity and asymmetry. It was a battle plan of long-standing and the treaty was another act in a war of patience. It seemed to Popoford to have had no distinct beginning. Certainly, it would have no distinct end, but little actions could slow it down. Little efforts, individual deeds, could worry and distract the enemy. Little deaths could delay many things. His actions could cause the enemy's patient achievements to slip and even slide away.

Popoford's continued driving, stopping only for gas as he continued east. It was dark by the time he'd left the lights of Salt Lake City behind. He had less than forty-eight hours left. It was plenty of time if nothing went wrong. He only had to get to eastern Nebraska. If he could stay awake, he could be there on time.

He had filled his tank but had underestimated the capacity of his stomach. He would have breakfast in the morning. In Colorado. Until then, he would distract himself by listening to the driving rain trying to get inside the car and by tuning in a local radio station.

The weatherman reported that the rain was spread over the entire country. There wasn't a dry spot in all the land. The news didn't make him feel better. Popoford preferred misery without company, and above all, he preferred that the rain should quit for the day. It would make driving a lot easier.

The radio had told Popoford something else. Hendricks' death hadn't been reported. It didn't matter. It was only that Popoford would have preferred that something had been said. Now he wasn't sure how to interpret the lack of news. It could be nothing, just the usual suppression for security reasons. At any rate, the president would know everything by now. The girl would pass everything along. He would know that Home Office had lost its number two man. He would also know that Popoford hadn't been killed and to expect his assassin. Popoford would have to take extra precautions. He wouldn't be able to drop by as one of the boys, a brigadier with special clearance. His old covers wouldn't work, not the reporter bit, nor the repairman front. He would have to melt even more thoroughly into the precise network of systems and individuals that protected, disguised, and blurred the movements of the president. As he drove, he struggled to create a new plan that would easily bring him in direct contact with the president. By sunup, Popoford was drifting with the car into Nebraska and no new plan had materialized.

He was exhausted and was on the verge of losing consciousness. He ran his hand continuously through his hair. From time to time he saw visions - distinct, solid, three-dimensional - vying for his share of the road. He pulled over into a ditch when he realized he'd end up there anyway if he didn't rest for a while. Better to choose one's own time, and he fell into a deep sleep in which he dreamed vividly of a voice that moaned without cessation. When he awoke, a muggy March 25th afternoon had arrived on the Great Plains. He was behind schedule, and events would now choose time for him.

CHAPTER TWELVE

The rain had stopped about the time that he was passing through the Sand Hills, and the morning had smoothed a creamy, tan light over the plains. The road wound as if by necessity through the softened mounds. The brown grasses of winter were beginning to green. This would be an especially short spring, and soon the welcomed new sun would grow old and tiresome. Soon it would scorch the grass blades back to brown. In the distance, a small herd of bison ran toward the horizon. They scattered a flock of roosting sandhill cranes from their breeding grounds. From Popoford's distance, there was no sign of the large beast's passing. He had spied them by chance, and now he found it hard to keep sight of them. In dry weather, the plume of dust would have pointed to them even after Popoford had left the hills. But the ground was soaked. There was no dust. Popoford lost them for good when the road dipped into the next wash.

The road from the Sand Hills to Omaha was essentially straight, and Popoford settled back and drove easily. He kept a sharp eye on the road, but he saw nothing suspicious. Traffic was normal.

At noon he stopped for gas and watched the road while the attendant filled the tank. No one faltered when they drove past his car. No one pulled off the road a few blocks further on. The girl wasn't driving one of the cars and Popoford concluded that she had flown ahead. She knew where he was going. He could relax until he got to Omaha.

"You a government man?" the attendant asked when he gave Popoford's credit card back.

Popoford froze for the briefest of instants. "How did you know?" he said, without looking into the man's eyes.

"Well hell, mister, that there's a government plate on your car. I ain't no idiot, ya know."

"No, of course, you're not. I just wasn't thinking. Sure, I'm a government man."

"Next time you see the president, you tell him something from one of the people, will ya?"

"I don't think I'll . . ."

"Don't be putting me off. You just tell him that Gerald Casper is sure happy he voted for him. Got that?"

"Yes, I've got that," Popoford said as he got back into the car. "I'll be sure to give him the message if . . . when I see him."

The attendant closed Popoford's door for him. "Thank you, mister."

He had a wide grin on his face. "Remember. It's Casper, Gerald Casper."

"I sure will, Mr. Casper." Popoford drove away. The attendant stood in his driveway and waved the government man on his way. He was happy. He thought that his voice would be heard. Popoford was saddened that the man considered himself a player when he was only a pawn. It made Popoford sad to see men like Gerald Casper, men who thought their opinions counted and that the president cared and could be swayed him. But Popoford had a new idea dredged from his confused memory: the country might well survive the death of this president. The systems, agencies, and customs might be unshakable. The country could survive its horror and it would go on to prosper. It could maintain a new martyr, a new, one-dimensional symbol of a past that had never been, a symbol worthy of the adoration of impotent citizens like Gerald Casper.

Popoford glanced at his watch. It was 7:30 p.m. He was crossing the Elkhorn. The water was high in her banks, nearly flooding, racing to the Missouri River. He could see the trees of the big river and Omaha as the road stretched out of the lowlands. Popoford slowed the car and pulled over at the top of the highest bluff.

Behind him, he could see the Great Plains stretching to the horizon. Out of the western sky, another storm was coming, building rapidly into black and billowy clouds, racing on a howling wind, driving the calm away. In front of him, he could see the Missouri River Valley and the bluffs of Iowa. He could see Omaha resting in its three-year time lag, working a parallel time frame pointing west, yet accepting the hand-me-down innovations of others. As one old fellow had told Popoford once, you can't just jump into new things with both feet. Let other folks have the screwy ideas. If any of them are worth a damn, we'll be using them soon: just you wait and see.

Popoford had once thought the good people of Omaha, had the right idea. Now he wasn't sure. He was only sure that he was glad to be back again. He wished he could stay. He wished that he had three years to slow down, to catch up. Even the isolation of Whimsy wasn't as comforting as the sight of Omaha. Popoford wished that he hadn't been assigned to kill the president. Omaha would suffer for his deed.

Popoford looked down the road for the girl. He sensed she was somewhere close, somewhere in Omaha, but she wasn't on the road. He scanned the hills and the valley, and then he got back into his car and drove the rest of the way down I-80 into town.

It was a familiar way. I-80 turned into Dodge Street and passed Boy's Town. Straight away it went up and down the small hills, past 90th Street and the memories it held, past the university and the breath of progressive narrowness, three beats lagging, that filled its halls. Past the quiet, tree-lined streets it went, its old brick still laid in parts, its potholes huge from the leverage of a hard winter. Popoford passed Tiny Naylor's on that road and continued into the downtown.

Omaha had changed. That was the only thing that Popoford could see in the new buildings. He didn't like it. The town hadn't waited for his return. He was angry that she'd grown up a little without him. But it didn't matter. It couldn't matter. He had come back to Omaha to do a job. There was no time to fret about memories. He was no favorite son anyway. What the hell could he expect? What had he expected?

He turned south and drove through the Old Market area. He only allowed himself a glance up the street. The bar, Mr. Toad's, was still there. Nate, Rusty, Al; everyone would be there still. If they were still alive. If they hadn't moved away. If things had stayed the same. But, no. Popoford knew that they hadn't. He drove on, past the temptation to find out. He had a job to do.

It was 8:30 p.m. Popoford would be on the road out of Omaha in less than four hours. He hoped. In the meantime, he had to find the president and avoid being spotted by a highly trained Secret Service team who knew exactly what he looked like. He then had to inject the president with a special, time-release poison, and then he had to get away. His odds weren't the best, but he'd survived other assignments which were themselves dangerous propositions. This assignment was, however, very much different. It was the most dangerous thing that he'd ever attempted. It was too dangerous for a sane, average agent to pull off. As he drove past the entrance to Offutt Air Force Base he knew the job was suicide. There was no way to get out of it alive. He'd been lucky over the years. He'd also been exceptionally good. Despite the crap that Home Office was dishing out, he was the best agent they had. When he'd been put on cases in the old days, the enemy would have been better off just surrendering. Then again, those were the old days and Hendricks had colored his memory. Those were the old assignments: the deeds of the Popoford-of-old, a younger man, a more intrepid man, a boy, a fool.

"Dammit!" Popoford gritted through his clenched teeth. "I'm still a bloody fool. I can still do it!"

His outburst startled him and he fell silent. He was having doubts. He reconsidered his chances and prepared to die.

He drove another two miles, then pulled over to the side of the road. The entrance to the bunker was still half a mile ahead. He would wait in the car until dark. It would only be a few hours. He might get some sleep. He closed his eyes.

Suddenly he realized what a stupid decision he had made parking so near the bunker.

"Don't move! Stay where you are!" an amplified voice blasted through the car windows and sat Popoford straight up. He looked around. A group of five Marines was charging the car. They were a hundred yards behind him. Another group was headed toward him coming from the gate. They were carrying machine guns. Popoford considered jumping out of the car and diving into the brush. He thought better of that plan when he heard a helicopter hovering overhead.

He started the car's engine. He considered waiting for the men to get close so that he could run them down. He reconsidered. The other men would blow him right out of the car. Popoford stopped thinking then and drove his foot into the floorboard and blew the crap out of the souped-up engine as he redlined it and filled the street with dust and gravel. He aimed the car for the men in front of him. They all stopped and calmly took up firing positions. Popoford tapped his brake pedal. He turned the wheel and spun the car's rear end at the men. His rear window disappeared in splinters. He bled, but he didn't know it. But he was that he was alive. No direct hits. He lived. He had stopped thinking but knew he lived.

Popoford drove bent low beside the steering wheel. He peered over the dashboard to see the road but didn't aim at the men who had been approaching from the rear. Though he hadn't aimed at them, he did manage to hit a Marine. Popoford's gut wrenched. He hated injuring the man. The two of them were alike in the way they would embrace sacrifice. They worked for the same country. They fought the same enemy. Popoford often thought, in times of reflection, that it would always be the same for his country. The armed forces would defend her even when the enemy was at her head. The men who died today would die foolhardy, ironic deaths. His fate would be the same if he failed.

The helicopter dipped in front of Popoford. A man was hanging out of the cockpit. He had a rifle pointed right at Popoford's head. Popoford jerked the wheel again. Bullets plunged into the seat next to him. He accelerated and saw the road ahead. It went straight for several miles, paralleling the river. He drove as fast as he could. The helicopter kept pace with him, as was to be expected, but it didn't overtake him. The man didn't shoot at the car anymore. They would tag along until Popoford made a mistake. Then they would come in for the kill. They knew who he was. They would respect his ability, but if they wanted him alive, they didn't respect it enough. Such a miscalculation could save his life and let him get away.

Popoford looked at his gas gauge. He was almost out of fuel. That was good. When the car crashed, there would be little chance of a fire. He took a quick look around him. Several cars were racing down the road behind him.

Popoford looked to the front again. He saw a side road that led down to the river. This was his chance if ever there was one. He pulled onto the dirt road without letting up on the speed. His hands were off the wheel; his foot was driving the car. Gravel was again flying everywhere. He saw the dock. He saw the people just getting out of the rowboat, back from a wet day of bottom fishing. He saw the looks on their faces as they realized that the car was headed right for them. He saw their instant movements as they twisted in unison away from the dock and pitched themselves into the river. He saw them as he passed them. He saw the river waiting for him. He took a great breath and relaxed as best he could, in an instant, so that he could better take the impact.

The crash came. He felt the cold river surround him, and he began to swim. He swam out of the car through the rear window. He swam hard for the opposite shore. He had to stay underwater, had to swim upstream, had to do what they least expected. He had to survive.

When he got to the other side, he slowly came up for air, letting his lips break water first. He took the first, welcome gasp of air as slowly as he could. He had to be quiet. He looked up through an inch of water toward the sky. He saw the overhanging brush and knew his luck was holding. He poked his head out of the water, staying close to the bank, hidden as best as possible under the brush. He saw the helicopter hovering over the dock. He saw the cars that had been following him. He saw the uniformed air police pulling the fishing party out of the water. He saw the plainclothes men pointing to the place where the car had gone in. He saw that they had radios. He saw them waving to the helicopter, and he saw it fly slowly downstream to search for his body.

Popoford grabbed another lung full of air and slid beneath the surface. The sun was setting. It would be dark very soon. He would swim in small segments, underwater, to the riverside of the bunker. He would have no time to catch up on his sleep.

CHAPTER THIRTEEN

Popoford examined the situation. From the water, he didn't have the best view of the bunker, but he could see the main building over the crest of the bank. He could see the head of a six-foot man who walked guard along the building's foundation. Anything below five feet was hidden. That wasn't good. Neither was it good that he hadn't had a chance to prepare for the stalking. He'd needed a little time, a little sleep, to consider a subtle approach. His plan now would be blunt. It would be very risky.

Dusk had settled on the stream. There had been no rain for several hours. Popoford couldn't remember the sun shining that day, but there was a warmth about that hinted of sweet spring.

Downstream, the helicopter had long since turned on its spotlight. Its Sun Gun swept the Missouri where the river widened gracefully into a long, left turn. Troops rummaged in the underbrush on both banks. That was good. No one seriously considered the possibility that he might have gone upstream.

Popoford looked back at the bunker. Lights spread against its gray, stucco walls. The guard's head floated back and forth on the edge of the bank. They may not be expecting him, but they would be ready for any intrusion of the compound.

He began swimming breaststroke fully clothed toward the bunker.

It was a narrow bit of light sparkling in the tall grasses up shore that first caught Popoford's eye. A tiny flashlight had been turned on for an instant. It hadn't been meant for his eyes. Someone else was stalking the bunker. It had to be the girl. Popoford was certain of it. He also knew that she was unaware of his presence so close to her. He swam silently toward the bank, keeping one eye on the guard and another on the darkness where the light had been.

Suddenly he realized that he'd underestimated the girl once again. He saw a brilliant flash from the brush upstream. He heard a quick splash just in front of him. Another flash. Another splash. He was being shot at. There was only a modest report from the blast. The girl was using a suppressor on her rifle, and it was probably equipped with a night-vision scope sight. She was a pro, and she seemed to know where Popoford was going even before he knew himself. She was always in the most strategic positions when he arrived. She'd always gotten the drop on him. He'd always thought that she was incapable of being clever, even though each time that he'd run into her she'd always outsmarted him. He'd been a fool.

She could have killed him at any time. An agent that good who didn't kill, who didn't take advantage when she could was very strange. There was danger in her individuality. There was danger in that Popoford couldn't read her. There was danger in that he'd been a fool.

He let himself sink beneath the water. He hoped that the lung full of air could help him get upstream of her. He swam strongly upriver even though his soaked clothes boughed him down.

The water was black and laden with fine silt from winter's exceptionally heavy flooding. He closed his eyes. He tested the current so that he could stay close to the river's flow. When his chest began to ache for air, he turned toward the shore. He swam with great caution then, but still, he ran into the bank. He was startled and lunged with a great splashing from the river.

Popoford blinked rapidly, trying to clear his eyes. He squinted through the sparkling blur. He slowly let out his breath.

His eyes had focused on a shaded flashlight. Its pinpoint back-lit the barrel of a rifle. The muzzle was inches from his face. He'd done it again.

"Come out of the water. Come out slowly. I want to get a good look at the greatest agent Home Office could muster."

Popoford rose and walked from the river. He had a fleeting, disgusting thought. He saw himself at that moment from another point of view. He was a soaking beast who had bungled another day's work. He was a hound, sodden with disgraceful error. He should have been shot. In the real world, he would have been shot. Why had the girl let him live? If for no other reason than he made too many mistakes, she should have shot him.

"So shoot," he said, as the water from his soaked clothes rapidly forming a puddle at his feet.

"Oh, stop whining. You would have been dead long before you ever left Whimsy if we wanted it that way. You're still alive. I'm not the one who will kill you."

"Really?" Popoford sat down in front of her. Even through his clothes, the grasses of the muddy bank scratched at his neck and back. Dead, stubled stalks jabbed his legs.

He could hear the sounds of a still pool just upstream. There were frogs there anxious to begin the belated spring. They croaked their mating calls as a fresh wind blew up the fragrance from the near-derelict stockyards. "Why do you let me live? If you mean to stop me, why not kill me?"

"You're of too much use to us."

"Oh come on. Nobody's too much use."

"We don't want you for your special abilities as an agent. You just happen to be the only one there is who can do a certain job for us."

"That's nearly what H.O. said. Certainly glad to know that I'm so much in demand."

"Let's get to the point," the girl said, her precise enunciation cutting through the dark. "You're used up. Once you were good, not great, but good. You were good enough to stay alive. That's about all. Home Office had to get rid of you when you killed your hottest lead. We've never been able to understand why they ever hired you, let alone kept you on for so long.

"But none of this matters except for the fact that Home Office has selected you, their last agent, to perform a treasonable act. We not only will stop you, but we'll have you working for us very soon. We have a job for you."

"So who the hell are you?"

"All you need to know is that we're loyal countrymen."

"I'll need much more than that, darling," Popoford hissed as he suddenly lunged at her. He grabbed the rifle barrel as he swung his right foot up high and caught her in the face. The barrel burned his hand. He shoved the rifle aside and whipped his fist across her cheek. He could barely make out her features in the night, but it didn't matter. He'd knocked her cold.

Popoford caught his breath. He'd made too much noise. He crawled up the bank and peered into the compound.

The bunker remained quiet, but there were no guards. They must be on the other side of the building, he thought, as he slid back to the girl. She hadn't moved. She would be out for a long time. Popoford scrambled in the grasses and found the rifle. Then he searched the girl's clothing and found her ammunition.

"So long, darling," he muttered. "When this is over I'll try to come back for you, but don't hold your breath."

The girl lay unconscious as Popoford began his attack.

He checked his right sock for the syringe. It was there. It had remained tucked away through the river crossing. That was good. At least one part of H.O.'s plan was working, but the rest of it, the subtlety that would blend him into the bunker's operation was useless. His would be a gross and violent attack. There was nothing at all subtle about his soaked clothes.

Popoford moved along the bank back to where he should have come out of the river. He checked the rifle and reloaded it. The night vision scope was excellent. He peered through it and pointed it downstream. He could see the helicopter hovering low along the bank. There was a boat beneath it, and several men pointing toward the banks. Popoford allowed himself a brief smile and then crawled up to the edge of the bank.

He worked quickly. He looked through the scope and centered the cross-hairs on the tall guard who had returned to his dutiful march. The guard was walking the path close to the building, and his body filled the eyepiece with negative, bright green light against the dark field of the lighted bunker.

Popoford took a breath, let it out partway, held it, waited for the pause in his heartbeat, and pressed the trigger like he'd done so many times before. It was an act that no longer even needed rationalization, but it did require a certain test. In this particular sort of murder where the relatively innocent are involved, the victim must be given time for more than thoughtlessness.

The guard clutched his throat for a second, surprised, and then slowly sank against the building and to the ground. Popoford followed the guard's face. The .226 bullet had been well placed. His dying eyes glistened slightly, and Popoford thought that he glimpsed a tear. The kill was clean. Popoford's ritual had been satisfied. The guard had been given a moment to recollect. It was a requirement of incidental death that Popoford found to be pretentious at all times except at the moment of the actual killing. It was an involuntary necessity for him. He couldn't remember when he'd first imposed it upon his work, but it had remained a slim verification of humanity's goodness. Whenever he could observe the last moment of his victim's thoughts and could imagine that his victims had seen the error of their ways, he would once again confirm his consciousness, integrity, and ability. This slow death was especially beneficial to Popoford given the poor reviews that H.O. and the girl had felt obliged to offer. As a killer, he was good. Popoford worked quickly, but he tried not to kill too quickly.

When he saw that the guard was indeed dead, Popoford jumped over the top of the bank and ran hard for the corner of the bunker.

Suddenly he heard the report of another weapon. He was being fired upon. He dove into a rolling tumble on the ground and caught a glimpse of a short guard about thirty feet in front of him. Popoford swung his rifle up as he rolled to a stop. He jerked several rounds into the guard's head. Self-defense wasn't the same as killing, and it required no special test. The second guard died instantly.

Popoford jumped to his feet again. Great floodlights popped on. The light was very bright. Nothing was concealed. Popoford ran for the corner of the building. There was no place to hide. A group of guards was running out of a door. They saw him and started to charge. Popoford knelt at the edge of the building and rapidly killed each of them as they came. He held his breath for a second. He listened. Somewhere within the bunker, a siren was wailing. Somewhere on the outside, a small herd of guards pounded that path in search of him. The faraway drone of the helicopter grew louder. Popoford ran past the pile of dead guards and ducked into the little door from which they'd emerged.

He was inside. He waited again, listened again, and reloaded the rifle. The siren was still sounding, and great havoc was being raised somewhere beyond this little guard station. He removed the night scope from the rifle. He left the silencer in place. He looked around the room.

There was a table, gray plastic laminate, government issue. There were six chairs and three beds. Six long overcoats were hanging on the wall. Popoford grabbed one and put it on. His wet body was covered. He ran his fingers through his hair. He glanced in the mirror that was attached to the back of the inside door. He could pass for one, he thought as he moved the syringe to the overcoat's pocket. The plan would be followed as closely as possible. If he could somehow inject the president, if the president would keep to the original schedule and go on the air at just the right time, then Popoford would do his best to follow the plan. If something went wrong, he would shoot him, assassinate him, but not too quickly.

Popoford opened the guard's door. The inside halls were cluttered with military and civilian personnel running to their assigned battle stations. Soon they would all be still again, standing watch for the intruder. Popoford had to find a place to hide until the right time presented itself. With President Bjoonic scheduled to go on the air at 11:00 p.m., Eastern time, he had to give the injection at 10:05 p.m., Central time. That was less than an hour away, but he couldn't take the chance of trying to blend into the ranks for that long. Not in his condition. Not for a while. He needed a hiding place.

With one hand grasping the rifle behind the overcoat, Popoford darted into the flow of alerted men. He ran with them down several corridors, following the man in front of him, keeping his eyes open for a place to hide from the havoc. He turned a corner and saw a pair of men shining flashlights into a closet. Finding nothing, they closed the door and moved on to the next possible hiding place.

When he got to the door, he stopped and opened it. He didn't go in and close the door behind him. That would guarantee that he would be captured. Someone else would be sure to look into the closet. So, instead of standing in the dark with a bucket and a mop, Popoford stood in the hall and stared at the cleaning tools. He stayed there until the search parties were called off patrol. He stayed there until anyone who had wanted to look in the closet had found him already there attending to it. When the call came to return to alert posts, Popoford glanced up and down the corridor and ducked into the closet. He squatted next to the bucket and waited.

CHAPTER FOURTEEN

The cramps in Popoford's legs were worse than he'd expected. He stood with great effort. The pain was determined to impede him. He tried to relax by repeating the rhythms of the relaxation exercises he'd been taught. He let concerns pass through his mind, denying them recognition. Yet, though he begged his legs to be heavy and warm, to relax, to be still, they would only obey in their own time, and he had to stand the pain until it subsided on its own. It was a bad sign that his body had acquired a will of its own; he was losing a bit of his control and skill. His body was aging, slowly, to eventually become the means of his demise.

Popoford shook his head violently. He wouldn't allow sneaky thoughts to take him. He fought aging's seductive whisper, sloughing off his fears. His body might be falling apart, but his mind was still good. He would get this job done.

He shook his head again and leaned closer to the door. It was quiet in the hall. he wanted to be certain that the hall was empty. It would be deadly to be caught coming out of the closet. But he had to get moving. There was no time to waste. Above all, he had to find a clock.

Popoford took his chance. He cracked the closet door and peered into the corridor. It was a neon blue-lighted hall that looked like the halls of Home Office. Popoford had always thought it ironic that the government made a point to decorate in the precise and sterile hues that represented an uncluttered efficiency. This even though, according to the people's wisdom, the government could be defined as inefficiency personified. It would best be contained, this morass, in a hovel, unpainted and rough. But the real irony was that a mind couldn't possibly excel in sterility. But the government continued to think that it could. They continued to build dead halls for the living.

In a moment Popoford's eyes had adjusted. There was no one in the hall. He opened it further and stepped out. Still, there was no one in the hall, so he stepped back into the closet. He didn't close the door all the way but kept his eyes in the light. He waited and kept his focus in the hallway. He waited and was tense, ready to spring.

Then he heard footsteps. Several men were approaching. Popoford pulled the rifle from under his overcoat. The men were coming from Popoford's blindside. That was just as well. When he was ready to jump them, they would have passed the door, and they would have their backs to him. He waited, holding his breath.

The men were talking softly as they approached the closet door. They weren't whispering. They didn't seem to have anything to hide or to fear. Popoford waited. The sweat hadn't begun to form under his collar. He was glad of that. At least some of his control had stayed with him. His finger rested on the trigger of the rifle. He kept the silencer pressed against the door jamb. He kept his muscles taut. He waited, and the men walked to the door. He waited for them to pass. He waited, but they didn't pass.

Suddenly the door opened and Popoford stood face to face with three janitors. They had on light blue overalls that were the usual government uniform for the help. They saw Popoford and froze.

Popoford froze too. For a second he made no decision. Then he released the rifle from the door jamb and shoved the muzzle up and through the chin of the janitor on the left. The man's mind was too occupied with trying to figure out who Popoford was to notice that he'd been struck unconscious. His eyes rolled to the back of his head as he fell.

The second janitor stood just as dumbfounded, as Popoford leveled him with the rifle butt.

The third janitor had been allowed too much time to think. As he began to turn to run, Popoford swung the rifle around and shot a silenced slug through his heart. The man died with a warning caught in his throat.

Popoford had no words of remorse for the man, even though he'd died without a noble moment of recollection. There was no time for such consideration. Popoford hurriedly pulled all three men into the tiny closet, stacking the bodies so that the dead man was on top. He closed the door. Then he stripped the dead man and put on his overalls and his watch. It was 9:30 a.m. It seemed to take him forever to get into the suit but Popoford hurried as best he could in the cramped space.

When he finally got the suit on, he listened again at the door. There was no one coming. He didn't wait longer but opened the door into the corridor. He quickly stripped the silencer from his rifle and tossed it into the bucket. Then he drove the rifle's butt into the skulls of the two living janitors. They would be of no further concern. Popoford tossed the rifle into the closet. He stuffed the syringe into his new overalls. He closed the closet door on the men. He didn't acknowledge the trickle of blood that linked the three bodies. He had a job to do.

Popoford walked the halls as if he owned them, as if he had an acceptable reason for being there. He was too seasoned a professional to be conspicuous. He played the role of a janitor on his way to an important chore. He played a man of such singular concentration that no one even noticed him. By walking briskly, his eyes staring straight ahead, Popoford managed to reconnoiter the bunker.

The floor he was on was designed as a maintenance floor. The signs on the doors all referred to mechanics, storage, cleaning, and stores. The halls connected in a square so that they surrounded a central cube of rooms. It was a common design. The elevators were also located within the central structure. There was only one button to call the elevator. He was on the top floor. The public entrance floor would be the next one down. Below that, the war rooms, the president's quarters, and the president himself. Popoford pushed the button.

The elevator door opened immediately. Popoford stepped into the car and stood between two huge guards. The guards were grim. They carried their rifles in their hands.

"Your pass!" one of the guards said sharply.

Popoford froze, his back to the men.

"Now!" the other guard urged, sticking his gun into Popoford's back.

Popoford stuck his hands into the jumpsuit's pockets. There was something there. He pulled it out while he took an instant to recover and to read the name tag that was pinned to the suit. He fumbled with the papers.

"Give those here!"

"Yes, sir," Popoford's voice was humble. "I'm just a little nervous. You guys get a little crazy when we're on alert."

"Shut up, buddy!" The guard eyed Popoford. "This is no alert. There's been a breach of security. Where you been?"

"He's the breach," the other guard said as he looked up from the papers. "Don't turn around. Bob, put your cuffs on him. We caught ourselves a spy."

Popoford felt the gun barrel against his spine. His body counted the split second that passed before the handcuffs touched his wrists. He didn't calculate his chances. He acted.

Swinging around as fast as he could, he pulled the old trick that he'd seen matinee cowboys pull. His right arm shoved the one guard's rifle away and into the other's stomach. The guard's trigger finger twitched and his partner's guts sprayed against the wall.

Three men in an elevator with their eyes bulging. One man was dead and still staring. One was about to die. One was about to kill again.

Popoford rammed his knee into the guard's groin. He pushed against the rifle, holding the man back. He rammed again, and the guard doubled over. Popoford released his pressure on the barrel. The guard fell to the floor and Popoford smashed his skull.

He glanced at the floor numbers. The car was on the twenty-third floor below the ground. It would stop soon. There were thirty floors indicated. He reached over to the buttons and pushed the number thirty. He held the guard's rifle against his leg, hiding it in the folds of his jumpsuit. He waited for the seconds to pass. He waited for the door to open. This was a priority elevator: once it had passengers and a command to move to a certain floor, it wouldn't take commands from outside the car. It would only stop on the floors that the passengers wanted. It was a typical security measure meant to help the president escape if need be, but when the car came to a stop, he had no time to think about security. The doors opened and he swung the rifle toward the dead man.

"That's him," he shouted. "That's the spy."

"Move out of the way." The first guard into the elevator yanked Popoford from the car. "Let me have a look at him."

"Hey! Not so rough. I'm on your side." Popoford was pushed out of the way, and all the men crowded into the car. They seemed desperate to have a peek at the spy.

Their unprofessional behavior disgusted Popoford. It gave him pleasure when he kicked them and watched them fall in a pile on top of the other two. He thought it appropriate that he was leaving government men stacked all over the place. He reached into the car and pushed the button for the service level, and then he stepped away and watched the doors close. The men were on their way up. They would be of no concern for a while.

Suddenly Popoford turned around. Two crouching men were silently stalking him, their guns trained on him. He pulled the trigger on the rifle twice and killed them both. They fell wondering why they were dying. Popoford controlled his ego. He realized that the game had profoundly changed. There would be no surprise. There would be no syringe, no special timing. Everybody knew where he was. He would have to proceed quickly and, in gross moves, kill the president any way possible. His own life wasn't worth a damn. The certainty that he would die gave him the strength to abandon caution.

He started running. He was on the right floor. The president was somewhere on this level. He was probably in a high-security office. He was undoubtedly heavily guarded. He wouldn't be afraid. He wouldn't be waiting for his assassin. He would be sure that no man could get to him. He would be preparing for his television broadcast. He would be preparing to sell out the country, but Popoford would stop the sale. He ran down the halls searching for the special door, the little hint that would tell him which way to go. Then he realized that he was alone in the hall. There were no guards. There was no attack. There were no defenses. Popoford was worried. It was another unexpected turn. It was like the girl's unexpected behavior. Something was very wrong.

He slowed to a walk. He listened. There was no sound. It was an eerie stillness. Not even the air conditioners made a noise. He waited, transfixed by the quiet, and then he saw in front of him the clue he needed. The brass handle on the door in front of him was well-worn. All the other knobs on all the other doors weren't worn at all. This door was the one he was looking for.

Popoford turned the handle and pushed the door in with his shoulder. He rolled into the room, his eyes wide open, his weapon aimed into the room. He rolled to his feet, hunched and ready. He looked around and realized that he was still alone. He was in a small office with a desk, a dark green wastebasket, two uncomfortable-looking chairs, and another door.

He stood up straight, astounded. The bunker was the most important building in the government's network of defense. It was the stronghold where the president could safely hide from all forms of attack. He was protected from a direct hit of a nuclear weapon. No airborne poisons or biological agents could find their way through the filters and air conditioning that screened the lower floors. The perimeter of the bunker was or should have been, the most carefully guarded ground in the world. This was the stronghold of wartime decision making. This was the bunker from which the country's last stand could be controlled. This was the bunker that Popoford had entered with relative ease. This was the building that surprisingly had only a handful of men guarding it. Even counting the men who were downstream looking for him, Popoford couldn't understand how he'd been able to get so far into the president's inner sanctum without being stopped.

He quit thinking for a second and kicked the other door down. The room was dark, and Popoford knew that he was in an extremely dangerous spot. He was backlit and anyone on the inside could see him clearly. He dropped to the floor and leveled the gun at the darkness.

"You're early, Mixer," a deep, self-assured voice chided from the dark. "Perhaps things were made too easy for you?"

"Who is it?" Popoford asked. It was a stupid question.

Suddenly the great light of four Kliegs was switched on and the richly appointed library was illuminated in the strong, hot light that old television cameras required. There was one camera, and it didn't have an operator. There was one person in the room. He sat behind the old, massive desk. He smoked the cigar that had become associated with him. He was the president, and he seemed old. So did his cigar.

"We still have five minutes to airtime, Mr. Mixer. You're so early."

"I'm surprised to see you so unprotected, President Bjoonic."

"Unprotected from what?"

"From me."

"Mr. Mixer, someone was bound to come. We expected H.O. might try himself. I thought that he was out of agents. I thought that he was out of funds. But I see that he dredged you up from somewhere. Hell, you probably agreed to kill me just on the grounds of national interest, without solid evidence, without substantiation. You're perfect for your function."

"My function is to kill a traitor."

"Yes, to kill a traitor, nothing more. You never consider that your responsibility is to think. You never think that you're nothing but a tool. You know nothing about the world, but you're willing to kill to keep it as it is."

"What is this righteous bullshit. You're deceiving the country. Treachery is not the way to change things. That's not acceptable where I come from."

"God spare me your provincial hogwash. Why don't you give me a few minutes before the camera comes on to tell you what is really happening in the world? Give me a chance to show you why this treaty must be signed. I might be able to save this nation. Hell! I might be able to save my own life. Give me at least that much, Mixer."

Popoford stared back at the man. He was balding much more than his publicity shots had admitted. He was such a short, ugly man that Popoford couldn't understand how he'd been elected. True, there hadn't been a handsome man in the executive chair for at least thirty years, but President Bjoonic had especially distorted features that were repulsive to anyone who saw him. Though the press had never printed a direct slander of his heritage, still the papers and the television were filled with nasty allusions. It wasn't just Popoford. Bjoonic was truly ugly. He reminded him of H.O.

Popoford slowly circled the desk. He stayed behind the lights and the camera. He didn't speak. He moved without noise so that he might hear anyone that waited in hiding for him. He watched the man searching through the glare for him. He watched his prey become frightened. He watched the little ugly man start to sweat. He felt his anger for the traitor build, and he turned all his hatred to him.

"Mixer! Where are you? Mixer! Let me explain. The treaty must be signed! Mixer!"

Popoford waited. Finally, the president reduced himself to silence. He sat staring. A certain calm had come to him. He was prepared to die, and it made Popoford angrier to think that such a traitor should be peaceful in death.

Popoford glanced at the clock. It was 11:00. The red light on the camera lit. President Bjoonic stared into the lens at over eighty million people. Popoford announced the show.

"This is going to be short. The president has confessed that the treaty he was about to sign is traitorous. He has been found guilty by a jury of his peers. The sentence is death."

Bjoonic smiled weakly. "You're being led by the nose."

"You damned traitor! You'll never sign that treaty!"

With that, Popoford pulled the trigger and gave the dulled minds of the viewing audience a startling and disgusting story to tell those who were fortunate enough not to have watched. Popoford looked away and let the camera peer at the ugly little man who stared and smiled into it, dead. The television camera shut off.

CHAPTER FIFTEEN

Suddenly the room's interior lights snapped on illuminating Popoford. He heard the door to the inner office close. He spun around and down to his knees. He pulled the trigger of the rifle. It was empty. He heard the camera being dollied away. He put his hand over his brow and squinted at the president and the president's desk as they were wheeled away. It was Hollywood. The efforts of the moment were over, and the set was struck.

"Well done, George! Well done. That was exactly the feeling we needed. Magnificently done. Don't you think so, Hendricks?"

Popoford heard the name, and his mind flashed back to his getaway when he saw Hendricks's mirrored image blown away by the sawed-off shotgun, the one the girl used. Connections were being made. "What the hell is happening?"

"You're quite right to be surprised, George," Hendricks said. " H.O., here, told me that you'd never be able to understand what has happened. Not in a million years, I think he said. But you're catching on, aren't you George?"

"Is that you, Hendricks? Come out of that spotlight glare. Let me see you."

"It is I, George. Truly, it is. I'm here and very much alive. We can't say as much for the president, can we? But he did die a patriot; and thanks to you, George, he's the greatest martyr this country has ever had."

"What? You bastards! You've used me!"

"Damn, George, you're slower than I thought you were. H.O. always did say you were stupid. I'm beginning to understand what he means. I think perhaps we were lucky that you were able to complete this little task after all."

"What an understatement, Hendricks," H.O. said. "I told you he was almost incompetent. Damn, he outdid himself today. Mixer, you outdid yourself. Again, well done," he said scornfully. "You're free to go back to Whimsy now."

"What? I want some answers. I've been used by you, and you're planning to dump me like I'm shit. You owe me. I want payment now: I want answers."

"Hendricks. Take over. I want him out of my hair for good."

"I'll see to it."

Popoford heard footsteps moving away from him.

"Oh, Mixer," H.O. said as he walked away. "You weren't exactly shit; you were a convenient tool. You thought like I wanted you to think."

A door opened and closed and Popoford couldn't hear the steps anymore. Hendricks walked out of the glare and smiled at Popoford.

"You bastard!" Popoford swung the rifle as hard as he could, but Hendricks caught the barrel and took it away.

"Now George, let's talk like civilized men."

"What a laughable thought," Popoford said, and as he did, he willed himself to relax. He would have to be patient. He would wait for his time. He would find out all he could. He saw the confidence that filled Hendricks. It was false and Popoford saw Hendrick's unmistakable weakness. Popoford would be like that weakness, would hide like that weakness, would wait in ambush for Hendricks to let his guard slip, allowing the weakness its inevitable, rushing conquest. Popoford relaxed and let his mind fill with confidence.

"George, you wouldn't think it so laughable if you knew more of what is happening. If you could be allowed to see the big picture, you would understand. What we've done is good. Bjoonic died a hero. It was a good death and will enable our beloved country to be saved."

"You still think I'll believe that you're doing good deeds just because of your super patriotic speeches? We can talk, Hendricks, but let's get past the bullshit right away. You're a slime bag no matter what your cause. Perhaps we could get on with it without you telling me how wonderful our country is. I remember how wonderful it was before your friends started their little games."

"H.O. was absolutely right about you. You're only a fool. You can't understand, can you? We *are* the country. You are not. We can advance the concepts of community. You would keep our people chained to old, worn-out ideals. Our way is the only way, and it doesn't matter how we achieve our ends. The future is ours. Our country will slip gently into that future. You've helped us ensure that."

"No speeches, Hendricks, just give me some answers before you have one of your men kill me."

"George? How can you say such a thing? We aren't murderers. We don't want you dead, we want you to go back to Whimsy and pick up your life where it left off."

"Why me, Hendricks?"

Hendricks rolled his eyes a little. He took Popoford by the elbow and gently guided him out of the inner office. They walked into the hall and then into the waiting elevator. The bodies of the guards were gone. Hendricks didn't seem to notice Popoford's irritation.

"George, you're like a child. I have to explain everything. Now listen. You're so unbelievably valuable. You're one of those rare agents who can be convinced to do anything. You'll work for anyone who claims to be doing something good for the country.

You'll work for any 'righteous' cause. Hell, George, who else could be so easily talked into assassinating the president?"

Popoford bristled inside at the insults. He'd had all he could take of Hendricks, but he held back. He needed to know more.

"So I'm a sap? What about it? You got what you wanted. How about the girl? How about her mother? How about Bjoonic?"

"George, it's so simple that I hate to tell you. We're all willing players. Bjoonic was willing to die. When we orchestrated the election and got him into office, he knew what the possibilities were. He knew public opinion would either be swayed with subtlety, or it would require direct action to bind it to our needs. He died just as he was about to sign the treaty. It was a treaty that hadn't garnered much support amongst the population. Believe me, George, it now has the strongest support. Hell, with our agitators in the streets right now, it'll only be a matter of hours before Vice-President Rosiva will sign the treaty himself. The people will demand it. The outrage they saw on their televisions has drawn them together in crisis. They'll soon demand Bjoonic's sainthood. The treaty will be signed with the blessing of the people."

"What perversion!"

"Don't be harsh, George. We did try to be subtle. It never works, but we tried anyway. For the people's sake. For the sake of free choice."

The elevator doors opened and Popoford was led out into the main lobby. This was the floor directly below the maintenance floor. This was the only floor that had windows, and Popoford could look out from the bunker and see the river drifting in the moonlight. Even from behind the glass, in the sterile air of the secured lobby, Popoford could see that warmth held the night.

He could see that life was raging in the open air even while men like H.O. and Hendricks played with death and domination.

"What about the girl? Where is she?"

Hendricks pointed to a group of men standing off the side. The girl was standing with them. She didn't seem to notice Popoford.

"The girl is one of us," Hendricks said.

"Her mother?" Popoford asked without emotion.

"Yes. She was ours. She was truly dedicated."

Popoford glanced at Hendricks. The comment wasn't meant to be ironic. He had merely meant that such loyalty was commonplace and expected.

Popoford looked at the girl and smiled briefly at his stupidity. "It looks like you have everything under control."

"We do, George," Hendricks replied. "We have everything and everyone under control. And George, that includes you. There's nothing that you can do to stop us. Soon the treaty will be signed. The people and the press will be too busy searching for the man who killed the president to even care about what the treaty means. You have served Home Office well, George, but now the job is done. You need a quiet rest out of the public eye. I don't want to have to call on you again, George. Do you understand? You'll be out to pasture until you die. I do hope you'll relax and enjoy growing old."

Popoford didn't miss the warning.

They'd reached the front doors of the lobby, and Hendricks handed Popoford over to four large men. He told them to escort Popoford safely to Whimsy. They didn't respond with words, but the biggest of them grunted as if he were an animal, obedient and thoughtless.

"Is this your idea of a sendoff?"

"They are the best for the job. Don't tempt them, George. They have orders to kill you at the slightest sign of trouble."

"That is the first thing that you've said that makes sense."

"So long, George." Hendricks turned away. Popoford called out after him. "What can you tell me about Gretchen Stricklin? Is she really dead?"

Hendricks didn't answer but entered the elevator and let the doors close without turning back toward Popoford.

Popoford had no time to fret over unanswered questions. Two of the men grabbed him by the arms and walked him out of the air-conditioned lobby and into the warm evening. He would have to act fast before the vice president signed the treaty. He must stop the signing at all costs.

CHAPTER SIXTEEN

The trip was relatively uneventful. Popoford sat in the front seat of the bullet-proofed car and passed the quiet ride without speaking. The four men were occupied with their task of removing him from service. They drove and watched and listened and watched some more, each, in turn relieving another throughout the long trip, remaining silent, allowing Popoford a chance to sleep and to think through his confusion.

When they pulled onto the road leading to Popoford's house in Whimsy two days later, he had thought through his concerns for the girl and had cast them aside. She was nothing. He had more important people and things to consider. Hendricks hadn't responded to his questions about Gretchen Stricklin. There was a possibility that she was still alive and he would find out. Now, he wanted to get that opportunity to find her.

He was let out of the car. Two of the men stayed behind, two of them accompanied him to his front door. When they got there, one of them gave him the key. Popoford opened it and turned back to look at the men as he went in and closed it to their silence.

"Damn!" he whispered. "The future sure ain't going to be much fun."

He locked the door. He thought of changing locks all around but knew better than to waste his efforts. They could always get in, and he wouldn't be there long enough to worry about breaking and entering.

Popoford would be on the road soon. He would wait until dark and then make his way to the airport. He would be watched, but it wouldn't matter. He couldn't let anyone get in his way. He had a mission, and for the first time, he could see through the deceptions that had been wrapped around his mind. He saw the threats that remained and understood the tragedy that awaited an unsuspecting people. They would react to the president's assassination just as Hendricks had predicted. The populous would rise up and demand President Bjoonic's killer; they would rejoice at the signing of the treaty.

Still dressed in the janitor's work clothes, he turned on the TV and sat in his favorite chair.

He found out that he was right as he watched the massed, mindless individuals, their feelings hurt, their ignorance left intact. Popoford saw himself in the mournful faces. He'd been a stooge all these years. Hendricks was right again. He was some kind of fool who could be led around by the nose.

"Dammit!" Popoford slammed his hand down on the end table. "That bastard! I've been their plaything. Well, you sons-a-bitches," Popoford called out to the television. "I'm not going to end up dead because of it, and neither are you. I don't care who I have to involve in this thing."

Popoford had poured himself a drink, and he downed it in one large gulp. He got up from the chair, stood in front of it for a moment, and then he sat down again. The oddest thought had come to him.

"Damn. There's no one to help me." Popoford picked up his glass and tried to suck another swallow. The glass was truly empty. He shook his head. "Damn!"

Popoford got up and poured himself another. "Boscwell," he said aloud. "That bastard. He's probably sitting his fat ass back in his chair and enjoying how smoothly everything has gone. Hell, this must be his greatest triumph. That slime."

Popoford finished his second drink. He'd thought about Boscwell during the silent drive home. At first, the idea of Boscwell as a traitor seemed ridiculous.

Boscwell had always been one of the most patriotic and outspoken supporters of protectionism. He'd served the country well for nearly five terms in the Senate. He was the one politician who truly seemed to be above politics. He seemed to be one of the people. He could be trusted. He always told the truth. He warmed the collective hearts.

It was on the trip from Omaha that Popoford had suddenly understood that it wasn't at all ridiculous for Boscwell to be involved. The roly-poly senator was a perfect choice. H.O. had picked his traitor well. The senator could tell any lie, and it would be believed.

Popoford put the glass on the table. He thought of packing an overnight bag but decided that he didn't have time for the details of cleanliness. He would have to move fast now. As soon as he started to run, he would be committed to running until it was all over. As soon as he started, the men who had brought him would get ahold of Sarah in her Home Office shack and the chase would be on.

The only preparation he made was to get out of the janitor's work clothes he was still wearing and put on his own pants and shirt. Then he made sure that he had the syringe transferred to his pocket.

"Well, dammit, here we go."

He walked straight to the door and went outside. He could see no sign of the four men, but they were somewhere nearby and watching.

Popoford went to the garage. He opened it. His car was there. Someone had returned it: Evidence of Home Office's attention to detail had motivated the return, not of any consideration for Popoford's needs.

Considerate or not, Popoford appreciated the car. It made things a lot easier. It made him think that perhaps he had a real chance to beat the odds. He fired it up and backed out onto the driveway. No one tried to stop him. He would be given the freedom of Whimsy tonight, but he would be followed.

Popoford drove out onto the gravel, and slowly let the road take him out of the woods. He came to a turn. The village was just around the bend. He would have to break away now.

He looked in his rearview mirror. A glint of moonlight reflected from the chrome of a bumper. Indeed, he was being followed. He stepped on the accelerator and sped through the curve onto the main street of the quiet, sleepy dream town of Whimsy.

The airport was ten miles on the other side of town. He would have to speed as fast as he could. Once outside of Whimsy, there was no cover. His only hope of getting away was speed and deceit.

He peered into the darkened street ahead of him. Ancient cast-iron streetlamps illuminated the curb. The yellow light they spilled was avoided by everyone and everything that roamed late in the night. This wasn't an exceptional town. Popoford knew that even a quiet town like Whimsy had murderous shadows.

He was snapped back from the urgency of his escape by a double thump under his wheels. He'd run over something that had been hiding in the shadows. There was no time to stop. Without having to analyze priorities, he pressed his foot even further into the floorboard. His life was the most important thing now. His was the most important life in the world.

He glanced in the rearview mirror. The car behind him had still not turned on its headlights, but he could see that it swerved in a late response to danger.

When the car swerved Popoford knew that the driver had made a blunder that was more than he could have hoped for. Popoford suddenly ripped the wheel of his car to the right. Muscling his way around the corner, he raced between the town hall and the community church. One block and he made a sharp left. He slowed slightly and shut off his headlamps. He made another left and looked up the street into the glow of a streetlight as it momentarily silhouetted the racing car passing his position.

Popoford smiled. He'd done it. He'd finessed the driver and was following him. He braked for the corner and drifted back onto Main Street. He slowed further, not wanting to get too close to the other car, straining to see it.

He'd been in situations like this before. Sooner or later they would give up. Sooner or later they would turn on their headlights. When they did, Popoford would win. He looked up the road for the spot where they should be. He drove with more caution than before. He could afford to slow down a little to protect the life of the most important man in the world.

Suddenly there was oncoming traffic and Popoford realized that a plane had landed. It was the daily prop jet that still made the milk run from Oakland. It would be taking off soon, returning to Oakland International. He would probably miss it. He shrugged off any disappointment. It didn't matter whether he caught that plane or not. Any plane would do as long as he got away clean. What mattered was the stream of cars whose headlights briefly lit the road in front of Popoford's car and sporadically revealed the car he was following about a hundred yards ahead. The driver hadn't caught on yet. He still thought that he was in control. He kept driving in pursuit of Popoford, and Popoford kept driving on the car's tail.

Popoford knew the other driver would soon have to make another move. He wasn't so stupid as to just go away when he realized that Popoford wasn't in front of him. He would at least go on to the airport to see if he'd made it on the plane.

Popoford reached over and opened his glove compartment. It was an instinctive move. He was looking for the pistol that he kept there. It was missing. He patted his chest just below his left armpit. That was also an instinctive move, and he was almost certain that he could feel a gun pressed against his chest, snug in the holster that he'd worn for so many years. But, no. There was no holster. He had no gun at all.

Popoford cursed his stupidity and was then caught by surprise as the headlights of an oncoming car began to wildly flash. Popoford yanked the wheel to the right. He had allowed his car to drift into the other lane. He caught his breath and sat frozen as he drove past the car. He could hear the driver yelling at him. When he once again looked into the night to try to see the car he was following, it wasn't to be found.

This was a complication that he hadn't counted on. He pulled off the road onto the shoulder. He waited and watched the road. There was no car in front of him going to the airport. As suddenly as he'd outwitted them, they'd done the same thing to him, and he'd lost them. Popoford started to heave a great sigh but caught himself and held his breath.

"What the hell am I doing?" he said. "They turned around!"

He snapped on his headlights and stepped on the accelerator. There was no time now to imagine where they were. He had to get to the airport as fast as possible and get out of Whimsy. He would have to consider them to be hot on his tail at all times. That was the only wise approach to take.

Popoford cursed himself again. He'd been smug; an overly confident ass who had simply underestimated his pursuers. An agent didn't live long making mistakes like that. It seemed to him that he always made the same blunder. If ever he got out of this mess and could settle somewhere, he would never again misjudge the competition. He promised that to himself as he crossed his fingers briefly for good luck. Then he stepped on the gas and sped on to the airport.

A look in his rearview mirror shattered his fantasy. The other car was following him again. Close. Headlights on.

CHAPTER SEVENTEEN

There was no time left for subtlety. No time to fool around. Popoford had to shake the men in the other car, and he had to do it right away.

There was no way to tell how long he had before the vice-president would sign the treaty himself or if he ever would. Surely Bjoonic had been replaced within minutes of the assassination, and perhaps Vice-President Rosiva had a mind of his own. And he may have been kept in the dark about Bjoonic's and Home Office's plan. He would, of course, know the general details and the propaganda that Bjoonic had dished to the press. But once in power, he had to make decisions for himself; to become his own man.

Popoford had heard such platitudes mouthed long enough that he could almost put his hope in the notion. The question was just how long did he have to find David Konklin, the intelligence officer, and force him to help stop the signing. It had already been almost seventy-two hours since he'd killed Bjoonic. Hell, the damned thing could already have been signed. The treaty could already be in the hands of a sympathetic Congress prepared to ratify it without hesitation. He would find out, but first, he had to dump the car that was following him.

The airport was just ahead. It was only a short landing strip, but the people of Whimsy were proud of the community airport that had sustained continuous service since before the Second Big War. Continuous service now consisted of the Oakland run and the infrequent comings and goings of several private pilots.

The milk flight had already departed, so Popoford would have to rely on one of the private planes.

He turned into the airport driveway, but instead of heading to the front of the clapboard terminal, he kept going straight and drove onto the tarmac. He hoped to confuse the men. He looked in the mirror. They were just turning into the driveway. Popoford looked out on the strip and found what he wanted. There was a private plane sitting on the field preparing to take off. Popoford aimed his car right at it and began to flash his lights on and off. He couldn't imagine what the pilot was thinking, but it didn't matter as long as he waited.

He looked in the mirror again. The other car was just turning onto the runway. At the same time, Popoford slammed on his brakes and skidded his car to a stop in front of the plane. He jumped out and waved his arms at the pilot, who backed off on his engine's revs. The pilot would be forced to get these bastards out of his hair before he even thought about getting off the ground.

"Open your door!" Popoford yelled above the noise of the single-engine. The pilot couldn't hear him. Popoford ran to the cockpit door and wrenched it open as the other car screeched to a stop.

"What the hell are you doing?" the pilot screamed. "Get those cars out of the way!"

Popoford swung himself up into the cockpit. "Move this thing around the car. Get us off the ground, now. Government Security! Move it!" Popoford flashed a twenty-cent blow in coupon he'd found in a magazine and had stuffed into his jacket pocket. The pilot saw the colorful paper and took it for the real thing. He nodded his head.

"Sure. What's going on?"

"Simple. That car on the runway is full of men who killed the president. Get this heap off the ground. Now!"

"Roger!" the pilot said, getting into the spirit of the danger. Let's do this."

The pilot didn't bother to contact the tower. He gunned the throttle while pushing hard on the right pedal. The tail spun toward the oncoming car, and a great shudder vibrated through the plane and Popoford. There was a sharp thud from behind as the plane picked up speed.

"Bastards have shot my tail! We have to check for damage before we take her up."

"The hell we do! Stop now and we'll be killed for sure. Get this thing off the ground now!"

Popoford had reached into his jacket as if to threaten with a concealed weapon. It worked, and he briefly wondered at how easy some things were when stereotyping led the way.

The pilot didn't answer Popoford's last demand but obeyed.

"Hold your breath," he whispered.

The engine strained for a second, and then the plane was racing down the runway.

Popoford sat still. He did hold his breath. Watching the pilot looking out the side window, he was astounded to learn that they couldn't see the runway straight ahead while they raced along. Neither he nor the pilot.

"How the hell can you see to get off the ground?"

"Shit! I can't until we get up some speed."

Popoford held his breath harder and began to sweat. He had no confidence in the plane at all. He'd never been in a small, private plane before. Strange that he'd been one of Home Office's agents for all these years and had never learned to fly. The idea had long fascinated him, but now that he was actually in one of the things, he recognized was scared to death of flying in a plane that small.

Popoford grabbed hold of the vinyl seat between his legs and froze.

"Once we get in the air, we'll be all right. I think."

Popoford squeezed harder. His palms slipped on the sweaty plastic. "Get this thing off the ground!"

"Shut up, dammit! Let me be," the pilot yelled as he opened up the throttle.

Popoford's reply was swamped by the roar of the engine. The radio, which had kept up a nerve-wracking jumble of nasal reports and static, momentarily lost its frenetic hold on the thick atmosphere and gave way to the engine's power.

"Come on!" Popoford pleaded. "Come on!"

It might have been a blessed moment for a man who believed in God. As Popoford pleaded, the plane left the ground and leveled off at a low altitude just skimming the treetops of the Whimsy Forest.

Popoford forced himself to relax a bit. "You do this often?"

The pilot heard the fear in the agent's voice and gave him a sidelong glance. "You sure you're with the government?"

"Yes. Of course. I don't fly if I can help it."

"Oh, one of them."

Popoford wondered to just which "them" he referred when the pilot backed off on his throttle and the engine quieted enough for the radio to grab their attention.

"...I repeat. This is Whimsy tower. Come back to me on this frequency. What are you trying to prove? Alpha 7465, report your intentions!"

The pilot picked up the microphone, and he spoke his nasal pilot's voice into it.

"Ah ...Whimsy tower. Ah ...This is Alpha 7465 ... Ah ... requesting permission to take off. Over."

There was a moment's silence. "What the hell, Bill, you're not being funny. Dammit! The president's been killed!"

"I know that Lou, you idiot. Stop swearing on this thing. F.C.C. will nail you. I'm telling you they'll hear you and kick you out on your butt."

"Bill! Shut up! Get that damned plane back here. Now!"

"Go to hell," the pilot said with a sweet lilt to his voice. He put the microphone back on its hook and turned the knob on the radio to change the channel.

"That guy is so damned dumb. What the hell! This is government business we're on. We don't need him for clearance out of this dump. Ain't that right?" he asked Popoford.

"That's right," Popoford answered, looking back at the pilot and considering that perhaps he would be of benefit in the future. "You're a pretty darned good pilot, aren't you?" Popoford thought a little positive reinforcement wouldn't only draw the man into his confidence, it would also distract Popoford from his fear.

"Yeah. I'm fairly good. You don't have to worry about my flying."

"I'm not worried. I just wondered why you're flying so low?"

"I'm keeping her under the radar."

"Of course," Popoford replied. "I see."

"I'm not kidding, mister. There's an alert been slapped on this country like I ain't never seen. Shit, there for a while everybody thought that the big one was on its way. Damn! Where you been? Ain't you been watching TV? I thought you knew all about the alert."

"I know more than many," Popoford said, and then realized that he was sounding far too dramatic. "I don't know about flying, that's all."

"You did say you're with the government, didn't you? I mean, I wouldn't want to be stuck up here with one of the bad guys. That might be dangerous."

"I'm one of the agents assigned to the case. That's all I can say about it."

"I understand."

"I knew you would."

The pilot relaxed a little. "You want to listen to some of the stuff on the radio?"

Popoford nodded without answering. He didn't care as long as he could think for a while. The radio noise turned up, and he considered the pilot. He was a short man with a slightly balding head of brown hair. He appeared to be about fifty and was strong. He seemed to be patriotic. He appeared willing to cooperate, and at the same time, he was susceptible to the right kind of lie. Popoford thought that the pilot might be helpful over the next several days.

"Will you be able to pull this plane up a little?"

"No, afraid not. I'm telling you there's a radar net over the whole continent. We've got to stay under it. No need to excite the boys flying the interceptors."

The radio was an endless, rhythmic report of the fears of the nation. If there was one horrible effect of President Bjoonic's death that a listener might not consider, the announcer was sure to speak of it. Thereby, Popoford thought, would H.O. raise the panic level of the whole country until public opinion could be easily swayed. Popoford would have the pilot, and Home Office would have the people.

Suddenly the drone on the radio was interrupted.

"All citizens are warned that a private plane took off only minutes ago from Whimsy, California. It's believed that the president's killer is on board. All are asked to watch the skies for this plane and to report any sightings to their local police. I repeat. All citizens are warned..."

Popoford reached over and shut off the radio.

"I've killed many men. Don't become the next," he told the pilot. "Just close your mouth and fly this thing."

The pilot looked out of the windshield; his ashen face taut against his skull. Popoford had lost his stooge.

CHAPTER EIGHTEEN

"Where can you land this thing? Where can we land and not be seen?" Popoford said, half turned in the passenger seat, leaning toward the pilot. The cabin was small. They were already so close together that Popoford's menacing face was nearly pressed against the pilot's head. The agent's lips warmed the pilot's ear with humid words. The pilot's whole body was wracked by an uncontrollable shiver. "Calm down. You'll live if you pay attention to the flying. Set us down where I can use the telephone undisturbed, and I'll spare you. If you fail, you'll die."

The pilot nodded.

"Good," Popoford said.

The pilot nodded again. "I...I'll get you a phone."

"Good," Popoford whispered, his tongue clipping the 'd'. "How long will it take?"

"Ah...I'm not sure. What time is it?"

"It's around eleven," Popoford replied, looking at the watch that he'd taken from the janitor. "Don't you have a watch?"

"Of course. Just checking on the assassin."

"Don't get smart. Be calm or you'll end up dead."

"For the time being, friend," the pilot said, his tone suddenly cold and harsh, "I seem to be in charge."

The pilot turned and looked Popoford directly in the eyes. "Get back with your hot breath, and you may live to see us land safely. Hurt me and you'll be killed in the crash."

Popoford eased back into his seat. He turned to his right and looked out his window. Beneath him were a thousand lights that meant that people were alive back on earth. He wanted to join them again and get the hell out of the skies. He'd thought he could do it with a show of power, but as long as he was in the air, the pilot was the intimidator.

"Just get us on the ground. Soon."

The pilot smiled but said nothing.

Popoford scowled. He had only a little time to get to the vice-president. Though Rosiva was known for his stance against international government and would probably not embrace a policy that involved the control of America by a global collective. Nothing was certain. He had to buy time, for he couldn't depend on Rosiva. Still, his hopes began to rise a little, for if the vice-president remained true to his character, he would put up a fight. And even though Home Office's techniques were effective, a single-minded, arrogant man like Rosiva could slow what might well be inevitable cooperation.

Popoford decided that he indeed might have time. Getting out of the plane and back on the ground was the first step and, right now, it was the most important step.

"Bill?" Popoford asked with a meek voice. "Are you afraid to die?"

"Without a doubt, but I try hard not to think about it. You should spend a little time on the subject. Might do you a bit of good where you're going."

"How do you mean, Bill?"

"First of all, I'm taking you in. The Feds will be happy to see you. Secondly, I expect you'll burn in Hell."

"You're a religious man, is that it?"

"In my way."

"Good, then you'll understand what I'm about to say."

Popoford suddenly grabbed Bill's throat.

"Now you listen to me! I'm not going to stand for any more of your heroic crap. You take this plane into San Francisco. That's a good place for me to go, but you get us down without anyone knowing it's us, or you're going to have a long time to discuss death with God."

Popoford gave Bill a sharp squeeze. The pilot nodded his head. Popoford relaxed his grip but kept his hands where they were.

"Now, you fly, Bill. You fly really low, and you fly really well. I'm going to sit right here and watch how you do." Popoford smiled a little, but Bill couldn't see him. The pilot was too busy thinking about dying.

Popoford looked down toward the darkened earth beneath him. He hated the feeling of disorientation. When streetlights started to show themselves, he started to relax. Before long, the plane rose over the Oakland Hills and drifted above the flatlands across from San Francisco. The pilot still flew the plane low as he turned a few degrees toward the south and then back again when he was over the Pacific turning to the Northwest, aiming the nose directly at the runways of San Francisco International. The little plane skimmed above the water only a few feet from the surface. Still looking out his window, Popoford could see a passenger plane landing at Oakland International. He quickly glanced around for any planes that might be landing on top of them and saw that the pilot had flown between the public airport and the more private strips of the Navy's base.

"I sure hope other planes can spot us," Popoford said.

"They probably can't. But don't worry. They've been warned that we're in the area. The towers and Oakland and SFO have certainly spotted us by now. They're probably going crazy on the radio."

"You said you could get us down undetected."

"I lied."

Popoford stared at the pilot. "Bill, you're a dead man."

"Hell," the pilot said calmly. "I figured that out a long time ago. You can't afford to let me live. I just figured that I'd get you caught before I die. Do a little something for the old Homeland."

"Oh, hell! Cut the crap and get us down."

The pilot smiled openly. Popoford wished that he were as sure of what he had to do himself. It would be great to have such a clear understanding of one's required deeds. The ignorance that Popoford knew was needed to be decisive and sure of one's self shone like sunshine on the pilot's face. His rationale was intact. He was prepared to die for his country. But then so was Popoford, even though he aware of more corruption in the world, in the country itself, than the pilot would ever believe.

Behind them, the sun was rising. It was 6:12 a.m. Beneath them, the choppy Bay waters turned suddenly quiet. They flew over the tide line. Then the almost nonexistent shore passed under the little plane. Scrub brush trying to dominate the meager soil dotted the land-filled strip that followed. Then suddenly, the earth was all gray with black streaks beneath them. They were over the runways of SFO.

The pilot brought the plane in for a perfect landing.

"Taxi in as close as you can to those buildings over there," Popoford said with a short, firm squeeze of the pilot's throat as Bill parked the plane where Popoford told him to.

"Wake up, Bill. You're still alive, and you're going to stay that way as long as you do what I say. Now get out."

Bill looked at Popoford but didn't move.

"Get the hell out of the plane!" Popoford demanded.

The pilot blinked once and opened his door.

Popoford shook his head and got out, too.

With his hand stuffed in his pocket to indicate a nonexistent pistol, Popoford gestured Bill around the plane.

"Now listen to me, Bill. I'm getting a car and getting out of here. You're going to help me. You'll stay alive if you help. Get it?"

"Yes, I get it," the pilot said, suddenly having found his voice.

"Great. Here on the ground, I'm the boss. Now walk beside me. Walk calmly. There's no hurry. When we're approached, let me do the talking. Understand?"

"Of course."

They walked together toward the open doors of a warehouse. They climbed the concrete steps at the end of the loading dock and walked inside. There, two men in plainclothes approached them. Popoford squeezed the pilot's elbow and walked on as if the two men weren't there.

"Hold it you two. This is airport security. You're under arrest." Popoford stopped. He looked back over his shoulder at the men while still holding the pilot's elbow. The look on Popoford's face was one of utter relief. "Thank God!" he exclaimed, and suddenly pulled the pilot's arm into his own gut. Popoford doubled over as if he'd been hit. As he did, he spun the pilot to the ground, making it look like he'd been thrown off balance. The two airport guards saw their advantage and leaped on the pilot. Popoford jumped to his feet and clasped his hands together into a pommel and brought it down on the back of the first guard's neck. The guard fell to the floor, unconscious. The second guard joined him within seconds, as Popoford's heel sank into his temple.

"You two should have called the Feds," Popoford said as he patted them down. There were no concealed weapons. He picked up the two pistols from their hands. "Bill, you're still alive. Thanks for being my stand-in, and thanks for the flight."

Popoford quickly looked around the nearly empty warehouse. The few men that worked the early morning hours were standing in a group by the wall. They weren't going to get involved. Popoford smiled at Bill and ran to a small door at the opposite end of the huge room.

He went out through a wooden door and closed it behind himself. He fell back against the door for a moment and took a deep breath. He was surprised that he'd gotten away with that trick. It meant that Home Office hadn't released his photograph, which was odd, and that only a few people knew what he looked like. Also, he could walk the streets without fear that some ordinary person would recognize him. That made things a little easier, but he hesitated to think that Home Office had made a mistake. He shook his head to get rid of the cobwebs that wanted him to stop thinking, that wanted him to be confident, that wanted him to fail.

He pushed himself away from the door and took a step down the alley. He heard a car's tires squealing just before he saw it careening around the corner of the building. It was a determined mass of chrome and black painted steel charging at him, raging, in total control. Popoford turned quickly on his heels and lunged back for the door. He grabbed the handle and twisted it violently. But it was self-locking and wouldn't move. He slammed his shoulder into the door. His eyes had been focused on the car. It was only a few feet away. His legs wouldn't work fast enough. He was weighted as in a heavy dream, and his effort was stretched throughout an endless second. The car kept coming, but suddenly huge brakes grabbed and rubber stripes a quarter-inch thick were smeared on the asphalt alley. The huge car screeched to a halt as Popoford broke through the door. Back in the building, he turned his head and straightened up to stare into the double barrels of a sawed-off shotgun.

CHAPTER NINETEEN

Her makeup covered her bruises, but not her anger. "Get back out here!" She snapped. "Get into the car! Now!"

The rage in the girl's eyes made Popoford move quickly. He turned around and ducked into the back seat of the car. The girl followed him and sandwiched him against the bony body of a thin, little man. The man motioned to the driver and the hired hand obeyed by taking the huge car on an aimless route among the numerous airport warehouses.

"Welcome, Mister Steven Popoford. I've waited a long time to meet you. It's too bad that we couldn't have met earlier. We might have spared everyone a lot of trouble." The little man's voice was deep and resonant. He had a look about him that welcomed Popoford, but the girl wasn't extending the welcome. Popoford felt the shotgun pressure increase.

"Get that thing out of my side," he snapped at the girl.

"Lorain, please relax a little. Steven is not going to get away from us again. He won't want to get away. He'll be one of us."

The girl did as she was told. Popoford glanced at her. Her cheek was black from where he'd hit her. Her childlike face was set in a pout, but her eyes flashed more than hurt feelings. She was angry, and Popoford decided not to provoke her further just then.

"How did you know where I'd be? How did you find me?"

"That was quite easy, my friend. Your actions are not hard to predict, and with the help of our tables, we've been very accurate."

"What tables?"

"You wouldn't be interested in that, my boy. It's just a bunch of probability charts generated by my technicians. Nothing special. But I dare say that you should study your habits a bit. You're becoming rather an obvious man in your middle age. Even my daughter knew what you would do next, and she was able to do that before the computer had made up its mind." The little man broke into a rolling laugh that belied his thin body. Even as his voice was one that would best have been generated by a fat man's vocal cords, so too was the rumbling joy that escaped his gaunt throat. But the laughter ended as quickly as it had started. "There are more important things to discuss, Steven. I'm terribly sorry we didn't get to you before this."

"What the hell do you mean by that? *She* certainly got to *me* enough. Why didn't you shoot me right away, or turn me into Home Office? What more could you want from me?"

"Be calm, Steven. We thought Lorain was enough to keep you away from Home Office's grasp. We thought her warnings would keep you away."

"So much for your probability charts," Popoford said.

"They were most accurate. It was a human miscalculation. We should have come to you directly, as we're now doing. That is the best way for men like you. Don't you agree, Steven? Isn't honesty the best way?"

"You did come to me directly," Popoford replied, and then he turned his head toward the girl. "The shotgun! You were told to relax a little."

"Please, Lorain, remove the gun from his side. We don't need to be so cautious,"

"Don't count on it, Mister. I'm caught, but I'll sure as hell try to get away."

"But why, Steven? We're with you. We know what has happened. We've been trying to stop it from happening. Although I agree that we haven't been very effective; still there should not be hostility between us."

"No hostility? You bastards used me to murder the president so that your public relations package would be more palatable. You made me sell out the country, and you think there should be no hostility? Damn your egotistical ass."

"You seem to have things a little backward, Steven. You don't know what you're talking about."

Popoford looked at the man's eyes. They were steady; clear. Popoford faltered at seeing that the man might be telling the truth.

"Ask her. Ask Lorain. She was there when I was taken out of the compound. She was there, dammit! I saw her!"

"That is hardly possible, Steven."

"Ask her. She's from Home Office. Hell, so are all of you. What's the use of all this crap? You've got me. Let's just get on with it."

The little man was staring at Popoford. He had a scowl on his face. He was thinking hard; he was unsure of his answer. Then all at once, his face spread out into a wide-open grin, and that deep laugh bellowed from his scrawny belly.

"Lorain. Do you believe it? He thinks we're from Home Office. Can you believe it?"

Lorain was laughing now. Popoford was puzzled.

"Steven. Steven. There could be nothing more humorous. Don't you see it? We've been trying to stop Home Office from the beginning. You and I are on the same side. It's us against them. Our considerable resources against their vast resources. No government agency or bureau or law could have stopped what

Home Office has done. There might have been a time when it would have been possible, but not now, not since the plot was first acted upon. It was too late even then, except for you, except for the long-shot possibility that an old agent who had been fingered as the most susceptible tool at their disposal could be used to jam up their machinery. You were the last hope we had. I admit that we bungled the job terribly, but that doesn't matter. What matters is what must be done now. We have to act with what we have."

Popoford was incredulous. He looked back and forth between his two unlikely escorts. He shook his head. "I saw her at the bunker."

"She has been with me since we picked her up on the riverbank. You hit my daughter awfully hard, Mr. Popoford. Under different conditions, I would be very offended."

"Your daughter? Who are you? What agency are you from?"

"Get this straight right away, Steven. We are not from any agency. We are not the government. Far from it. You didn't see my daughter inside the bunker. You think you did, but you didn't. They may have a double there. They want you to be confused. They want you to go into hiding, to forget that you killed the president. They want you to be silent until they need you again. You're on the hook, and they figure that you'll never get off. And when they've convinced the vice-president to sign the treaty, they'll merely say it didn't work. You'll still be on the hook, and your efforts would have been so fruitless, so futile."

"Lies. You're a liar, and not particularly good at it. She was there, at the bunker. She was at the safe house, too; I saw her kill Hendricks. She blew his head off. I saw it."

"You did?" It was the girl talking.

Popoford glanced at her. "You know I did. You waited till I had a clear view before you pulled the trigger. I saw it all."

"Not from me, Popoford. I was never at the safe house. I don't know what you're talking about."

"There were four contacts with you, Steven," the little man said. "Two in the village, one on the river by the bunker. All three encounters with my daughter. The fourth contact was in the field outside Whimsy. That meeting was with my wife. There were no other meetings, no other contacts."

"She was your wife?"

"It does not matter now. The point is that you had no contact with us at the safe house. You saw a double there. You saw her again inside the bunker."

"She killed a man I thought was Hendricks, and she killed two guards, two of their only men. Would Home Office have done that?"

"Of course. That's what Home Office wanted you to see. The man who was killed instead of Hendricks was a decoy. You fell for it. You didn't see what you thought you'd seen; you only saw what you wanted to see. The two guards were of no real value to Home Office. He only needed you, and he got you by showing you an enemy, a girl who was ruthless enough to kill the number two man in the agency. That would spur you on. You would be theirs. You were theirs. And to top it off, you thought Lorain was theirs. Home Office is good. You must know that. We certainly do."

Popoford thought about what the little man had said. There was a strong element of truth to the story. There was a strong feeling of truth in his passionate delivery. There was truth in his face. "Who are you?" Popoford asked.

"My name is Mous. P. Y. Mous," the little man said and paused.

"Who are you?" Popoford insisted.

"I thought you might have recognized the name. Times have changed more than I thought." The little man leaned back in his seat and took a deep breath. He looked out on the passing hills crowned with the rolled tube of unseasonably early fog. He was trying to find the right words.

"I'll know if you're lying, Popoford said.

The little man turned to Popoford. "There's no reason to lie, Steven. I'm merely trying to anticipate your reaction. But it doesn't matter. I am P. Y. Mous, industrialist."

Popoford looked at the little man. "So what?"

"I'm an industrialist, Steven. I'm not a politician. I'm outside the government, yet that is only part of the truth, because, like all men of business, I'm very much involved with government on all levels. It's not currently popular for men such as me to be too influential. If the public had its way, business would be segregated from the whole process. We would be entirely removed from the system, but that is just the public's ignorant and passing fancy. We *are* the system. The government cannot operate without us, and in truth, we cannot operate without the government. It's a symbiosis that has served us all very well over the years, but it's a relationship that we all have denied to varying degrees. These past few years have been a time when the government has seen fit to be particularly antagonistic towards us. H.O. has been instrumental in the great effort to denigrate business as a whole and big business in particular. Public sympathy for business has never been lower. In contrast, the government has never enjoyed a higher level of trust. It's this great imbalance of power that has allowed H.O. to pursue such extreme tactics to reach his end goals. Big Business has been cut out. We're as much on the hook as you are. We are to keep quiet or to be blamed, whichever is more convenient at the time for H.O."

Popoford shook his head. "That is rather hard to believe."

"Not at all, Steven. H.O. would be king. He will be if we don't stop him."

"How do you propose to do that?"

"With your help, Steven, and with the help of certain influences which we can still peddle behind the scenes."

Popoford thought he understood the meaning. Lobbying had been outlawed less than a year ago. Special interest groups that had been a key element for influencing politics since the country's beginnings and their questionable tactics had been so tainted that the public cheered when they were made to keep quiet in the cloakrooms of every legislative office throughout the land.

"What could you possibly need of me? You seem to have your little army right here," Popoford said, indicating Lorain.

"I do have my army. As for Lorain, she's good, as you know, but she's only one person, and she does not know the ways of Home Office quite as well as you do."

"Oh, I doubt that," she said with a contemptuous look at Popoford.

Popoford was startled by Lorain's outburst.

"Don't be unkind, dear. You must work together, you and Steven."

"Do as your father says," Popoford replied with as much sarcasm as he could muster. "What's in this for you, Mr. P. Y. Mous?"

"Everything, Steven: my country, my business, my hope for the future, my daughter's future, everything that freedom allows me. I won't lose my freedom without a fight."

Popoford looked straight ahead. "How do you know so much about Home Office? How do you know about the treaty?"

"There was a time when I was approached to be part of it. Home Office sent the man Hendricks to me. I was a supporter of Bjoonic during the primaries. Home Office thought that I might be willing to give his efforts some financial aid. I didn't agree. I didn't like the sound of his plans."

"You mean that Hendricks just came right out and told you that they intended to kill the president?"

"No, not at all. Hendricks was much more subtle than that. He informed me that Bjoonic was a dying man. Cancer. He only had a few months to live."

"He didn't drop out of the race."

"No, he didn't. That would have been the proper thing to do, of course. Hendricks said that he wanted me to talk the candidate into withdrawing. I told him to go to hell. If Bjoonic was ill, he would withdraw himself. I advised Hendricks to keep quiet about any illness until he could show some proof to the whole world. I then called the candidate myself. He denied the report. He even offered to send me a copy of his latest physical exam. I refused, and I was even more determined than ever to support Bjoonic in the election. I did just that, and because of it, he won."

"Yes," Popoford responded, "and he took office last January."

"I'm afraid so. Since then," Mons continued, "I've found that Bjoonic really was dying. He knew it all along. He even sent me his medical charts. He and H.O. were rubbing my nose in it. I don't take that without a fight. They thought that I was ineffectual. They thought that I was too vulnerable to speak up. They were right about that, but they underestimated my anger. They underestimated my ability to work behind the scenes. I'm after them, Steven, and I won't rest until H.O. is stopped."

Popoford sat silently. He had nothing to say. H.O.'s sickening arrogance made his blood boil. Even more sickening was the knowledge that H.O. was laughing at him, just the way that he was laughing at P. Y. Mous. Popoford and the industrialist had both been used, their pride played with, a complete disdain shown for their considerable talents. Popoford understood what Mous was saying. He looked him in the eyes once again and saw what he wanted to see. P. Y. Mous was telling the truth. "How will you stop him?"

Mous smiled at the agent and patted him on the leg. He put his weapon away.

"Lorain, he's with us."

"Only for the time being. I do believe you, but I may not be working with you. I prefer to work alone."

"That is understandable, Steven, but we have the means to help you. Together we might be able to stop that treaty from being signed."

"Perhaps," Popoford said. "We'll see. You haven't told me how you found out about the treaty, about the plot."

"I told you that I won't be used. I got angry and started looking into Bjoonic's past. I looked into it very thoroughly. I found H.O. there. One thing led to another as it must, and I found the treaty. It was quite simple once I was angry enough to set my whole operation to the task."

"What kind of operation, Mr. Mous?"

"My business, Steven, my international business."

"Which is?"

"It's of no consequence."

"It is for me. What is your business?"

Mous hesitated.

"Tell me, Mous, or I won't play along. I'll do just fine on my own."

"That is very unlikely, Steven, but it's just as unlikely that we could do very well without you. I had hoped to keep this from you. My business is weapons. Manufacturing and distribution. Clandestine operations."

Popoford's whole body tensed. The girl snapped the sawed-off back into his side.

"Be calm, Steven. I can assure you that I do not sell weapons to our enemies. My main concern is the elimination of terror. I'm as patriotic as they come, Steven. I've mellowed a bit since childhood, but not terribly. I'm kind of like an old-time physician. I do what I do in the hope that I'll someday be put out of business because there's no more business to do. Can't you see, Steven? Someone has to try to stop the terrorists. Someone must stop them and people like H.O. who would turn us over to them for our own good."

Popoford's body remained tense. "Who the hell do you think you're kidding? I've been out there in the field. There are no suppliers like you. An ethical international weapons broker? Get off it."

"Take it or leave it, Steven. I won't try to prove myself to you. You have my story. You've said that you believe me. I'm sorry if we can't work things out. Whatever you think of me, we have a common goal. But if you've made up your mind, we'll waste no more of your time."

"Samuels," Mous said to the driver, "Pull over, and let Mr. Popoford out."

Lorain opened her door. She got out and motioned for Popoford to do the same. Popoford looked at her for a second and then turned back to P. Y. Mous. "Is she one of your agents? Is your daughter one of your employees?"

"Naturally, Steven, I have said so. I like to keep things in the family."

Popoford hesitated. "Get back in the car, Lorain," he said. "I'll be sticking around for a while."

CHAPTER TWENTY

Samuels pulled the Cadillac up to the airport exit where a security checkpoint had been established. There were two lanes: one backed up for three blocks as regular folks were slowly cleared to leave; the other for high-security clearance officials to cut through the inconvenience. They were second in line and were cleared in a matter of minutes. They traveled out of the airport property onto the freeway and proceeded south until he got to the Half Moon Bay exit, Route 92. He drove to the west, toward the Pacific. Popoford thought of the headquarters of Home Office, only a few miles behind them across the bay. He imagined H.O. himself sunk in his leather chair, gloating. Popoford's anger grew stronger.

There was no further conversation. This might turn out to be a temporary arrangement; that would depend entirely on Mous.

Samuels had driven along the tree-lined road for only a few minutes when he pulled the car sharply into a narrow driveway obscured by thick brush. The Cadillac eased onto the gravel road and was immediately concealed, covered by the dense thickets. The road was an arbored tunnel, a tube of leaves, and filtered light. They drove for several hundred yards through the dimness and then the car popped into an immense clearing.

They drove up to an exceptionally large stone house situated in the middle of the open space. It was a rustic fieldstone and wood building that harmonized with the forest, even though the woods had retreated and stood back from it on every side. Steel Quonset huts surrounded the main building. Popoford looked around and couldn't find another exit.

Samuels parked the car and got out to open Mous' door.

"Welcome to..."

"Your distribution operation?" Popoford asked.

"Yes, Steven. Rather impressive, don't you think?" Mous replied as they got out of the car.

Popoford took a full look around the circular compound, noticing that every building was flying the American flag. "Yes. Impressive."

"We'll look around later if you like, but now, please come in. You're looking very tired, Steven. Perhaps something to eat? Come in, come in."

Popoford walked up the stone steps behind Mous, up to the porch where a deferential man was waiting.

"Get some breakfast going, will you John? And a pitcher of Bloody Marys for me. This is Steven Popoford. Please welcome him as my guest until further notice. Steven, John. My butler."

Mous spoke to him without breaking stride and Popoford followed. As he passed the butler, Popoford nodded and the butler returned a slight bow, and Popoford noticed the pistol bulge under his coat.

Mous led him into a large office where there were several desks, each with a terminal, each with a two-way radio, each with an empty chair. There was one larger desk to the rear of the room. Mous walked to it and sat in the chair. "Take a seat, Steven. Lorain?" Mous said as he gestured his daughter to another seat. "Now, Steven, while we wait for your food, we had better catch up on the world news."

Mous winked as he turned on the television. Popoford didn't see the humor in Mous's remark. The news was all about the assassination of the beloved president, a man so dearly loved that people were saying there would never be another like him. There was an intensely somber tone to every voice that told each part of the story. The tape of the killing was played over and over again until it surely must have been memorized by the whole world. The details of the massive search for the unidentified killer were described. Sobbing people on the street were interviewed. None of them could understand how such a horrible thing could happen. The commentators wanted to know how the killer got away. People calling into the station wanted to know why he hadn't been caught, and Popoford wanted to know why H.O. hadn't released his name.

"It's mighty odd that he doesn't tell the police who I am."

"No, Steven, he may need you again. Sooner or later H.O. will want you dead, but when does, he'll want to do it himself."

"But if the police knew who I am, they would shoot me on sight. He would be rid of me. I wouldn't have a chance to tell the police anything. If he doesn't see that, he's made a mistake."

Mous was silent for a moment. He was thinking. "Yes, but he still wants you himself. It fits his egotism."

"You know H.O., then?"

"No, Steven, we've never actually met, but it certainly fits. The man is egotistical as hell. Who else would think that he could give this country away and still keep control over it?"

"But he must have a deal with the enemy."

"Then he's a fool. H.O. must believe that they'll honor their contract, that he'll be put in charge with no strings attached. He's naive, and that's his mistake."

A commercial for cold beer blasted over their conversation. Mous reached over and turned down the offensive jingle.

"So. Where do we go from here?" Lorain asked as she followed her father's hand to the television set and shut it off. "How do we stop that treaty from being signed? We know how things are. How do we change them?"

The three of them sat around the desk for the rest of the morning. Breakfast was brought and consumed. The pitcher of Bloody Marys all went into Mous. It was noon by the time they'd talked over the situation completely.

Vice-President Rosiva had been sworn in within minutes of the telecast. He had made a statement that indicated he'd taken control of the government, and that the populace could rest assured that strong security measures were in place. He assured the people that a mad man had killed President Bjoonic. There was no conspiracy, and no foreign government had been involved.

"I hope he believes that," Popoford said. "He could already be under H.O.'s control. Shit! It couldn't be more perfect."

Mous replied that Vice-President Rosiva, now President Rosiva, would show his loyalties soon enough.

By the time lunch arrived, they'd discussed Senator Boscwell and his connection with David Konklin, the espionage agent. They'd discussed what Mous could offer Popoford in the way of supplies, money, contacts, men. Steven had formulated a plan which would require Mous to establish a group of agents to keep track of the events in D.C. Popoford wanted to know anything that Rosiva did. Mous would take care of those details. Popoford and Lorain would visit Senator Boscwell in his Hollywood house and ask a few questions. They would take a plane to L.A. that night. By the time lunch was over, Popoford had grown very tired, and he was grateful that he had a safe place to sleep before he had to catch that plane.

He was led to a second-story bedroom by Mous.

"By the way," Popoford asked, "Is there another exit? You must have to get trucks in and out of here."

"I have my ways," Mous replied without emphasis. "Rest well, Steven. You may have little chance to sleep in the next few days."

Popoford nodded. There was little time for them to stop the conspirators. He should have tried to catch a plane out of SFO right away, after lunch. But he had to be alone for a while to sleep, and he had to think. He had to re-evaluate what he'd done and why he'd done it. Also, another problem was nagging at him. He had to understand why he had killed Gretchen Stricklin. If he had killed her. He had to remember the details of who Gretchen Stricklin was. He remembered that she was his lover. At least he thought he had remembered her, at some time, before Home Office had made him forget. They'd been lovers, but somehow he couldn't see her in his memory. He couldn't remember how she looked. Her face was without distinction. Her body unknown. The whole experience that was theirs was a phantom. He could remember her, but not her touch, not her lips, not her scent, her words. There were times that he wondered from whose imagination Gretchen Stricklin had come. She may have been real, but she wasn't a part of his imagination. He fell asleep trying to think about her formless image. He dreamed of how he killed a ghost.

He awoke to a darkened room. His fists were thumping fear, muffled silently into the quilt-covered mattress. His clothes were soaking, the sweat rolling off his brow. His jaws were clenched hard. He heard his teeth grind. He forced himself to relax, and the dreadful noise of his dreams subsided. Slowly the room quieted. He tried to think clearly again.

Popoford saw himself in his thoughts and wondered at how a rather good government agent had been coaxed into killing the president of the United States, how he had come to be snared in an ugly international trap.

From what he could piece together, his role depended on one thing: his mind had been tampered with. Just as he was duped into thinking that the president should be killed, so then too he might have been lied to about Gretchen. It was possible, even probable. Popoford knew that there were long stretches that he couldn't remember. There were days at Home Office, under the drugs, lost days - the fog days he called them - the dark days of debriefing. Those were days in which the subtle suggestions could have been whispered into his sleeping brain, his mind trained. He could have been washed clean. He could have been remade. Gretchen could have been a figment; the ghost of his dreams.

He wondered also about Mous, about his daughter. They were a pair that was hard to accept without laughing. They were the truly absurd twist to a rather straightforward if traitorous, crime: he the betrayed maker of presidents, she the seasoned guerrilla warrior.

Popoford wondered about their real motives. He reviewed his conversations with them, and in the end, he could not see that the treaty would impact Mous' business, whether or not it was signed. There was always going to be a market for weapons. With or without the treaty, Maus would profit. And if the treaty were signed, the shift of global power might mean, if anything, better sales for him. There was no advantage to Maus in getting involved.

There was a soft knock on the door and the butler came into the room before Popoford could respond. "It's time, sir."

Popoford rose slowly. His body had grown stiff. He was aging far too fast for this work. He couldn't remember when he'd last put his tired body through so much. He couldn't remember when death had been so near. A cold fear shot through him. He couldn't remember his last assignment.

"Mr. Mous has provided you with these clothes," the butler told Popoford, laying them on the bed. "He trusts they'll be suitable."

"Yes...yes," Popoford said without interest.

"Miss Lorain will meet you at the car in fifteen minutes," the butler said, looking at Popoford for a word of agreement.

"Yes...the girl...fifteen minutes. I'll be there."

"Very good, sir."

The butler left the room. The door closed, and suddenly Popoford's last assignment came back to him. It was that surveillance of the Canadian embassy. Gretchen had been involved. Now he remembered her distinctly. Distinctly, but not her face. A body. No, not a body, just the clothes. Only an outline.

The sharp memory rapidly dissolved, and Popoford got dressed. He went downstairs and joined Lorain in the car. Her father hadn't seen them off, but Popoford barely noticed. He was too involved in getting his feet back on the ground. He was too busy trying to concentrate on the job at hand.

They were driven out of the woods and back to SFO. Once there, the Cadillac was directed onto the runway. A private, unmarked jet was waiting. When they landed in Burbank fifty minutes later, a similar Cadillac picked them up and took them to the driveway of Everette Boscwell, United States Senator.

CHAPTER TWENTY-ONE

They'd been driven up into a canyon on the north side of the Hollywood Hills, and they saw the Boscwell home beneath them in an old creek bed. The land was an alluvial meadow cut from solid rock. The erosion had created a hideaway lot where the home of a senator could be nestled. Eucalyptus and pine sappy scents drifted into the soft breeze. The sky was clear with no promise of showers. The peaceful scene of filtered moonlight on the wooded property abruptly died when bright floodlights snapped on, and Popoford and Lorain were caught walking down the senator's driveway.

Loud barking came from a kennel that was attached to the house. Then lights began to come on in the house itself.

"We tripped an alarm system," Popoford said to the girl.

"Without doubt," she replied. Popoford thought that he heard a note of sarcasm in her voice. He glanced at her but didn't see any sign of it. He tried to shake off a feeling of paranoia. Fear was a dangerous excess.

"Was your father sure that Boscwell would be home?"

"I'm sure," she replied with a tone of emphasis. "Father called and told him we were coming."

"He did *what*? Christ! H.O. will be waiting for us. He'll have us shot right here."

"I don't think so."

"You don't think so? You were so sure of yourself a second ago. What do you mean you don't think so? You're out of your mind."

"No, Steven, I'm not." She was calm, completely controlled. "I feel that he'll be cooperative."

Popoford looked at Lorain. He shook his head slowly. "You take too many chances. Hell, these people are fanatics."

"Again you're wrong, Steven. They are not fanatics. The senator, in particular, is no fanatic. He's very cautious and very opportunistic. If we can show him the danger he's in, then we can convince him that he should cooperate with us. You haven't been involved in this long enough to understand its true nature."

Popoford shook his head again. He didn't understand why she and her father should take such chances.

They approached the door and rang the bell.

"What is it?" a man's voice called out.

"P. Y. Mous told you we would come to speak to you."

There was silence for a moment, and then the door opened, and standing there, with a rifle pointed directly at them, was the senator.

"State your business. I haven't had any rest since Bjoonic was killed. Say what you have to say, and then let me get back to bed. I must return to Washington in the morning for the funeral."

"Let us in," Popoford said.

"Bullshit, fella. You can talk right there."

"I'm with Home Office," Popoford protested. "We're investigating the assassination."

"My ass. Talk out there or get the hell off my property."

"It's a little uncomfortable talking to you like this. This lady would like to sit down."

"Again, so what? The cops are on their way. You'd better stop wasting your time."

"Senator! This is official business. The police can't get involved. What are you going to do, have them arrest a federal agent? Wise up, Senator. Let us in. We don't need much time."

"And I don't *have* much time, Mister. Speak your piece and stop this crap."

The girl jabbed Popoford. "Talk to him. Hurry up."

Popoford looked back at the senator. He couldn't remember a time that he felt more incompetent. Where was his aggressiveness? Where was his sharp mind, his strategically subtle mind, his trained mind -- his *mind?*

"Ah...right...Ah, Senator, you've been the principal supporter of the Freedom of Intelligence Treaty, is that right?"

"Yes, and damned proud of it."

"With due respect, Senator," the girl interrupted, pushing Popoford out of the way, "we don't give a damn about your politics. We have a job to do and we need information. First, has the treaty been signed?"

"No, not yet," Senator Boscwell said. "President Rosiva has not signed it yet."

"Why not? He's had enough time."

"He's not taking our advice," Boscwell said, a note of contempt in his voice.

"Meaning what?" the girl asked.

"Meaning that he will wait until after the funeral to review the treaty. He's never read the full text. He says he'll make up his own mind. It's to be expected."

"Too independent for you?"

Boscwell's eyes twitched.

"Everette?" The voice of a woman filled the silent look of loathing that passed between Lorain and the Senator. "Is everything all right, Everette?"

"Yes, dear," he called over his shoulder. "I'll be up in a minute."

"Hurry, darling."

"You want to know anything else?" he asked, looking beyond the girl at Popoford.

"How do you intend to act if Rosiva vetoes the treaty?" the girl responded.

"That's my business."

"Forget that crap," Popoford said. "The good of the country is *our* business. You're obliged to give us the information we want."

"Go to hell," the Senator sneered. "You'd better let the girl do the talking."

"Well fuck yourself, you pig!" Popoford snapped as he lunged for the senator's throat.

The girl was instantly between the two men.

"No harsh stuff, Steven," she said, looking quizzically into his eyes. "Excuse my partner, Senator. He has had a difficult time."

"Get him out of here. Now!"

There was a siren howling up from the valley floor. The police were on the way.

"The treaty is a mistake," the girl said. "Consider what it will do for our enemies. Consider what we'll lose, Senator."

"There's nothing to lose, young lady. Freely exchanged information is a benefit to all nations."

"Try to pull that on someone else, OK? I'm not about to buy that kind of crap. Let's go, Steven."

The girl grabbed Popoford by the arm and yanked him away from the door. She ran up the driveway, pulling on him all the way. They got into the car and were driven away just in time. Just after they were back on the road and had rounded the next corner, a squad car's rhythmically flashing lights lit up the road in front of them. The siren penetrated Popoford's head as the police car raced passed them towards the Senator's home.

Lorrain turned on him. "What the hell are you trying to prove? I thought you were supposed to be some kind of professional. Looks to me like you don't know a damned thing about interrogation."

Popoford sat slumped against the car door. His head hung on his chest. He couldn't understand the way he was behaving. He couldn't understand the way he was thinking. He was afraid. He was out of control. He was indecisive, inconsistent, unprofessional. It made no sense. His actions were confused, irrational. He was acting hotheaded, like an amateur.

"What's going on?" he mumbled.

"That's what I'd like to know. What was the rough stuff all about? Boscwell wasn't going to give us anything with you being tough. I expected more from you."

Popoford didn't answer. He had no answer for the way his mind had changed. Somewhere, deep within him, he felt there was a reason for his mind faltering, the feeling of anguish, the feeling of fear. He would reach the answer. He could reach it. Just a little further. Reach a little further, a little deeper. It was there. The answer was there. Reach it. Touch it. Harder. Try harder to reach it.

"Wake up, Popoford. What the hell is the matter with you?" Lorain was pushing on his shoulder. "Wake up."

"I am awake," Popoford said, unsure if he really was.

"You were mumbling, Steven. You look like you're on drugs."

Her words were a lifeline. Drugs. He'd been drugged. When? Who had done it? Had to think. Who could have done it? The senator? Of course not. It had to have been Lorain, or Mous himself. Of both of them. He'd been drugged. She might not know. She might not know what her father had done. He would have to find out. Subtly. Quietly. With finesse.

"You drugged me," he blurted out, unable to control his mouth.

"That's absurd."

"I've been drugged, dammit." His voice wasn't strong, his tone uncommitted. "Someone did it."

"Be quiet, Steven. I'll get you back to Father. He'll know what to do."

She leaned forward and spoke to the driver. "Get us back to the airport right away. I can't take this much longer."

The driver nodded and did what he was told.

The flight out of the San Fernando Valley and back to SFO was a short trip back to unaltered consciousness for Popoford. Lorain held him in her arms. It was the comforting, soothing embrace of a friend, but in the fragrance that filled Popoford's nostrils, in the warmth that touched his skin, he smelled the thick, sexually laced air, he felt the wet friction of her skin, and the comfort and soothing turned to lust and desire in his dreams. He dreamed, and he tasted her salty flesh on his tongue. He heard the soft groan in his own throat spread in the air until it filled his ears and his thoughts tapered to ecstasy.

"It's all right, Steven," she repeatedly whispered. "It's all right." She rocked him in her arms. "I know how it can be. In a few hours, it will go away. Until then, lie still. Be still." She rocked him in her folded arms, and he bit his lips, and she worried more over him.

Then gradually everything began to change as the drug wore off. All that had stimulated Popoford was still there, but his mind led him to clearer, more reasonable thoughts.

Popoford was sweating. He felt sticky. He could smell his fear on his skin. It overpowered her skin's perfume. He could hear her whispering too loudly in his ear. He was groaning from deep within his throat, and the animal sound knotted his guts. He felt nauseated. His head ached.

Popoford bolted from the seat. "What is happening?"

He was raving, swinging his arms wildly, then holding his head. He glared at Lorain, staring as if he couldn't see her. He tried to punch her, but he missed and fell to the cabin floor with the momentum.

"Steven!" Lorain yelled and slapped him hard.

Popoford froze for an instant. He had regained his sanity, and he responded as the trained agent that he was. He struck out at her, his instinct strong. She was much too quick for his recovering reactions, and she easily dodged his fist again. As Popoford tried to hit her a third time, the copilot, who had been alerted by all of Popoford's noise, grabbed him in an embrace that was meant to crush the life from him.

"Let him go!" Lorain ordered. The copilot sat Popoford roughly back in the seat. "I appreciate it," she said to the man. "Thank you. I have him under control. Thanks." The copilot returned to his other duties.

"Steven, you're coming around. You were drugged. You're coming out of it. Calm down."

Popoford looked up at her. He blinked and then closed his eyes and felt the welcome relief as he squeezed his lids together. A single tear hung in his lashes. A weariness, ancient and heavy, took him for a few minutes, and he slept like he need never wake up.

"Wake up, Steven. We're here. You must get to the car."

Popoford opened his eyes. "I want to see your father!" he said quietly, but with a determination which the girl could only answer with a nod.

CHAPTER TWENTY-TWO

As the Cadillac pulled to a smooth stop in front of the Mous mansion, Popoford bolted out of the back seat and leaped up the front stairs. P. Y. Mous was waiting for their return, standing at the top of the stairs, a broad smile across his face, his little body enhanced by a fine silk smoking jacket that he wore draped from his shoulders. The butler was with him, a few steps to the rear, holding a silver tray filled with the refreshments.

"Welcome back my boy," Mous blurted out, his reddened face beaming with joy. "How did it go?"

Popoford didn't answer but grabbed Mous by the arm and wrenched him through the front door. The butler, laden with the tray of drinks reached for his pistol and three martinis smashed to the porch. He ignored the slippery mess as he lowered the gun on Popoford.

"John! No!" Lorain yelled. The butler looked at her. "It's all right, John. He won't hurt Daddy. Put the gun away. Now!"

The butler hesitated and then complied. He put the pistol back, but he hurried inside the house to be with Mous if he did need protection. Lorain followed him.

Popoford could hear Lorain yelling at him to stop, but her words meant nothing to him. He would get the truth out of Mous if he had to beat the little man to death.

He dragged Mous into the sitting room and swung him around into an overstuffed chair. He yanked on his collar, drawing Mous up by the scruff and leaning into his face.

"Talk to me! Why did you drug me?" Popoford kept his voice low but firm and the intonation of his voice threatened more than pain if he wasn't obeyed. "John!" he called to the butler. "Don't interfere. Touch me and he's dead. Lorain?"

"Yes." Her voice was muffled. Popoford looked around at her. He saw her standing against the doorjamb, her hand against her mouth pressing back her terror. Her other hand was on the butler's arm. For a moment she wasn't the hardened guerrilla, she wasn't the daughter of the munitions peddler, she was merely a girl scared to death that her father would be hurt.

"Don't worry, Lorain. I'll only kill the bastard if he lies to me." He turned back and stuck his face right against Mous' reddened temple. "Speak to me, friend. Tell me why you drugged me. Tell me what you were afraid I'd learn from Boscwell."

"I'm innocent. Steven! I'd never do that!"

"Liar! You slime!" Popoford jerked the man's neck again. He stared into the little man's eyes. "You're dead."

"No, Steven! I didn't have you drugged. Damn! Why would I? Steven! Why?"

"You answer that one. It has to be you. This is where I ate. Your hospitality is in question."

"Steven! Please!" Mous sputtered. "It would have done me no good. Steven! It would have been so much easier to turn you in. Or to have you killed. I would never use drugs on you."

Popoford squinted. He had to consider what Mous said.

"You wanted me to stay away from Boscwell."

"That's not true, Steven. I helped you see him. Don't you remember that? I helped you. I even called Boscwell and told him you were coming."

"Yes. That's what Lorain said," Popoford said hesitantly.

"Boscwell is quick on the trigger. He might have shot you if you'd gone on his property without warning."

"Don't try to distract me, Mous. You were the only one who had the opportunity. I was drugged while I was at your house."

"You can't prove that, Steven. There are too many time-released capsules on the market. There's no way to tell when it happened. You should know that."

Popoford relaxed his grip again.

"Dammit, Steven," Mous went on. "Let go of me! Let me up. We're on the same side. I want that treaty to be stopped. I thought you did too. Let me up!"

"Tell John to mind himself," Popoford said. "Tell him to back off, and I'll let you up."

"John! Relax. Please leave us alone and don't touch Mr. Popoford. All right, Steven. Get off me."

John reluctantly left the room and Popoford slowly stood erect. He took a deep breath to calm his heartbeat. Then he stepped back so that he could see both Mous and Lorain.

"God, Steven," Mous said. "You're so damned touchy that I think you ought to get a little professional help. It's paranoia. You shouldn't be working."

"Under the circumstances, there isn't much choice. It wasn't my idea to get involved in this thing at all," Popoford said.

"It wasn't anybody's desire to be involved in it, Steven, but we're here because there's no other way. We can't have any more of this behaviour. It just won't do," Mous smiled gently up at Popoford as he might have smiled at an errant child. "Promise me, Steven, that it won't happen again."

Popoford didn't like the tone in Mous' voice, but he promised him anyway.

"Good boy, Steven. Good boy," Mous said and broke into one of his deep, rolling belly laughs. No one else joined him. Popoford looked at the little man, then at his daughter. He considered the obedient butler and adding it all up, he wasn't convinced that Mous was what he claimed to be. He wasn't convinced by anything that he saw surrounding the little man. His daughter was of questionable innocence. The little man seemed fearless, yet he thought it wise to keep John around though not use him when the need arose. What was the point? And there was supposedly a large weapons business operating out of the Mous complex, but Popoford hadn't seen any proof that such an operation existed. Aside from the Quonset huts, there was no evidence of any industry in the woods. He couldn't trust Mous for anything.

"I'm taking over this operation," Popoford finally said. "After this, you don't call ahead to anyone and let them know I'm coming. From now on I give all the orders. And if you don't get any orders, that means that you're to stay put and shut up. Understand? We've wasted too much time already with you two playing cops and robbers. I hope I make myself clear."

"You make yourself very clear, Steven," Mous said. "But I'm afraid that your terms are not acceptable. You're the one who can't be trusted. You're the one who has put the whole effort in jeopardy right from the beginning. Hell, we haven't accomplished a damned thing yet, and you've already destroyed our spirit of trust. No, Steven. I'll remain in charge. You'll do your job and do it well, or we may be forced to eliminate you as an unaffordable burden. Remember, you've assassinated the president."

Popoford glared at Mous. The little man still had the trump card. Too many people had trump cards. Everyone held a winning hand except him. His only leverage was his ability, and he wasn't certain of that. He decided to retreat and wait for a better time to deal with Mous. Anyway, there might not be any need later on, and he could still run his own, secret show.

"You wouldn't dare turn me in. Your illegal operations would be discovered."

"Steven, the illegalities of my operations are all in your mind. Like I told you before, what I do may not be morally acceptable to many, but everything is legal. You see, Steven, you're the only one here who has reason to fear the law. You're the only one who needs to be kept in line with blackmail. It's a pity, really, but it's a necessity. You understand. I'm sure."

"Too well," Popoford replied.

"Good. Good," Mous laughed again. "Then we can forget this unfortunate...conversation and get on with our efforts."

Popoford didn't answer Mous. He'd retreated in appearance only, outwardly making a show of being licked. Inside he sharpened his senses and prepared to work alone. He still had so many questions that needed answering, but they would have to wait. For now, he would act and watch and give his trust to no one. The only thing that was certain for him was that he had finally come completely out of retirement.

CHAPTER TWENTY-THREE

Popoford fell into a worried sleep. After a few hours of exhausted slumber, he woke to his nagging thoughts and the haunting pictures in his mind. He had to act. But what should he do? Nothing seemed to make sense. The events of the days since Whimsy had a rough edge. Indefinable questions kept waiting to be asked. There was something wrong. Something was missing. Popoford knew that he should have no worries. He never had worried over any other killing, but this time it was different, and it wasn't just because it was the president.

When he finally got out of bed, his thoughts began to clear. He realized that he'd never before been made a fool of by the agency.

He wasn't so naive as to think that espionage was an activity of purity. America's interests and those of Home Office were often entangled, if only in the subtle slanting of certain reports. But one difference was present in the death of Bjoonic. Popoford had been made a fool. He'd been told about his error. H.O. and Hendricks had made a point of rubbing his error in his face. They had no understandable reason to do that. They wanted him to be angry. That could have been the reason for his humiliation. He didn't know, but he *was* angry that H.O. had manipulated him like this. H.O. might still be working him. Pushing him quietly. Using him. He would have to find out somehow, somewhere along the way. He went downstairs to breakfast and announced that he was going to catch the next plane to Washington D.C.

"Naturally, Steven. What else can you do? The signing must be stopped," P. Y. Mous replied, looking up from the morning paper. "I'll have the car brought around right after breakfast."

"Bring it around now. I can eat breakfast on the plane."

"As you wish, Steven. Lorain will go along to assist you."

Popoford scowled and stood up. He grabbed a cup and gulped down the steaming coffee. He looked over at the girl, who was buttering a piece of toast. Popoford couldn't understand how she could be so calm.

"Let's go," he snapped.

Lorain looked up at him and slowly smiled. She put the toast down, rose from her chair, kissed her father, and preceded Popoford out of the room. She didn't say a word.

"I wouldn't push my luck with her, Steven. She might not take kindly to mistreatment."

"I don't like her being along. I don't like either one of you being involved with this. As far as I'm concerned, I'm on my own. Your threats of exposing me are enough to make me take her, but when this thing is over, Mous, I'm going to ask you a few questions that I don't think you'll be able to answer. That's something I'm sure you won't like."

"Steven, you're a mistrusting man. I've done nothing to warrant your abuse." Mous stood up. "I went too far when I threatened you, but those were just words. There is no enemy except H.O. We work together against him - against his actions, not his words. Go to Washington and do your job. Your threats are boring me. Go do your job, and when you're done, don't bother to come back here. We needn't work together again."

Popoford turned and left the room. He was still hot about Mous when his plane landed at the Dulles Airport. Lorain still gave an effortless smile whenever he glanced at her. He hadn't spoken during the flight. He didn't intend to speak to her at all. He didn't need the girl. She would only get in his way. As if in response to his thoughts, she spoke to Popoford.

"Steven. You know that I won't be in the way. You know how I work. You know I'm not a problem."

Popoford turned and walked briskly away from her, wishing that he could be rid of her, knowing that the best he could do would be to keep her at arm's length and perhaps even get her out of the way.

Security presence at Dulles was as high as it had ever been. In every direction, Popoford saw pairs of armed federal officers, most with police dogs at their sides. His tension was heightened as they surveyed the passengers coming, going, and loitering.

As he walked through the terminal, he gazed into the eyes of arriving passengers who were marching away with their own burdens, following deceptive melodies. He saw a sadness that at first startled him. It was a sadness that he had rarely seen, a gaze of mindless hurt mixed with panic. Everyone seemed to be afraid that something was lurking in their private lives for the dirge to end and for the onslaught of panic and terror to recommence. They were dulled, but they were oddly watchful.

All at once, it hit him. What he saw was grief. The murder of a president had clutched the imaginations of the American people, and with melancholy felt in common, terrible events had struck a lifeless minor chord.

This unsettling feeling stopped him abruptly. Popoford could almost hear the groaning from within the passengers. He could almost hear them questioning everyone they saw. The suspicion they radiated was, thankfully, too broad to focus on one man, even him, the true assassin. He turned away and walked quickly down the ramp to a newsstand.

Popoford bought a copy of the *Post*. He had to overcome his feelings. He couldn't let the pain reach him. He had a job to do.

Grief and fear could come later when it was safe to feel again. Such emotions were only an extravagance now.

He glanced at the paper. The front page was fit for the occasion. The ink was excessive and thickly black. It nearly glistened on the page, and it spread its smudge to everything it touched.

"NATION GRIEVES!"

It was an order. The rank and file had obeyed. But Popoford couldn't pay any attention.

He was working, and the several undercover agents that posed in the open while their nonchalant uniformed companions stood in the shadows were more important than an ignorant nation's misdirected grief. In a way, he wished that the world knew the truth, but it was too late in the game for any good to come of it. He was on his own.

Popoford listened to the conversation of three men standing nearby. They were only one group of several in the main gallery of the terminal. He sensed their words were similar to the words of so many others at the airport. The thoughts were the same, the pain the same.

"So, where were you when it happened?"

"In the elevator down at the office."

"You didn't see it then."

"I saw the taped replay."

"That wasn't the same."

"No, of course not."

"It's just as well."

"Still. I wish I'd seen it."

"I know what you mean. It was so horrible. I saw it, and now I feel like there's just no hope. What in God's name is this country coming to?"

"Yeah. I know what you mean. So where were you?"

"I was in the pub down the street from my apartment."

The conversation dwindled as Popoford walked out to the sidewalk and hailed a cab.

Suddenly the noisy gloom was shattered.

"Steven!" It was Lorain.

He felt the rage swell up his back. He focused on the heat it made.

"Steven! Don't be stupid. You can't do this without me."

He reached for the cab door.

"Steven! You know you need me!"

Popoford slowly turned his head and looked at her. He glanced at the guards that had been stationed at the doors. He allowed a bitter smile to show.

"Bullshit," he said. "Be a good girl and shut up. Get into the cab."

They got in. Popoford first. He told the cabby to get them to the White House from the south along Constitution and then through the Ellipse. The cabby drove east, and Popoford pulled the plastic window between them and the cabbie closed. It would provide some privacy. He found a piece of paper in his pocket and started crumpling it and unwrapping it. It would help to muffle their words.

"I have a use for you, Lorain," Popoford finally muttered. "You'll play the part of my wife for a while. We're tourists, understand?"

"Certainly, Steven, but just what do you expect to do? Do you want to grab the president when he comes strolling out the front door for his daily constitutional? You going to whisper the ugly truth in his ear?"

"Hardly."

"Then what the hell do you have planned? Do you think we can just take the tour?

"Knock it off. I don't need your shit. We're going to have enough to worry about without it. This town is scared. Everybody will be looking for the assassin, watching for him to try again. They are all immersed in themselves, but a part of each of them is looking for the assassin. They are looking for me."

"Oh stop spouting the obvious. What's your plan? It had better be good. Damned good. The secret service will shoot you just for getting too near the damned building. Hell, you don't even know if Rosiva is in there."

"He's in there. He can't afford to go far. He has to establish his leadership. The world is watching him. He's there."

"So how are you going to get to him. It's impossible."

"Perhaps you're not as smart as you think you are," Popoford said without emotion. "But you're going to be useful. You'll be my diversion. Tonight, just after the sun is down, you're going to make a loud assault on the White House. The obvious scene will follow. You'll be captured, and I'll join the Secret Service boys as they pour into the Rose Garden. We'll both be taken inside. I'll get to Rosiva."

"And I'm to be sacrificed."

"Perhaps we both will be."

"That's bullshit."

"It can work."

The cab had been traveling along Dolly Madison Boulevard for ten minutes. Popoford turned to see out the back window, to see if they were being followed. He tried to memorize the faces of the drivers behind him. He would look again in a few minutes.

The massive security worried him. The normal precautions that are established for the protection of the president would have been hard enough to outwit. But with the whole city locked down, there was only one way to get to Rosiva. Once again he would have to become an assassin. He didn't need elaborate plans: he only had to accept that he would probably get caught, to clear his mind, and act without care for his safety. By being simple and without fear, he might outwit the system that was attuned to complex and magnificent attacks. Popoford thought he could pull it off. He had to do it.

He turned back in his seat and glanced at Lorain who was watching him. He ignored an urge to smile, and he picked up the paper.

On the bottom of the front page, there was a story pleading for the capture of the assassin. The story was a rehash of the killing. There was no more information today than there had been from the start. The grieving nation had seen their beloved president killed "in their living rooms." They cried, these people, for the slain man, for the outrage done the office, for the disgust and contempt with which they held the fugitive. They screamed in unison for the piked head of the beast. Great statements were uttered and duly recorded. Men who thought that they had a destiny and a responsibility to comment upon every moment of the human condition did so, and loudly. It bothered Popoford. And it bothered him that the press roiled the crowd and printed as much of the wailing and protesting as it could. The details of nearly every moment since Popoford had entered the bunker until this morning's printing of the three-star edition were treated with equal weight. Throughout every word and every argument, however, Popoford recognized the lack of spirit and conviction. Even though the newsboys had ferreted every detail even vaguely connected to the killing of President Bjoonic, they had no idea who had done it. The security at the bunker had been thoroughly scrutinized, but there was no indication in the paper that anything was known about who had entered the building. No one seemed to know anything. Yet throughout the paper, the assassination was the only story.

Popoford smiled at that. H.O. was a genius. He had managed to cover everything up. The dead janitors were never mentioned. The dead guards had been removed, the elevator cleaned, and Popoford had been neatly removed from the events of that day. Everything had been sterilized. For a second Popoford felt cheated of notoriety, but at once shook off the perverse idea.

The cab had come to a stop. They were on the Theodore Roosevelt Bridge about halfway across just above the southern tip of T. R. Island. Knowing that security was heavy, and he figured all vehicles entering the District were being inspected. He slid the plastic window open.

"How long is this going to take, cabby?"

"About twenty minutes. Everybody gets the once-over. At least it ain't martial law. Traffic's bad enough as it is without these Secret Service boys slappin' a state of war on D.C. I don't think he's here anyway. The guy's got to be crazy. You know he's got to be. But he's not that crazy."

"They're hoping to get lucky. They're looking for a quick arrest," Popoford said.

"What was that?" the cabby asked.

"I just said I hope they make a quick arrest."

"If the bastard is here, they'll get him soon."

"Yeah. Let's hope so."

They waited for a while without talking. It was hot: one of the early, humid, hot days that are the only kind that many people can remember about Washington D.C. Popoford opened the window. Lorain did the same thing on her side, but there was no wind, and the still air hung on them, isolating them further. Popoford looked around at the faces of the drivers and passengers in the other cars. There were ordinary-looking people in various states of distress. None of them were paying attention to the inspection ahead of them. Each one was gazing about, doing as Popoford was doing, looking at the other people who shared such dangerously close quarters. They had suspicion in their eyes. Popoford could see it. They all were looking for the killer among them.

Popoford looked behind the cab at the three rows of cars that backed up over the bridge and out of view toward Arlington. All the people behind him were looking too. All with the same hope of heroic retribution. Popoford looked at them for a long time. He marveled at the mutual hope in their faces. Then he saw something that made him gasp.

Quickly he opened the cab door.

"Behind us. Three or four cars back," he whispered. "The brown Ford with three men. I'm going to give them the slip. You stay here and cover for me. Pick me up at the Ellipse just after dark. I'll find you."

He slipped out between the stalled lanes of traffic and quietly closed his door. He moved away from the cab, crouching low, listening for evidence of discovery. He heard Lorain's door open. He didn't understand it. What was she trying to prove? He had told her to stay there. He needed her to distract the men. He wanted to scream. The damned bitch was too unpredictable. She had no discipline. Dammit!

Popoford didn't dare call out. He didn't dare look back for her. He had to keep moving, had to get over the bridge; had to keep out of the security net for a few more hours. He couldn't afford to wait and see what the headstrong Lorain would do. Time was wasting, and he had to take action. He had enough experience with her to know that she could get in the way, and he had a sense of foreboding that was only getting stronger. The unresolved question of the drug he'd been slipped, Mous' threats, and all his other questions crowded his mind. Popoford had better toe the line himself or else the world might find out who killed President Bjoonic. Popoford knew he was taking a lunatic risk. His plan was insane. But sanity wasn't important now. Disciplined action was everything.

He sneaked closer to the roadblock. As cars were searched and released, the traffic jam inched forward. Popoford stopped and waited for a second. He took a few minutes to think of the best way off the bridge.

Squatting near a railing, he caught his breath and tried in vain to calm his heartbeat. He tried desperately to remember the particulars of his last assignment, but he found the details impossible to retrieve. And then he found that he'd wasted too much time trying to think.

"What ya doing, Mister?"

The voice made Popoford flip over on his back and reach for a pistol that he didn't have. He stared at the curious face of a little boy.

"Daddy. A man is lying out there on his back. Daddy?"

Popoford didn't wait for the child's father to take the boy seriously. He stood up in a panic, afraid of being caught, and yet willing to show himself to everyone. He stood straight up and glared at the boy. His mind skipped over logic and discretion, and he started to run. He ran hard through the several, close lanes of traffic. A horn followed his weaving path. Then every nearby horn joined him, pointing at him, aiming at him, giving him away. Popoford didn't look behind him as he ran. He didn't think. He saw the treetops at the edge of the bridge. Without another thought, he leaped. As he landed in the muck of T. R. Island marsh, he could smell the oily diesel in the water. He could taste the waterfront jetsam. He could hope, as he hit the mud and sank up to his ankles, that he could escape. He could hope against reality and the odds. He could hope that he was a damned good agent.

But Popoford sank further nearly up to his knees and his heavy shoes and soaked clothing bogged him down. He felt that some mysterious force was grasping him, making him feel the weariness of stress, making him think for a second of himself, making him want to give up, give in and die.

Suddenly darkness surrounded him. A black cloth hood was slapped over his head and a drawstring yanked tight about his throat. He sucked in his own dead air, and four hands grabbed him under his arms. His captors said nothing. They forced him to stand and yanked him out of the mud. Then they forced him to walk quickly up a rise and onto a paved path soft from the hot day.

Popoford could smell his breath mingled with the sizing of the new cloth. He could hear traffic noise increasing as the roadblock was lifted. Soon he was transferred to some kind of electric cart and he was driven away from the bridge. Finally, he was taken off the cart. His head was pushed down, and he was coaxed into a car. There was no violence. The grip of four clamped hands was warning enough. Popoford would cooperate. He was a professional in the hands of professionals. They understood his decisions, his resolve, his honor. There would be no malice.

Popoford was driven for a short distance. He noted that the car stopped within seconds of starting. The door was opened, and Popoford was removed. He was marched a few steps to an opening door. He was taken inside, the door was closed, and he was alone. The lock was turned, and Popoford removed his cloth hood.

He found himself in a simple, concrete-block room. There were no windows and only one door. A single light fixture was attached to the ceiling and gave the room a yellowish, incandescent cast.

Popoford smiled. feeling that he was on the brink of fulfilling his destiny. He had only to survive. He was getting closer all the time. He began to pace the little floor. He was a survivor. Survivors won. He was winning. He was alive. He had survived the past. He would survive the present. He had been successful in his previous, forgotten missions. He would be successful now.

The lock clicked and the door opened. Two men, young and obviously Secret Service agents, peered into the room. Their three-piece suits were the same, and, instead of allowing them to blend into the crowds, the expensive uniforms announced their presence to even the most naive. Their faces were scrubbed so that their skin glowed, and their hair had been cut by the same unimaginative barber. Popoford smiled at them, but they only looked him over. They were making sure that the goods were correct and in one piece before accepting delivery.

Popoford tried to see who was behind them. Someone in the group behind them might give him a clue to his captor's identity.

The sight of one man froze Popoford -- froze his feet, froze his idiotic smile, froze his mind momentarily as he wondered at his horrible misfortune.

The man caught Popoford's eye and winked. Popoford turned and tried to run. He struck a wall, and in the ensuing clamor, he again felt the four huge hands grabbing him from behind. Popoford was spun around. His arms were yanked hard behind his back. He could smell the peppermint breath of a third man whose face was shoved up close against Popoford's nose. The man slapped Popoford hard in the gut. He jammed a pistol into his ribs. He reached under Popoford's wet jacket in search of a weapon. He stared into Popoford's eyes and called to someone to give him a hand. The man pushed Popoford away from him, and Popoford could look over the offensive man's shoulder into Hendricks' eyes.

"Steven?" Hendricks asked. "Can this be you?" Hendricks smiled. "Tut, tut, my boy. What brings you to this part of the world? Get tired of Whimsy?"

Popoford didn't have time to respond.

He was instantly blindfolded, and he was roughly tossed on the concrete floor. No one spoke to him. He heard the door close.

Popoford held his breath. He heard the men leaving. He noticed a slight whisper of furnace air coming through a floor vent. He added his breathing to the sound. For a good agent, perhaps a great agent, he felt that he wasn't living up to expectations. He pulled off the blindfold and sat up. The overhead light was off, but he saw the light under the door. He would know when Hendricks was coming. He would be ready to jump him. He felt good to have a plan. He felt that he certainly would survive.

Without warning, someone snapped on the lights.

"For a great agent, George, you certainly are a bungler."

Popoford turned his head slowly. He forced himself to be calm.

"Since I'm no longer in service to you, call me by my own name."

"Right, you little bastard," Hendricks said, suddenly changing his tone. "I'll just do that. You just shut your mouth, *Steven*. You've got to be the worst excuse for a spy that ever existed. Damned if H.O. wasn't right all along about you."

Popoford looked up at Hendricks. He didn't blink. He didn't respond. He sat perfectly still. Saving his energy.

"Look, Popoford, don't get any ideas of escaping from here. I have men stationed throughout the building. They know who you are. You would die." Hendricks punctuated his words with a finger jabbed at Popoford's face. "How can anybody be so stupid? How could you go to Boscwell? That in itself was the most idiotic move you've made. Don't you realize that I have his house under surveillance? I can't believe it."

"He didn't tell you what happened?"

Hendricks paused for a second. "Why should he?"

"How would I know?"

"What are you talking about, Steven?"

Popoford hesitated. He gave Hendricks a quizzical stare. "You mean that the good senator is not one of your boys?"

"What do you want to say, Popoford? Say it or shut up."

"Keep control, Hendricks. You're too jumpy."

"The point. What's your point?"

"I'm surprised that you had to watch your own boy's house. What's the matter. Doesn't he report everything to you?"

"Just the usual precautions of the agency. You know that."

Popoford looked at Hendricks. Popoford didn't remember that.

"Sure, the usual precautions."

"Right. Now, what's your point?"

Popoford hated the feeling that he'd forgotten so fundamental a procedure. It was like his memory of Gretchen. When someone explained the memory, he felt like he could almost remember the person and the situation himself. He felt that he was supposed to remember; that the memories would find familiar places in his mind, even if they weren't comforting when made clear. He'd forgotten so much. H.O. had taken his typical post-mission memory wipe too far.

"The point is, Boscwell didn't tell you himself that I had visited his house. He didn't tell you that I have his complete cooperation."

"You jerk! What the hell do you think is going on? This isn't a game. I'm not an idiot, Popoford. Get one thing through that thick skull: I won't be manipulated."

Hendricks stepped forward and yanked Popoford up by the shoulders.

"You're the prey, Steven. I'm the predator." Hendricks hissed the words softly into Popoford's face. "You've gone too far for your own good. You can't return to Whimsy. You must die."

"How very melodramatic," Popoford said.

Hendricks dropped Popoford's shoulders. He stepped back.

"We should have left well enough alone. You've been through the Run too many times."

"What does that mean?"

Hendricks smiled at Popoford as if the agent were an errant child. "I'm afraid you'll never know, Steven."

Hendricks turned around and opened a door that Popoford hadn't noticed. Two huge men, silk stockings over their heads, emerged from the darkness and took Popoford by the wrists. They stretched his arms out away from his sides and pinned his feet to the floor by stepping on them. Popoford could smell their expensive cologne. They wore blue blazers. They were overdressed for the occasion. They would help Hendricks kill.

"No stomach for it by yourself, Hendricks? Or can't you handle me alone?"

"It doesn't matter," Hendricks whispered as he slipped a pistol from under his coat. He didn't say a word as he screwed a silencer on the barrel. He gazed at Popoford for a second as if to say something final, but then he shook his head slightly as if from exasperation. He raised the pistol to Popoford's forehead. The men leaned away from Popoford and turned their heads.

"Your Resurrection Run is over," Hendricks whispered.

"Mous will stop you," Popoford replied and closed his eyes for death.

Hendricks didn't pull the trigger.

"What did you say?"

Popoford opened his eyes. The pistol barrel was still pressed against his head. The men were still pulling on him. Hendricks looked surprised.

"You'll be stopped," Popoford stammered.

"You mentioned a name."

Popoford had no idea what was going on, but he wasn't dead. "Mous. I said Mous will stop you. So what?"

"Let him go," Hendricks ordered the men. They obeyed without making a sound. Hendricks kept the pistol at Popoford's head. Popoford massaged his shoulders.

"What do you know about Mous?"

Popoford knew that this might be his chance. He could jump Hendricks. He could get the pistol back. He decided to wait. His shoulders hurt too much.

"Who wants to know?" Popoford said.

Hendricks nodded to the men, and a sudden, vicious punch sent him to the floor in a crumpled lump. His back felt like it had been broken. It had been an accurate punch, however, and no bones had been injured. The men held him down and Hendricks straddled his chest.

"P. Y. Mous. That his name?"

"Yes," Popoford replied feebly.

"Speak up, Steven. Why does P. Y. Mous want to stop us?"

"Who wouldn't?"

Hendricks slugged Popoford on his chest. Popoford felt that his heart had stopped.

"Talk about Mous, Steven. How do you know about Mous?"

"The girl," Popoford gasped. "The girl. Mous is her father. He's helping me."

Hendricks slammed his fist into Popoford's chest again. "That's a lie. How do you know about Mous?"

Popoford could barely talk. He looked up at Hendricks sitting on his chest in the darkened room. He saw what he thought might be fear. His vision was blurred, but he thought he saw fear.

"He's a gun-runner," Popoford said. "He's a maniac. Like you. He's crazy. That's all I know."

"Is he helping you?"

Popoford couldn't catch his breath.

"Answer me! Is Mous helping you?"

Popoford nodded. "I told you he was."

"Dammit!" Hendricks said.

Slowly, Hendricks stood up. He was lost in thought. He didn't seem to remember Popoford or the men. He paced along the wall and mumbled to himself. His head was stooped in worried thought. After several minutes Hendricks straightened up. He had made a decision.

"Pick him up."

Again the men obeyed without a word. They lifted Popoford from the floor, and they held him up. He wouldn't be able to walk for a while.

"Clean him up and get him out of here. Keep close to him. Take him to the hotel room and stay with him." Hendricks turned away and went out the door. He paused before he closed it and looked back at Popoford. "We may need you for another Run after all," he said, a slight smile of cynicism stretching his lips. He closed the door and Popoford passed out.

CHAPTER TWENTY-FOUR

Steven Popoford was a mess. His face was twisted with pain. His back was still hurting and his chest felt like Hendricks was still pounding on it. He slouched in the back seat of a big car, only half-realizing that the two men who had held him for Hendricks were sitting next to him. There was a driver, but Popoford couldn't see his face. The pain was interrupting his thoughts, and the constant static it caused in his head held his attention. He was being taken somewhere, but he didn't care where. All he could care about just then was that he was alive. The pain proved that.

Hendricks' boys did as they'd been told. They found a cheap room in the back of a run-down, guano-stained hotel. It seemed they'd been there before; had used the room before for similar reasons. The clerk was unquestioning as the two men half-dragged Popoford through the lobby and up the single flight of steps. Popoford guessed that the hotel was a safe house of sorts. Was it Home Offices', or was it a place of imprisonment for Hendricks' personal use? Popoford didn't know, but he began to care. He began to think, and gradually the pain began to subside.

The door to the musty room was opened and he was hauled inside and pushed down on a cot. One of the men made a cursory search of the room. Neither man spoke. Popoford lay back, grateful for the opportunity. The man who had looked around came out of the bathroom and picked up the telephone.

"Call him," he said, apparently to the clerk. He looked over at Popoford as if he were looking at the wall. There was no interest in the man's eyes. There wasn't a single hint of thoughtfulness. Popoford had seen so many men like this one. The vagueness of his memories still nagged him, but he recognized the stare in the man's eyes, blank and obeying. It was the stare of loyalty that allowed men to behave heroically or despicably with the same sense of honor. It was a stare that Popoford suddenly realized he'd seen most often in his mirror. It was the stare that he must have been wearing when he pulled the trigger on President Bjoonic. Popoford closed his eyes.

The man said no more, he only listened and then hung up. Popoford opened his eyes.

The seated guard glanced at the one who had called for instructions. They nodded at each other, and the seated man stood up. He pulled a pistol from under his coat and held it on Popoford. Then the other man approached Popoford and removed a syringe from a table beside the cot. He jabbed the needle into a little vial of clear liquid. The vial was sucked dry.

"Get that thing away from me, you bastard!" Popoford yelled and swung his fist at the needle. The man was very quick and managed to grab Popoford's wrist. He yanked Popoford's arm straight out and stuffed his knee into the agent's gut, flattening him on the cot. Popoford gasped and tried to struggle out of the man's grasp, but it was too late. The other man had already pulled Popoford's sleeve up, and the needle was poised above his skin, about to be driven into his arm.

Popoford heard the crash that came next. It took him a couple of seconds to realize that it wasn't the sound of his head bursting. It wasn't the sound of horrid drugs destroying his mind. It was the sound of glass shattering and something crashing to the floor. Someone had thrown a rock through the window.

"Lorain!" Popoford shouted. How could he have forgotten?

Suddenly the door burst open. Two sharp blasts caught the two men staring in surprise at the broken glass and blew great holes in their backs. Their bodies fell behind a beat as they continued to move even after death. One man spun toward the door and fired his pistol once and then fell on his face in front of Lorain. The other man looked back at Popoford and jabbed the needle at his bare skin, but Popoford jerked out of the way and the drug was spent in the thin mattress. The man slumped to the floor.

"Come on, Steven. Let's get the hell out of here."

"The clerk. He's one of them."

"He's dead. Let's go."

Popoford stood up. It would be days before the pain would be completely gone. Right then he forgot that there was any pain.

They ran out to the street together, Popoford leading the way, Lorain concealing her shotgun under her coat. Popoford hadn't seen the hotel clerk. He must have fallen behind the counter. There was no time to worry about details. There was only time to get away, to find a safe house of their own. Sirens were already echoing. The police would arrive soon, and someone would identify them. People were already peering from behind blinds. Popoford looked for a cab. Wrong neighborhood. There were none. He took Lorain by the elbow.

"We'll have to walk out. Come on. Be calm."

"I can manage for myself, thank you," Lorain said, removing his hand. She wasn't harsh, but she was firm. Popoford wouldn't get away with solicitous behavior, no matter what the circumstances.

"Yes, of course, you can," Popoford said simply.

They walked rapidly down the sidewalk until they saw the first police car pull into view, then they stopped for a second and watched the car pass. They walked on for a while until another police car passed. They watched it also. To the police, they presented themselves as curious bystanders. When no one was looking, they walked away from the neighborhood, leaving it a little more abused than it deserved to be.

They found a cab several blocks from the hotel. Popoford flagged it down and they got in.

"Where to, mister?"

Popoford hadn't considered where he could hide. He couldn't stay in any public place. Hendricks would find him in a matter of hours. But he had to be close. He still had to stop President Rosiva from signing the treaty. He still had to tell the president what had been happening. He still had to do something to atone for his own crimes. Destroying Home Office, seeing Hendricks and the old man destroyed would be gratifying, especially if he could kill them himself. He couldn't do these things if he was too far away.

"Just a minute. Just start driving, and I'll let you know where we're going in a minute."

"Right, mister. It's your money."

Lorain leaned into Popoford and lowered her voice so the cabby couldn't hear her. "You must know someplace to go, Steven. You've surely been assigned to Washington before. There must be a safe place to go."

Popoford shook his head slowly. "No, I don't think that I ever have been assigned here. None of it is familiar."

"What?"

"Oh...it's nothing, just a little memory loss. I'll tell you about it later. It was a gift from Home Office. But I'm sure I've never been here."

Lorain couldn't respond, she just looked at him like she was gazing at the subject of an experiment. She looked at him like he was a thing with unpredictable reactions; like he was a befuddled man, a fool.

"Don't look at me like that. I can't help it."

Lorain looked away. Popoford thought it was pity.

"Look," he said. "I know where we could go. My memory's not that bad. I just remembered that my brother lives here."

Lorain looked at Popoford again in her sterile way.

"Dammit. It's not that surprising. I haven't seen him in twenty years. Driver, find a telephone book."

The cabby pulled over and Popoford jumped out to look up his brother's address. He wasn't gone long. He came back running and jumped back in the cab.

"Take this!" he shouted to Lorain as he shoved a piece of paper into her hand. "I'll be there. Don't follow me. Just call me tonight."

Lorain nodded. Popoford talked rapidly. He felt like he was in control of himself again.

"Cabby," Popoford said. "Take this cash and drive quickly around the corner. then let me out. Get rid of the blue car that's following us a couple of blocks back, then take the lady to a good hotel."

The cabby nodded and spun around the corner and stopping suddenly.

Popoford spoke under his breath. "They don't know you're here, Lorain. I'm convinced of it. Hendricks didn't mention you. They won't hurt you."

"If they find me, they'll know what I've done today. I won't get off easily."

"Yes, of course," Popoford said. "That was foolish. Just get them off my tail."

He jumped out of the car, slammed the door, and ducked into a darkened stairwell. The taxi drove away fast. Popoford saw that same cold look in Lorain's eyes as she glanced back at him. It bothered him. The taxi turned the corner.

Two, three, four beats, and the blue car came into view and slowed for the corner where Popoford was hidden. He spotted Hendricks in the back seat. He was leaning forward pointing through the windshield, haranguing the driver. H.O. sat in the passenger seat. Popoford saw in a glance the old man's calm, ugly face. He was looking straight ahead as if he were dead. There was a trail of saliva running down his chin. The blue car rushed by and headed straight up the street. Already Lorain was free of her assailants. Popoford stepped out of the doorway and walked back the way he'd come. He found another cab and directed the cabby to take him out to a certain address in Bethesda. He would stay awhile with his nearly forgotten brother.

By the time the taxi found the house, the spring sun was within an hour of setting, and deep shadows had already concealed the architectural detail of the two-story tract houses. Electric fixtures had been turned on above the front doors, and they glared into Popoford's eyes, causing him to squint against their ironic, repelling light. The woods behind the row houses were a thick, black wall that caught the chilling north wind and howled at its touch. Popoford shivered at the sight and paid the driver. He would be grateful for the warmth that awaited him within his brother's home. He needed sanctuary, and his heart warmed to the notion that it was so close at hand even while his skin quivered in the frigid air.

Popoford walked quickly up the long, straight walk. He stood on the porch, bowing his head against the harsh light, and he pushed the doorbell button. A light rain began to fall.

He waited for a moment and listened to the roaring sound of the approaching storm, and then he heard a voice from behind the thick door.

"Who is it?"

"It's Steven."

"Who?"

"Steven. Steven Popoford. Jerry's brother." Popoford waited. There was no reply. "Jerry, it's me, Steven!"

"I don't know any Steven."

Popoford was astounded.

"Wait a minute," the voice continued. "Steven who?"

"Steven Popoford."

"Popoford? Yes, that's the name," the voice behind the door said. "What do you want?"

"For goodness sake, Jerry, it's me, Steven, your brother. Let me in. Open the door."

"What did you say? My brother?"

"God yes. Open up!" Popoford yelled and started knocking on the door.

"I don't have a brother. Get off my property."

Popoford stopped knocking. "What did you say?"

"Get out of here. We're calling the police. Now get out of here!"

Popoford pounded hard on the door. "God damn your ass. It hasn't been that long! You wrote me a letter in Whimsy! Open this door, damn you!"

The storm was gathering quickly. The rain fell harder, and even above the thudding of his fists, Popoford could hear sirens approaching.

Suddenly the door burst open. Popoford was grabbed by his collar. His head was filled with the hot, alcoholic breath of an enraged monster. The man's face filled Popoford's view with its ghastly features. The man's flesh had grown loose, his facial muscles slackened by gravity. His eyes were reddened, gleaming pools overly supplied from tear ducts that couldn't close. A rough stubble covered his cheeks. Popoford thought that he recognized the man. He wasn't sure. Liquor had so ravaged and bloated the man's face that he wasn't sure for a while if it was the brother of his memory or not.

"I don't have a brother, mister. Get it straight!"

Popoford knocked the man's hands away. He took a step backward, staggering in disbelief. Had he made a mistake? The huge man that glared at him wasn't his brother. That was certain. Even though it had been years since Popoford had last seen him, this man wasn't the man that Popoford remembered. Looking at the grotesque anger that filled the man's face, he found it hard to recollect the exact picture of Jerry Popoford, but this man wasn't even a close likeness. He turned and ran down the walk without bothering to apologize.

"Get off my property!" the man yelled. He'd stumbled out onto his porch. "Go back to where you belong!"

Sirens were getting louder. The police were closing in on the Bethesda intruder, and confusion was closing in on Popoford. He wandered away from the house, wondering if he was going crazy. He was doing things that didn't make sense, and too many memories had no definition. He was a hero of sorts in his memory, but there were no recent events that could prove it. He was a special, exceptional agent in his memory, but he'd been persuaded to commit to a hideous and questionable assassination. He had been manipulated by I.I.O., made a fool of in the field by Lorain, and was fumbling his way through ludicrous attempts to stop the signing of the treaty. In his memory, he knew who he was, but in the present, he was only a vague imitator who he could barely recognize. Something was very wrong. He had known it. How long had he known it? There was confusion and ineptness in everything that he remembered. He didn't have a memory of the repulsive man with his brother's name, but there was a vague, incomplete memory of another time when he'd known that his brother lived in Bethesda.

Somewhere in his head, he could almost see the memory. He could almost touch it, but it always slipped away when he tried. He'd had no specifics in his head since before Whimsy. Gretchen and Home Office, his every act as a man, the very events that must have occurred as he worked his way through the agency on his way to becoming an extraordinary agent, everything was lost behind a veil of translucent memory.

Popoford remembered Hendricks talking about the debriefing. He remembered how the debriefing had seemed to be the usual and acceptable procedure when an agent had been pulled from the field. But how had he remembered that? How could he have accepted that when now he couldn't even remember the specifics of his life? He was going crazy. There was no doubt in his mind about that. He had to stop the continuing slide. He had to find something that he could hold onto, some memory that could give him hope. He thought of Hendricks and how he'd been manipulated into returning to service. He remembered the strange phone calls in the hotel room when the clerk seemed to have been bypassed, the switchboard circumvented. He remembered Hendricks; remembered his face, remembered every detail he'd known before the debriefing, and before Whimsy.

"Hendricks!" Popoford cried. "My God! Hendricks! I can remember you. You were real!"

Popoford wandered along the sidewalk, talking to himself and grasping the one name that represented his sanity. The police sirens grew nearer, then the flashing lights on the cars cut through the heavy rain.

As Popoford walked away from the house in Bethesda, he was unaware of the commotion behind him. He didn't notice the police cars pulling to a stop in front of the house. He didn't notice his soaked clothing. He was too busy trying to understand why he was there in the first place, and why it was that the only thing he could clearly remember of his past was the face of Hendricks.

Popoford didn't notice the other car that cruised the wide curving street. He didn't pay attention to it as it slid up behind him. He was unaware of anything but his thoughts until the car stopped, the door opened, and Hendricks collected him in an overcoat and put him in the back seat.

CHAPTER TWENTY-FIVE

Popoford snuggled in between Hendricks and the other man. He shivered at the sudden warmth of the car.

"You're a sick man, Steven. A very sick man. We need to get you to a hospital right away. You need professional help."

Popoford was in a daze. At first, he didn't know where he was. He hung onto Hendricks' voice. It was the soothing tone of a shepherd: gentle and assuring. It was confirmation of his sanity, yet also proof of his insanity. Nevertheless, it felt so good to hear the words of someone who cared, someone who might prove that he wasn't crazy.

"There, there, Steven. Try to relax. You'll get used to the warmth in a second. Just try to relax and everything will be all right."

Popoford looked up at Hendricks. He looked in his old boss's eyes. There was a glint that brought a flashing scene to his mind. There was a sneering twinkle in the black center that caused the scene to stick, and Popoford clearly recalled the hideous moment when he'd been ridiculed by this very man. He could clearly see the president dying. He could even feel the great rush of adrenaline as the deed was done, and he could feel the tense knot that had grown in his stomach when he'd been confronted by his commanders and had been told of his disgraceful manipulation. He saw his disgrace in Hendricks' eyes, and the old rage returned. Popoford threw open his coat and took a wild swing at Hendricks.

"You bastard! I'll kill you!"

"Calm yourself, Steven," Hendricks said softly as if to a little boy. He had grabbed Popoford's wrist in midair. He held it there until Popoford gave in, and then he placed his hand back under the overcoat. Hendricks fell silent and looked away from Popoford. He acted as if his feelings had been hurt. Popoford relaxed. The man to his right remained silent. The car drove away from Bethesda.

Popoford sat still, looking straight ahead. Once again he'd been captured. Once more he was being maneuvered by Hendricks, and therefore by H.O. Once more he'd failed as the great secret agent of his mind. But something was different this time. He was still completely confused, and he had no idea what had actually happened to him. But at least he wasn't insane. There had been a man named Hendricks before he'd been recalled from Whimsy. The man next to him was that man. There was no doubt of that, and Popoford took heart at the knowledge. He took courage in the possibility that he could use Hendricks to get to H.O. and could then kill the old man. Even if he couldn't stop the treaty signing, he could still try to stop the organization that would deliver the country up to its enemies. Once he killed H.O., perhaps he still could stop the signing, perhaps there would still be enough time and a way for that, but for now, only one thing needed doing, and patience was his first step in the attack. He would have to wait patiently for his chance.

The car was driven along back roads that were ill-lit and didn't allow curious eyes time for identification. The three men in the back seat were silent. The driver said nothing and avoided Popoford's eyes in the rearview mirror.

When they'd driven several miles from Bethesda, the car was driven onto a gravel road. Its lights were switched off, then the ignition key was removed, and the car was allowed to coast to a silent stop. Popoford remained calm, but his heart sank.

"You're going to kill me. The obvious solution to your problems. I never thought about it."

"You're wrong. You represent too large an investment, Steven. We've overtaxed you, but you're salvageable. We just have to know a few things. We have to ask you a few questions. Then we can correct the errors we made with you, and you'll be as good as new."

"So you've captured me so that you can beat the answers from me. That's it. So let's get it over with."

"You're much too noble, Steven," Hendricks said with a gentle laugh. "We have no further use for force against you. You'll cooperate without force, won't you?"

"Very doubtful," Popoford replied.

Hendricks fell silent again, and together the three men sat squeezed side-by-side in the slowly cooling back seat and waited for something.

There was a sharp knocking at the window. Popoford jumped slightly. His muscles tightened. Hendricks rubbed his hands against the fogged window and peered out. Popoford couldn't see what was happening outside, but Hendricks could.

"Time to get out, Steven," Hendricks said, and he opened the door and got out himself. "Come on Steven, it's cold out here. Hurry up."

The rain had stopped, but the wind had remained and was growing stronger. They were parked on a country road, and there was no sign of life in any direction. There was no moon, and the stars that snapped on and off in the crisp sky provided no useful light. Popoford looked about in all directions and could see nothing. There was only a man wrapped close in a great, fur-collared coat who whispered something to Hendricks and then disappeared into the dark. Hendricks turned to Popoford.

"Over there, Steven. Walk in that direction." He indicated the way that the other man had gone. "There's another car waiting for you."

Popoford did as he was told. He walked away from Hendricks, expecting to be clubbed at any moment, expecting to be brutalized in some manner, not understanding the restrained and almost respectful tone in Hendricks' voice, not trusting it at all. In the dark, he came upon the man in the overcoat.

"This way. Hurry," the man said, but he didn't rush, nor did he give the appearance that there was any hurry, so Popoford kept walking at the same pace.

"Move it, dammit!" the man yelled, and Popoford jumped into a faster cadence. A few rapid steps and Popoford bumped headlong into the other car.

The man in the fur coat opened the front door. "Get in." Popoford did so, and the door was closed behind him. Popoford sat alone in the front seat of the dark car and waited.

"Don't turn around. I have a gun on you. I'll kill you if you threaten me. Understood?"

Popoford nodded.

"Speak up!"

"Yes, I understand, sir," Popoford said with an emphasized contempt. "I understand perfectly." It was I.I.O. in the back seat. Popoford understood only one thing perfectly. he had to keep his temper. Somehow, if he could hold back until just the right time, he would have a chance to kill the ugly little man. He understood this one thing very well as he listened to the regular breathing of the man whom he had to kill.

"Why are you here, Popoford? Why have you been so stupid? I warned you to stay out of the way. You could have been safe in Whimsy."

"I couldn't have just let you convince Rosiva to sign the treaty."

H.O. laughed. "You're kidding, of course. There's no way for you to stop that. It's over. There's nothing more to be done about the treaty."

"He signed it?"

"No, but there was never any need to coerce or to convince Rosiva to do anything."

"He's with you?"

"Always has been. Remember that Bjoonic chose his running mate. They'd lived together as children. They had the same stepfather. When Bjoonic discovered that he had terminal cancer, he decided not to get out of the race. He would run and eventually win, but there would be a change of plans. He would become a martyr and get the people to support his dying effort. It's working very well. The good citizens have been driven to mass hysteria. The papers are reporting overwhelming popular support for the treaty signing. We've planted so many stories that the voters are convinced that there's a demand for the signing. Following our suggestion, they are obliging us by falling into step. In a few days, the demand will be too much, and a reluctant Rosiva will be forced to sign."

Popoford could hear a smile on the old man's thin lips. In a way, he thought that stopping the signing would be easier now. He would have to kill Rosiva. It would be easier than having to convince him. In another way, H.O.'s words made life even more difficult. The assassin of a president is a loathed man. He had survived one such act unexposed. Still, the anger that was growing in the public forum would be pushed beyond outrage if he were to kill a second president, and without the complicity and influence of H.O. and his fellow conspirators, he could never escape detection. Unless there was an act of God, Popoford knew that he would soon give his life for his country.

"I see that you've had me in your control since the beginning."

"Yes, and we still have you," H.O. replied. "You're my highest achievement."

"What does that mean?" Popoford asked. "Can't you get on with the questioning? I've got a heavy date tonight."

"The girl? Don't be absurd Steven. Hendricks told you that she was with us."

"I can't always believe Hendricks."

Again Home Office laughed. "What an understatement, Steven."

The laugh annoyed Popoford. "Knock it off and get on with it. What do you want to know?"

"What do you know about this P. Y. Mous? Are you connected to him somehow?"

"He's a patriot."

H.O.'s voice hardened. "He's a smuggler and a crook. You know nothing of him."

"I know he wants you stopped. So does his daughter."

"So it seems. Maybe they do."

"So what do you want to know?" Popoford asked, not expecting an answer.

"There's one thing that I can't stand, Popoford. Do you think you know what that is? Do you think you know why a man of such great loyalty as yourself should be highly valued? Do you think that I created you just for the hell of it?"

"What are you talking about, dammit? Make sense."

"Loyalty, Popoford, like yours. I can't stand a traitor like Mous,"

Popoford caught his breath at the stupid irony. There was a sudden, loud crack outside, and a small hole appeared in the windshield. It happened so suddenly. Popoford was holding back a great laugh. He let it out with only the sound of escaping air. There was no humor left in him. He turned quickly and saw Home Office dying. There was a hole the same size as the one in the glass drilled into the old man's throat. H.O. didn't die suddenly. There were still words in his mouth, and Popoford leaned over the seat to hear. "Mous sent you to me...Resurrection Runner..." H.O. died.

Outside, a firefight started and was quickly concluded with a short burst of automatic weapon fire. The brief violence left the dark country road silent. Except for Popoford, the remaining intruders upon the road's usual calm were dead.

Popoford found a flashlight in the glove compartment. He cautiously got out and searched the road finding the body of a man wrapped in a fur-collared greatcoat. He found the car that had brought him. He found the driver, his head thrashed by a stream of lead, slumped halfway out of the door. But he didn't find Hendricks.

Leaving the rest of the scene untouched, Popoford took the keys from the driver's dead hand and yanked him out of the car. Then he took his pistol. Finally, he got into the car, started the engine, and snapped on the headlights. The barren closeness of the black night wasn't relieved. The lights were only yellow tunnels that narrowed the perspective of his confusion. He drove away from the scene without knowing in which direction to go. He would try to find Lorain. That would be the best thing to do. He couldn't trust her, but it would be safer if he could keep an eye on her. He had to keep moving.

He drove for several miles, and before long he approached the outskirts of town. He imagined Washington D.C. lit only by streetlights, waiting for him to return. Indeed, he would return and stalk his prey, and he would kill it swiftly, leaving only a moment for his victim's silent repentance. He had the skills to do what he had to do, but he needed help. It was a longshot, but perhaps Lorain could end up being that help.

He came to the main road. The sign said Washington to the south, Bethesda to the north. He drove north to stake out his brother's house and to wait for Lorain to come looking for him. As he drove, he thought briefly about his skills, and he wondered why he'd been trained as an assassin who couldn't remember his past. He wondered what Hendricks and Home Office had meant when they said that he was too valuable to eliminate. There were too many things to think about. What was meant by "Resurrection Runner?" Perhaps he would never know more than that H.O. died with that phrase and P. Y. Mous' name on his lips. When the treaty was torn up, before he was lynched for his crimes, he might force someone to explain everything. For now, time was wasting.

CHAPTER TWENTY-SIX

Popoford arrived at his brother's house while it was still dark, but he drove by because the police were in the driveway wrapping up some kind of investigation. As he drove, he saw a parking space on the other side of the street about a block away. Making a u-turn, he came back toward the house and slid into the empty space. There were several cars parked along on the road, but a cursory inspection didn't reveal any passengers in the cars.

He figured that if it had been Lorrain who killed H.O., it would take her about an hour to get there from Bethesda. He also thought that Hendricks would be on his tail as well. What was odd was that he hadn't been stopped already. Hendricks might have let him live, but he wouldn't have let him roam free to try to stop the treaty signing. If Lorain was involved, she would have made herself known to him, unless she was on his side. These things were bothersome, but the most bothersome question that occurred to Popoford was what even though H.O. had known about Mous, still, his name had been so startling to them? Popoford could understand all of H.O.'s talk about traitors. A man like H.O. had such a twisted mind that he must have genuinely thought that his own traitorous acts were of primary benefit to the country. Popoford was the traitor to H.O. He was the traitor to Hendricks, but what was the connection to Mous?

Just then there was a light rapping on the window. Popoford turned quickly. It was Lorain. He motioned her to come around to the other side of the car and to get in. She just shook her head, and Popoford lowered the window.

"What's going on?"

"Get out of the car. It's hot. Come on before the cops take notice."

Popoford looked at the house. The police were already in their patrol car and hadn't noticed him. They probably wouldn't do anything to him anyway. They couldn't know who he was. It was strange that Lorain should think that they would care. He decided to play along with her. If she were deceiving him, he would find out by letting her plans unfold. He got out of the car.

"Come on. I have another car over here. There's someone who wants to see you."

Popoford looked at her but didn't ask who would want to see him. It would be Hendricks. He knew then that Lorain had been involved with Home Office right from the beginning. She'd used Popoford from the start, and she'd drawn him into her web with little effort. Here he was again doing what she wanted done. It seemed that there was little else he could do.

Popoford walked over to the other car. There was a brilliant flash of lightning, and daylight returned to the street for a second. The car and its interior were lit up. A man was sitting in the back seat looking out the window at Popoford. Popoford looked back into the face of P. Y. Mous.

"What the..." Popoford said.

"When you sent me to the hotel the first thing I did was to call Father. I thought it best. He came right away."

Popoford didn't reply. Only about two hours and a half had passed since he'd last seen her. Mous hadn't been called in from California. He probably was already in Washington. Popoford didn't like it.

"I'm surprised to see you here, Mous," Popoford said as he got into the car.

"You need direction. I can get you into the Oval Office."

Popoford looked at the man. "You're telling me that you can get me in to see the president?"

"Yes."

"I have a gun on me."

"Give it to me. You can't get into the White House with a gun, You won't need it anyway. I'm known. I've made an appointment."

Popoford was flabbergasted. "You did what? Did you make an appointment? Tonight?"

"Yes."

"If you could do that, why in God's name have I been running around playing spy? Why didn't you just take me to see Rosiva?"

"I will now. Before, it wasn't the best way. Now it is. You should be able to understand that, Steven."

"Well, I don't. Why don't you explain it to me? Maybe your explanation will make sense. Nothing else does."

"Not now, Steven. Later, when we talk to the president. You'll understand then."

"Wait a minute. What's this about talking to the president? The only thing I need to talk to him about is the treaty."

"Now you're catching on, Steven. Don't forget your goal. Remember the assignment that you gave yourself. The treaty must be stopped no matter what. I can make it easy for you to get to Rosiva. That's all that you need to know now. We can discuss methods of operation at a better time."

Popoford thought for a second. Then, still needing to know much more, he nodded. "Right."

"Good. That's better. We mustn't lose our heads," Mous said. "Lorain, you may drive us to the White House now."

"But what about Hendricks? How did he know? What do you know about Resurrection Runner? Did you kill Home Office?"

Mous burst out laughing at Popoford's insistence. "Later, Steven. You'll understand everything later. Let's get the treaty taken care of first, Okay?"

Popoford nodded and set his resolve all the more strongly.

"Now, give that gun before you forget about it."

Lorain drove from Bethesda down into D.C.

The sun was turning the black, rainy night to grey when they arrived at the White House. They didn't bother with public entrances but went directly to the private reception area. The car wove through the concrete, anti-terror barriers. Credentials were presented to a stiff-backed Secret Service agent, his partner with the dog watching close by. The car was passed through with a smart salute. As they drove toward the White House, Popoford's trained eye noted the quiet signs of judiciously placed security. They were being observed, spied on with powerful scopes, followed up the slowly winding drive, tracked and mistrusted. They were met at the end of the driveway by other, equally stiff agents who escorted them through the doors and into the mansion. It was almost seven-thirty by the time they walked into the lobby. A young man, properly dressed in the gray flannel of his position and flanked by two Secret Service agents, welcomed them.

"It's good to see you again, Mr. Mous. The president is anxiously awaiting you in the Oval Office."

"Good to see you too, Robert. How is he tonight?"

"President Rosiva is prepared for the unexpected."

"Is he now?" Mous smiled.

"Though you're always challenging, he welcomes whatever you bring," John replied.

"How diplomatic, and flattering. You do make me feel welcome, Robert. Let me introduce you to my companions. This is my daughter, Lorain. Perhaps you remember her from several years ago. I think I brought her around when President Bjoonic was first elected."

"Yes, of course, I remember. How do you do?"

Lorain nodded. The trace of a smile crossed her mouth.

"And this is a business partner of mine. May I present Steven Popoford."

"Mr. Popoford. Welcome to the White House," Robert said, warmly. "And now, I must ask you to submit to a search. It's inconvenient but necessary. Security is much tighter since the assassination. I do hope you understand."

"Of course, John. We're happy to oblige."

Popoford noted the extreme familiarity that was shared by Mous and Robert. It bothered him. He could almost taste the cloying deference hanging like a cloud in the lobby.

Two more Secret Service agents had been sitting straight in hard chairs. They stood in unison and proceeded to search Mous and Popoford. Then they turned to Lorain. The process was over quickly. No weapons nor recording devices were found. The agents returned to their chairs without a word.

"All clear, Mr. Mous. You may go in."

"Thank you, Robert. We'll see you again on the way out."

"Yes, of course," Robert said and bowed slightly.

"You do seem to know your way around," Popoford said.

"Yes I do, Steven. That reminds me. I'm a long-time friend of President Rosiva. I think that if you let me do the talking, we can be done with the treaty problem in short order."

Again Popoford was aghast. "What do you mean? Dammit, if you could do something about the treaty before this, why the hell have I been going through so much crap?"

"Steven!" Mous said sharply. "Later! We haven't time for that now. Please!"

Mous opened the double doors and they went in.

CHAPTER TWENTY-SEVEN

Popoford walked through the doors. He was tense. He would stop the signing of the treaty no matter what it took. He was prepared to fight if he had to. He was prepared to die. If he had Mous' and Lorain's help, the signing would be stopped. He was sure of it. He would win this little battle. For once, at least, he would crush this traitorous political will. He was hoping that Home Office had lied about Rosiva's complicity. It would make his task a little easier. He walked confidently through the doors, and they were closed behind him. A second set of heavy doors slid down over the first. it was sheathed in thick steel. This wasn't the Oval Office.

Popoford instantly flexed his legs as he prepared for an attacker to leap out of the half-lit corners. Mous and Lorain moved off in opposite directions, keeping their backs close to the walls. Popoford waited quietly, listening closely for a sign of movement from the front. He sniffed the air like a wolf downwind of his prey. There was a faint scent in the air, but he couldn't name the tart aroma. It was someone's aftershave. They were certainly not alone.

Suddenly a glaring spotlight burst on. Popoford was blinded. There was a soft report of an air pistol. Popoford froze. He'd been hit. He brushed his neck wildly, knowing he was too late. The dart had hit home in his left carotid artery. His wild swiping quickly ceased. The tranquilizer had reached his brain almost instantly.

Popoford stood still. The tension left him. His muscles all relaxed. He didn't lose his resolve. He didn't lose his anger. He kept his passion to destroy the treaty and the traitors, and to accept death. But he couldn't move, but he listened. His brain was still alert.

The spotlight was shut off, and gradually Popoford's eyes grew used to the half-light. Then someone brought the lights up a bit more, and he saw others in the room.

"How are you feeling, Mr. Popoford?"

Popoford only looked at the man sitting behind a simple card table.

"Come, come, Mr. Popoford. You can talk. The drug allows you to talk. As you can tell, you can't move your limbs, but you can talk. Now, how are you feeling?"

"Horrible."

"That's to be expected, Mr. Popoford. I'm President Rosiva. I'm so happy you could see me tonight. I'll need witnesses for the signing of this historic document."

Rosiva waved a folder in the air as he twisted his waxed mustache between the fingers of his left hand.

"When that is done, you'll be put to the use for which you were intended, Mr. Popoford. This has already been a most interesting night. You may be surprised to know that the Senate of the United States met in a closed session earlier this evening and ratified this treaty by a vote of 78 to 22. A rather convincing result, don't you think?"

Popoford didn't reply. He found that he could move his eyes, and he looked around in the shadows for Mous and Lorain, and for any people who might be involved in the historic event. "I don't think that you need to be introduced to these men."

Popoford saw Hendricks leaning against the wall behind Rosiva. He looked away from the sneering face. Hendricks had lived. He had certainly been involved in H.O.'s murder. He couldn't bear to see him, confident and cocky, a traitor even to honor among thieves. He looked away to a man who sat in a straight-backed chair. This man wasn't smiling, but he met Popoford's eyes with his unyielding gaze. It was the good Senator Boscwell. So, he'd been in on the treason from the beginning. Some things that H.O. had told him had been true.

Then Popoford remembered Mous and Lorain. He looked further into the shadows to find his companions. To his left, he saw Lorain. She was slumped in another straight-backed chair. She'd been drugged and tied down with a rope. Her chin rested on her chest. She would be of no use to him. Then Popoford realized that he, too, was useless.

He looked to his right, and there he saw P. Y. Mous. The sight drained Popoford of even the tiny hope that had remained in his mind. Mous walked out of the shadows and took a place just in front and to the left of Popoford. He smiled broadly at Popoford, and then he turned to Rosiva and bowed. "We're all here. Let the signing begin."

Rosiva snapped his fingers and Hendricks stood up straight.

"The pen please, Mr. Hendricks."

Hendricks withdrew a black pen and handed it to Rosiva who bent over the paper and then looked up.

"You know, Popoford, your presence here for the signing is more important to me than you might imagine. I've been keeping track of you for almost fifteen years. You've been the primary weapon in our strategy since the beginning. It's necessary, for propriety's sake, that you be here. After all, you've put just as much effort into the treaty as anyone has. But above all, you're going to finish the job that you originally undertook. Isn't that right, Mous?"

"Yes, it certainly is," Mous said, without turning to look at Popoford.

The president smiled at Popoford. He had a devilish twinkle in his eyes. He had a secret, and he was looking forward to finally telling it.

Rosiva looked at the document. He put the pen to the signature page, and he signed it with a firm stroke. The treaty was now law.

Popoford felt tears welling in his eyes. Mous, Hendricks, and Rosiva shook hands. They were all smiling, and Popoford saw that the signing had allowed Mous to relax into the jovial man who had taken him in at San Francisco International airport. He was a strange man who would let his daughter be drugged and left tied in the corner. Then Popoford remembered that Mous had said that the woman who had died in the field in Whimsy was his wife.

"Have you killed your daughter, too?" Popoford asked.

Mous looked at Popoford. He was indeed in a jovial mood. "Steven, it's about time for you to complete your assignment. I don't want Lorain to see what is going to happen here. When you're removed, she'll take your place. We don't want her to be contaminated."

"What's he talking about?" Popoford asked Rosiva. "I won't do anything for you."

"There's no need to do anything, Steven. It's already done. Mous, please get on with it. We have a timetable."

"Of course, Mr. President," Mous said and took a deep breath. "Steven Popoford, you are the Resurrection Runner. You are the result of many years of work, many years of continuous effort. You are a human tool, perfectly programmed so that your inadequacies can be utilized in our favor. Through hypnosis and the reinforcement of pseudo-memories, we've controlled what you know and what you believe. Through the use of memory-wiping drugs, we've been able to mold and to eventually control not only what you do, but also what you remember. You remember training that did occur, but you haven't been allowed to remember everything. You are an assassin. You are the best in the sense that you'll not hesitate to pull the trigger. You are also the best because it only takes a little reminder to start your programmed responses. It's so very easy to get you going, to get your patriotism going, to bring America's current threat to a boil within you. Hendricks and H.O. formed you well. When they first offered your services to Bjoonic, there was no doubt as to your value, but it took a mind like Bjoonic's to formulate a plan that could best utilize your features."

Popoford fought his fear. Even the tranquilizer wasn't strong enough to keep it at bay. He might go insane if he were to accept these revelations. "How...how long?"

"You've been in service for almost twenty years. You've been very useful," Hendricks answered. He leaned on the card table as he spoke. "But these briefings do get boring. This will be about the thirteenth or fourteenth time that we've explained it all to you. Usually, it's necessary so that your mind can be cleared. There's no need for that today. Mous, let's get on with it. He doesn't need to know what he is."

"Perhaps he doesn't, Hendricks," President Rosiva said. "But I want Mr. Popoford to know why he's about to die. Mr. Mous?"

"Certainly," Mous said, and he turned to Popoford and stood in front of him though not so close that Popoford couldn't see the other men.

"We've arranged for you to be caught in the act of attempted assassination. You will die at the heroic hands of President Rosiva. You will be killed with a bullet from one of your guns."

Still facing Popoford, Mous stretched his hand behind him. "Hendricks. If you please."

Hendricks came out from behind the card table and came close to Popoford. He pulled a pistol from under his jacket, and he showed it to Popoford. He didn't give it to Mous. Popoford saw a slight look of consternation on Mous' face.

"Anyway, the president will shoot you dead with your gun, and the people will rise as one in favor of the president and every policy that he might propose. The treaty will be heralded as a breakthrough in East-West relations, and we'll go on with our plans to unify the secret services of the world."

Popoford was having no difficulty understanding what was happening. "You once said that this would be the worst thing that could happen to our country. You once said that by sharing our intelligence we would be destroyed."

"Yes, and I was right. I'm sorry that you won't be around after the nation's fall to see it rise again."

Popoford strained against the drug. He tried with all his might to force his neck to move, to make his legs and arms respond to his panic. Nothing happened. He didn't move, but he did manage to gather enough saliva in his mouth to spit on P. Y. Mous.

"You bastards!" Popoford cried. "Where is my life?"

"Gone, you pig!" Mous said. "Hendricks, give the pistol to Rosiva. Let's get on with it. The assassin must die."

Mous stepped aside from the line of fire.

"I have the pistol," Rosiva said. "Say good-bye to Mr. Steven Popoford."

Hendricks stood still, a smirk on his face. Mous looked away from Popoford. The president took careful aim. Popoford could see the barrel align with his eyes. He could see the steady gaze of the president sighting down the blued steel. He resolved to keep his eyes open as the slug hit his head. He would die bravely. He waited for death.

Suddenly Rosiva switched the sighting of the pistol slightly, and he pulled the trigger twice. There was a sharp, double report that was contained in the room by the steel doors. Popoford looked to his right. Mous was holding his chest. The look on his face was so desperate, so confused, so questioning. He stared at Rosiva without saying a word. Then he fell unceremoniously in a lump on the floor. All the questions that he had would stay inside his throat, stifled, and dead.

Rosiva smiled at Popoford. He touched a small box that had been sitting unnoticed on the card table "Come quickly. I need help!" he called into the box. Then he pushed another button and the steel sheathed doors rose. Hendricks hurried to Popoford and picked him up in his arms. He placed Popoford gently in the straight-backed chair that Mous had used. "No need to worry, Steven. You're not going to die today. Remember that I told you how valuable you are."

The doors burst open, and two Secret Service officers came flying into the room, landing on their feet, aiming their weapons at the people there.

"Thank God you were out there!" Rosiva said to the soldiers. "I was almost killed."

"Captain," Hendricks ordered. "Put your pistols down. The incident is over. Please remove the body. He was the one who assassinated President Bjoonic. Take him away."

"And Captain," Rosiva said to the Marine, "Get hold of my physician and have him take a look at these two. I think that Mr. Mous drugged them. Be sure to keep them in isolation. They have been delirious and have been saying outrageous things. The girl is Mous's daughter. She doesn't know what has happened. Best not tell her right now. Mr. Hendricks will take them off your hands shortly. Understand?"

"Yes sir," the Secret Service agent replied to his commander-in-chief.

"Arrange for a press conference," Rosiva said to Robert who had just entered the room.

"Right away, sir," the aide said and left the room.

Popoford felt the Secret Service agent lifting him into his arms. He was being carried from the room, and he looked back at President Rosiva, who remained seated at the card table and who still had a confident smile on his face. Rosiva looked up at Popoford for a final time. "He became expendable, Mr. Popoford. P. Y. Mous was a man who would be king. He was expendable," he said, and the doors closed on the strange, private room in the White House.

CHAPTER TWENTY-EIGHT

The events of the next few days confused Popoford. He was rushed to a tiny room where he was stretched out on a pedestal bed under a great overhead light. The Secret Service agent explained that it would be best for Popoford to stop talking, and his voice was filled with concern. Popoford, however, continued to jabber out all the questions that came to him. Popoford soon found the officer's hand over his mouth, and the agent prevailed.

Hendricks opened the door. He smiled and appraised the situation. He approved. "Good idea. Let's just see to it that he remains quiet for the next few days."

"Yes, sir."

"Here," Hendricks said. "Put this in his mouth," and he produced a gag. For the next few days, Popoford had the gag in place except at feeding time. His body was kept equally quiet with regular injections of the tranquilizer. During all this, he was flown to the west coast, and when his gurney was finally wheeled into the basement interrogation rooms of Home Office in Hayward, Popoford had long since stopped questioning what had happened.

All he wanted was sleep. The lights in the room were lowered, and Popoford wanted to beg for sleep, but he couldn't talk. A soft melody played, and he tried to cry for sleep, but there were no tears. Hendricks popped up by the gurney as he had so often done during the flight from Washington, and Popoford knew that even if he could talk, no amount of begging would help him, no amount of crying would keep the drug from affecting his sleep. The drug was one that he knew. He had a clear memory of it. It was a memory out of context, but it was a distinct and precise memory.

Hendricks rolled up Popoford's sleeve once more and injected the drug.

"Are you tired, Steven? Do you feel like you could die of wakefulness?"

Popoford could only answer with slow and involuntary blinking. He lay on the rolling bed for several hours, staring and waiting.

"Yes, dear Steven. I know it must be hard," Hendricks continued when he spoke again. He picked up the conversation as if he'd never left Popoford's side. "I assure you that it's necessary to keep you in this state for a while. In the long run, it's the easiest way."

Hendricks walked around the gurney from Popoford's right arm to his left. He kept Popoford's eye as he walked and even as he sat on a stool and leaned closer to Popoford's face.

"We've been through this before, Steven. I know that you don't remember any of it since all previous explanations are mostly forgotten. For you, only the special memories remain, but that doesn't matter now. We'll get into all that later. What matters now is that I've kept you like this before. It's the best way to keep your mind wide open. You need to accept so much each time we talk like this, each time you remember, and you need to remember. You need to remember, Steven. I will talk, and you'll remember. You must remember if you're to be Resurrected. You must."

The music was smothering him, producing anxiety that seemed to grab him in the small of his back. His mind made a rack for him to scream on, and the music cloyed at his ears and tried to replace his hopes with dread. "Please..." he gasped. "Please turn it off."

"I can do that, Steven. Yes. I can do that. You'll listen? Steven? Answer me. Will you listen?"

"Yes... I'll try."

"Good, Steven, that will be enough. That is all we ask."

Hendricks turned the music off.

"Who else is involved?" Popoford asked tentatively. "What do you mean, 'all we ask'?"

"Very good, Steven. Ask all the questions you want. Start slowly until you get used to the music being gone. But remember, Steven, the sooner you remember everything, the sooner we can let you sleep. Understand?"

Popoford only looked up at Hendricks and despised the man. There was no way to know where the session would lead. He fought to retain the hope that he would someday have all his memories. When he killed Hendricks he wanted to remember every detail of the man's crimes.

"Good," Hendricks continued. "I think you understand. We will begin. The 'we' began as H.O. and me, years ago. Today it consists of President Rosiva, Senator Boscwell, and me. Over the years a couple of others have joined us; most of them are dead."

"What the hell are you talking about?" Popoford asked. His speech was rapidly becoming easier. "I don't understand what you mean."

"I'll make it simple for you, Steven. After all, you're my first success. You're my first Resurrection Runner. I'll tell the story. If you have any questions, let me know."

Popoford shrugged: there were too many questions. Hendricks moved back and settled on his stool. Popoford stared up at the ceiling, and it gradually lit up with the images that accompanied Hendricks' words. He barely noticed the projection; it was so unobtrusive and yet compelling. As complete exhaustion took over, and as if in a trance, he forgot the pain and his mind absorbed the dream-like images as he listened to Hendrick's monotonous, soothing voice.

Hendricks started from the beginning when Popoford was recruited for service in Home Office. He reviewed the early days just after college when Popoford was wandering and waiting for some kind of direction to materialize. Popoford had been an average student in a small-town college, a child who got there despite his inadequate education. He might have done better not going to school at all, Hendricks said, if for no other reason than that he would have remained undiscovered: an average kid invisibly marching in place. Instead, Popoford had gone to school and had been duly recorded as the common student that he was. The records revealed even more to the analyzing mind of Hendricks. Popoford had distinguished himself as a dreamer, a boy with an astonishing ability to think more of his abilities than was remotely appropriate.

Hendricks talked about how Popoford tried to come up with alternatives to scholastic achievement. He talked about the many sports that Popoford had "gone out for." He showed Popoford images of varsity events. He spoke of failure and ridicule, of continued optimism, of inevitably hopeless attempts to prove himself, and of the repeated disgrace that finally drove Popoford to the school counselors. The counselors knew just what to do with such a desire accompanied by such inadequate skills. They recommended that Popoford join the armed forces. He considered their suggestion but tabled the whole decision until after graduation. He would have more time to think about those things after college. For now, he wanted to focus on track-team try-outs. Eventually, Popoford graduated without participating in any team effort, and he was cut loose from the student body, unarmed except for heightened expertise in denying all failures, no matter how obvious.

Popoford, the graduate, was just the kid that Hendricks wanted for his experiments on behavioral control. He approached Popoford in a chummy way, pretending to be an enlistment officer for the Air Force. He told Popoford that he was needed. He made Popoford believe that he was being asked to join the team. No one ever explained to the eager boy what team he was truly joining, and Popoford, hoping that he would become a pilot, never asked, but was immediately drenched in sweat, undergoing weeks of backbreaking training for an Air Force which had never heard of Hendricks, and had never sanctioned Popoford's induction. By the time Hendricks had identified Home Office by name, Popoford had already had his mind cleansed and programmed. When Hendricks finally told Popoford that he'd been chosen for a special assignment, an elite, internal spy team known as Resurrection Runner, Popoford's new memory justified his belief in himself as the perfect choice. He accepted without hesitation. He even told Hendricks that he'd always known he was a special person who had been chosen by God for this moment. Hendricks had agreed.

From that moment on, Popoford was trained alone. The first Runner never saw any other agents. He was told that his assignment was of such a special nature and that he was such a special person, that H.O. himself would be the leader of the field unit. Popoford should never expect to see H.O., but H.O. would always be his control. Hendricks would be the immediate authority, but H.O. would always pull the strings.

While Hendricks talked, the projections continued, and Popoford saw events unfolding that had only been vague memories to him. The moments of his controlled life cut quickly from scene to scene, and he remembered each of them as if they'd just happened. He remembered the first killing and the numbness in his head as he prepared for that first test. He would be a true member of the team if he could pass the first test. It meant everything to him. There would be nothing for him if he failed. Hendricks had said so over and over again. Failure would mean that Popoford would be cut loose from the team, and Hendricks would make sure that Popoford would never be able to live with that failure. But Hendricks also persuaded Popoford that he couldn't fail, and the young man's mind was numb not because of fear, but because he had to force the joy in his heart to stay put until his inevitable triumph was obtained.

For the first test, Hendricks had marked a young woman in a nearby neighborhood as the target. Her name was Gretchen, an unattached, undistinguished working girl who had nearly given up waiting for a man. Hendricks filled Popoford's head with trumped-up reports of her criminal record. Gretchen soon existed in Popoford's mind as an arch-villain bent on the destruction of the government. She was a master spy: the leader of a large ring of enemy agents in the latest plotting against the peace of the world. Popoford would kill her. Popoford would be the tool of the free world, he would be the master spy for liberty, the chosen arm of the team, the avenger.

Hendricks spared no detail as he retold the history of the making of Popoford the human-robot. He showed photographs of Gretchen's killing. The scenes were ugly, the murder messy. Popoford hadn't yet acquired the instincts of a hunter, and he'd taken too much time; had gone too far. Hendricks was reassuring, even in the retelling, and even though Popoford had nearly bungled the entire operation, Hendricks had managed to convince him that he wasn't incompetent, and was, in fact, one of the best operatives that he'd ever seen. Lies had been at the root of Popoford's training, and they'd become the whole organism before long.

An obscure woman by the name of Gretchen was dead, and an equally obscure man with the code name George Mixer would be forever grateful to her for helping him join the club. Popoford was ready to meet President Bjoonic.

Hendricks paused in his explanation. He stood up and got himself a glass of water. He offered some to Popoford, but the drug had too tight a grip on him. He didn't answer but continued to stare at the ceiling and the pictures there. Hendricks sat down again.

"Do you have any questions?" Hendricks asked. "Steven? Any questions?"

Popoford mumbled something which Hendricks couldn't understand, so the show continued. His life was being revealed as if for the first time, and every event was fresh and yet comfortably familiar. He had a nagging headache, but not wanting to miss a second of Hendricks' explanation, he ignored the irritation and kept watching.

What Hendricks then told Popoford was fascinating to the agent. Popoford had been presented to President Bjoonic. It had been an amazing meeting, where the elected official had displayed a remarkable capacity for far-sighted and complicated thinking. Hendricks told Popoford that even he, a seasoned professional, was astounded by the president's ability to grasp the tactical power that could be commanded with Popoford as the basic agent, and Popoford was reminded just how thrilled they all were when President Bjoonic whole-heartedly accepted Home Office and the special team as his personal project. With these memories re-enacted, the projector paused and the ceiling went black.

Hendricks spoke rapidly. He kept his eyes on Popoford. He seemed to sense the growing alertness in the agent's eyes.

"The president's plan was ironic. You would kill him before cancer did. His death would rouse the people to action, and Rosiva would play out the charade until the people's voices became too loud to ignore. It worked very well, as you know, but the best part of the plan was the utilization of your primary flaw: we would put you in a position of complete humiliation, and you would respond. And you did respond, though you were a little early, you responded just as predicted. You went after Rosiva to convince him that he should not sign the document. We sent you back to Whimsy knowing that you would finally end up in the White House. When you did arrive, instead of killing you and presenting your body to a public hungry for blood, President Rosiva decided to take care of an in-house problem and you were spared."

"I was spared?" Popoford said. There was anger in his voice.

"Yes, Steven, you were spared so that we could use you another day. You'll be returning to Whimsy as soon as your training here is complete. You won't remember any of this. It will only be another vague memory of a compulsory debriefing. Now please relax while I prepare a fresh sedative."

Hendricks stood up and turned to the nearby white Formica counter. Popoford watched him carefully tear the plastic wrapper from a new syringe.

"Has it been twenty years?" Popoford asked. "Twenty years gone?"

"Not gone, Steven. If that were the case I should think it would be more accurate to consider your whole life gone. I like to think of your life as having been one of total devotion. You've given, and you'll continue to give. You don't need to worry, you'll be contented. In a few minutes, even your questions about the past will be gone.

"You're wrong."

Hendricks turned his head and looked quizzically at Popoford. "Just relax," he said. "It will be over soon." He turned back to the counter and jabbed the needle into the rubber capped vial.

"I remember too much," Popoford said under his breath. He felt a wave of fear washing over him. He remembered the cluttered thoughts that he'd grappled with during the past weeks. He remembered how he thought that he was going crazy. He clenched his fist.

"There's no possibility that you remembered anything. Every thought was given to you. They were thoughts selected by me so that you would be programmed for the assignment. You had to kill Bjoonic, and then you had to try to stop Rosiva. It was a simple plan, but it required all my expertise to prepare your mind."

Hendricks removed the air from the syringe. A spurt of the drug hit the counter. "You must realize, Steven, that it took years just to get you purged. We've been at this project for a long time. As I told you earlier, you represent a considerable investment. We prefer to have you alive."

"You would have killed me if Mous hadn't been involved. You would have shot your investment."

"That was the plan. Plans change."

"Was it always in the plan to kill H.O.?"

"What do you mean?" Hendricks said as he approached the gurney. "I just told you that..." Hendricks paused. "Oh, God," he laughed. "I completely forgot."

Hendricks sat down on the stool.

Popoford was disgusted by the glee that Hendricks showed. Even the killing of H.O. required more solemnity than this. "You're sicker than I thought."

Hendricks laughed even harder. "Steven, you misunderstand. There are some things that you don't know." Hendricks put the syringe down on his knee. "We killed H.O., true, but it wasn't as it seemed." Hendricks controlled his laughter. "Let me ask you something, Steven. Don't you remember how you hated H.O. the first time you met him? He was a disgusting little man who ridiculed you right from the start. You wondered about him. You even wondered how such a disrespectable man could have become H.O."

"Of course I did. I even told you, and all you said was that he thought very highly of me."

"Yes, but that was all just part of the script. Don't you see, Steven? You were being run through a play. Everybody had lines to read. Everything was staged."

"So what does that have to do with H.O.?" Popoford asked.

"Simply this: H.O. had gotten too big for his britches. He'd intercepted you for a private job. He'd corralled you instead of letting the play continue as planned, and he'd twisted your loyalties. We had to kill him. He was a traitor."

"But I never saw H.O. after you and I drove out of here and went to the safe house."

"No, Steven, that's where you're wrong. That's why I'm so amused. The H.O. you know was an actor. We've used him several times. He was a patriot killed while sitting in the back seat of a government car. You were in the front seat. The car was parked on a quiet road outside of Bethesda. The actor was killed by a single rifle shot. He was killed by a girl named Lorain, Lorain Mous, daughter of P. Y. Mous: H.O."

"What?!"

"You heard me. P. Y. Mous is, or rather was, H.O. Senator Boscwell has recently been appointed to replace him."

Popoford lay silently, wondering at all the confusion that was being lifted from his mind. There were no proper memories to replace the muddle with which he'd lived, but a great relief filled him with hope for his uncertain future, and with anger at the loss of his forgotten past.

Hendricks again picked up the syringe, as if in an afterthought. "Mous was trying to betray us. He wanted you to kill Rosiva, but Rosiva outsmarted him. We've succeeded, and the treaty is signed with the people's blessing. They are so very happy to have a hero in the White House. How many presidents have killed an assassin? The people are proud. We are a strong nation once again."

"You scum," Popoford whispered. "You cynical scum. You've destroyed my life."

"Steven, calm down. You had no life. You were a loser."

"I had my own mind!"

"That's enough, Steven. I'll give you the shot, and you won't have to think about this anymore."

"The hell I won't!" Popoford shouted, and he swung wildly at Hendricks. He struck the syringe out of Hendricks' hand, and it fell undamaged to the floor. He rolled up on his side and tensed his whole body in a single punch that he aimed at Hendricks' face. Popoford's fist crushed into Hendricks' mouth, and he stumbled off the bed and fell on top of his boss. He reached out and grabbed the syringe, and in a sweeping motion that he could barely control, he plunged the needle into Hendricks' chest.

"You're going to die, you bastard!" he yelled, as he quickly reached under Hendricks' jacket and removed a pistol. "Not quite regulation," he spat. "But it'll do."

He held the gun to Hendricks' head. "Your muscles will soon be paralyzed. You're lucky. You might not feel the bullet ripping your heart apart."

Hendricks lay still under Popoford's weight. "This is all a waste, Steven," he said calmly. "The deed has been done. You're too late."

"Too late for what, you bastard?" Popoford screamed. His mind snapped. He dropped the pistol and began to pound Hendricks' chest. "Tell me what has happened! Tell me! Talk! Talk!..."

Popoford's fists slammed into the man's body. Each blow snapped his sternum a little more. Soon the blows were jamming ribs against his lungs, against his heart. Popoford stared at Hendricks' face. He was calm. His face was relaxed, he was at peace, smiling gently at Popoford as if some divine grace had touched him. Popoford was infuriated by the placid, rhythmic tempo that Hendricks began to mouth. The agent flailed away, but he couldn't take his eyes off Hendricks' mouth. By bits and pieces, a few words reached Popoford until finally, he heard the whole message. "I can't feel a thing...I can't feel..."

Popoford's resolve and anger collapsed. A terrible weariness instantly sucked the tone from all his muscles, and he fell in a wretched heap on top of Hendricks. Popoford's face was pressed to the smooth concrete floor, his mouth within inches of Hendricks' ear. "You...bastard," he stammered, trying to catch his breath. "You can't even feel yourself die."

"You're a child, Steven. I *can* feel death. Don't be mistaken about that, but I can't feel pain. The drug. It works like that. You know it does."

"You bastard," Popoford said. "Tell me the whole thing. Give me something."

"You *are* a child. My child in a way," Hendricks paused for a pensive moment. Popoford could smell the cold concrete in his nostrils. He could smell Hendricks. It was a clinical odor, and both the floor and Hendricks had it.

"What the hell are you talking about?" Popoford gasped. "Don't give me any sob stories. Just talk. You'll be dead soon, so talk."

"I'll talk, Steven. I'll tell you a little more. You'll die with me."

"Horse-shit!"

"Soon. Your death has already been ordered."

"Fine. Don't let it concern you. Just tell me more about Gretchen. Tell me about Home Office."

"What is there left to tell? When my body is discovered, you will be a dead man. The first Resurrection Runner will be killed. You're of no further use to us. You've gone too far; you've drawn too many conclusions. Your brain is no longer completely ours. It's such a waste. With each assignment, you got better. With each test, I learned how to make more of your kind and to make them better, faster. I learned how to discover the hook that would set them off on their obedient ways. With you it was Gretchen. Her killing was your proof of manliness. We switched things around a little in your head, and before long, Gretchen became your lover, and the confusion and self-hatred that would come over you when we reminded you that you'd killed her made you so pliable that you would do anything we wanted. You would become so depressed and ultimately so outraged at yourself. In your mind, she was so much a part of you that you even accused yourself of causing her suicide. You were a tool, a body into which we poured a new mind each time we needed you. We killed your memory between assignments, and then we refilled it and gave you a new life. You and the others were born again, Steven. The Resurrected became the tools of our plans. They are still at work."

"Tell me about them," Popoford said. "Give me more."

"I've told you enough. You should understand that. We've taken the government just as we planned. H.O. and his stand-in were killed in the process, but the results are even better than we had expected. Some things were bound to change in a plan of this magnitude and duration. It doesn't matter. We've still united the intelligence forces of the world. Peace will follow. We have started humanity down the inevitable road to salvation. We have a mandate."

"A mandate of fools."

"You're a dead man, Popoford. Lorain will kill you; one perfected Runner will kill the prototype. You're a dead man, Steven. Now, who's the fool?"

"We both are," Popoford said, and he listened to the ghastly gurgle of Hendricks' final breath. The creator of Resurrection Runner was dead.

CHAPTER TWENTY-NINE

Popoford became acutely aware of his surroundings. He could hear his regular breathing loud in his ears. He could feel the cold concrete hard against his ear, a warm draft of air whispering over his other. Hendricks' cadaver lay beneath him. The light, cool and uniform, pierced his closed eyelids and beckoned him back from shock. He opened his eyes and stared into Hendricks' ear. He studied the ear, the head, the hair. It had been Hendricks, a man that Popoford found he didn't know.

He rolled off the body and lay upon his back. He stared at the neon tubes above him. He didn't know the man who had violated him. And violated wasn't the right word. This man, Hendricks, had eliminated him, made him nonexistent. This dead man had made of him a hollow tool to be filled at the whim of conspirators. Popoford knew that in a true sense he, too, was dead. Without content, without memory, he was unformed, growing older without a past. But there was an important difference that took Popoford quite a while to discover, a difference that any other man would have taken for granted. He was still alive. His flesh was still alive. There was a future for him. He could make a past for himself in that future. He could survive.

He sat up and looked around the room. It was similar to the room that he'd been taken to when Hendricks had first called him back from Whimsy. It could have been the same one. It was an operating room, all white and hard plastic except for the floor. The door was covered with a layer of white Formica. The counters were white. The mirror on the wall reflected the opposite, white wall. Only the floor, the pistol, and the graying hands of the corpse weren't covered with white. Then Popoford saw the vial on the counter. He picked it up. Its label had no information printed on it, but Popoford remembered that it was the mind-stripping tranquilizer. He put it in his pocket. He opened a drawer and grabbed a handful of disposable syringes and stuffed them in the same pocket. He reflected on how odd it was to have been left in his street clothes. He picked up the pistol and took Hendrick's billfold and put them into his other pocket. His jacket was stuffed, and a glance in the mirror told him to rearrange his load. He removed the pistol and distributed the other gear throughout his several jacket pockets. He didn't know how many syringes he had. He would take inventory later.

Right now, he had to do something about Lorain Mous. He had to find her. He had to figure out if she indeed would try to kill him. He had to find out if she was like him. Was she a Resurrection Runner as Hendricks had said? Was there a hook that Hendricks could have activated to make her do whatever he asked, and if there was a hook, could Popoford make contact with her controlled mind and make her give up the vendetta? Perhaps the drug in the vial could help him.

He went to the door and listened. There was no noise outside; were no footsteps in the hall. He turned the knob slowly and wondered if he would be able to subdue Lorain when he found her. She'd an unnerving capacity to outdo him at every turn. But no, she'd been part of the Home Office plans all along and had been directed to where he would be. Popoford hoped that with his newly free mind he might now have a slight advantage over Lorain. He was no longer a Runner. He could think for himself. He opened the door.

The hall was as well lighted as he remembered. It was just as empty as he'd hoped. He made his way down it, keeping his back close to the wall, his pistol hand half-raised and preceding him out of the secret labyrinth.

He came to the stairs. There was a special room on the upper floor. He remembered that room. He remembered the poverty there. He remembered Sarah, the gatekeeper. He would have to get past her. She wouldn't be a problem. He took the steps three at a time but slowly, silently. He anticipated a haggard old woman but didn't know quite what to expect. When he reached the top of the stairs he crouched on the small landing and pressed his ear against the door. He listened to the silence.

Suddenly there was a great blast that almost knocked Popoford off his feet. The top half of the door blew away. Splinters and ricocheting buckshot bounced down the stairwell. The blast echoed through the empty, white halls below. Instinctively Popoford found the only cover available. He slid partially down the stairs and from his semi-prone position, he held the pistol at arm's length, aiming it at the hole in the door. He waited without breathing for Lorain to step through the breach, her sawed-off shotgun lowered for the kill. He waited there for her footsteps. He held his breath and wondered if he could kill her. He wondered, and he heard her steps. His finger began the slow pressing of the trigger. The steps came closer. They were soft steps and were taken with care. There was a long pause between each one. Lorain listened each time; listened before she took the next step. Popoford held his breath. He waited, his blood draining the stale air in his lungs of oxygen. She took another step. Popoford's lungs screamed for more air. She listened. Popoford couldn't hold his breath. She took another step, and Popoford gasped.

Everything happened rapidly. A second shotgun blast exploded through the bottom half of the door. Popoford jerked off four rounds. The echoes died away. He heard running. The dust settled. He waited and listened until the footsteps were gone. He blinked and wiped the sweat from his eyes. He listened again. There was no sound of movement. No sound. Then he heard a door slam, an ignition jolt an engine to life, a stream of gravel spraying against the dilapidated facade of Home Office. He had a quick memory of Lorain, the hallway, and death. He stood up and walked through the staged poverty. Sarah wasn't there.

Popoford walked out to the driveway. He saw nothing of a speeding car. Life along Castro Street was placid. No one was bothered by the sound of buckshot and racing engines. He was alone there on the road, and he would have to hunt for Lorain himself. He quickly rejected calling in any authority. He'd have to assume every agency was colluding. After all, the commander-in-chief was behind all orders from Home Office, from Boscwell.

Popoford was on his own, alone without a single tool except for his nearly blank mind. He turned away from the street and walked back into the ramshackle house. He closed the door. He would have to think. He had to make a plan. He had to develop some kind of attack. He had to destroy the whole rotten plot. Him. Alone.

In the darkened room, with only the reflected light from the exposed stairwell lighting the way, Popoford had a thought that would guarantee success. It was a plan, however, that wouldn't guarantee his life. Nothing could do that.

He was alone at Home Office. He was alone in the headquarters of the enemy. There would be names. Proof. He could bring down the whole government if need be. He still had to stop Lorain, but even if he couldn't do that, even if she killed him, he could arrange for the proper files to be discovered. Everything that he needed was in the rooms below, everything except the people who knew who he was, knew where he was, and knew that he must die.

Popoford went downstairs to find the file room.

He tried several white doors and found more interrogation rooms. Several agents could be programmed at the same time. Resurrection Run had gone into full operation. There were others like him and Lorain. Others perhaps more cleverly trained as provocateurs of State; as assassins and liars, perhaps traveling in groups, their minds artificially intertwined; an army of the secret government, of the supremely egotistical few who would have the world settle into a passive unity of their doing and for their benefit.

But one of them had mistakenly slipped from their grasp. Popoford knew the right thing to do. There was left in his manipulated brain a sense of morality that rebelled against their kind of protective guidance. Popoford wondered at his own sense of right and wrong. He couldn't understand how he'd been left with such a sure knowledge that they had to be stopped; that Rosiva, and Lorain, and all the Generals and the soldiers had to be destroyed. If nothing else, his intact morality had survived. He was the last of the Resurrection Runners to be allowed to retain a sense of right and wrong which differed from the party line. He saw proof of that in the files that he found.

The files were in a small room just off the office that the actor had used when he first played H.O. for Popoford. Before going into the room, Popoford had searched the office desk and its file cabinet. The drawers were all empty and, from the pristine cleanliness of them, he realized that no personal notes from the Director had ever been found there. He would have to go back to the munitions factory, Mous' headquarters, to find things like that. For now, there was only a table and a single file cabinet in the small room with three drawers of personnel reports marked "Resurrection Run - Unit Preparation." The drawers held the cross-referenced and intertwined notes that Hendricks had kept over the years.

Popoford glanced through the first drawer. He found his own file. He took it out, holding it delicately, not sure if he should disturb its secrets, not certain if he could keep a cold and dispassionate head while reading the details of his own forgotten life. He laid his file on the table that stood against the wall. He would first collect as many of the other files as he could. Then he would take them to a quiet place. He would take them to Whimsy. Somehow. He would take them to his house where he might find time to read them all, and also find a place to hide them. He couldn't be sure if there would be any safety in Whimsy, but it was worth a chance. He needed to go to Whimsy, if only for a short time, only for a moment to recover a bit of his personality and to prepare for his attack on the other Resurrection Runners. He needed Whimsy like an addict searching for peace that could barely be remembered.

He gathered as many of the files as he could carry in his arms, taking some from every part of the chronological sequence. He hoped that he had enough to reconstruct the whole treason, that the proof would be unmistakable.

He walked out of the room without closing the door. He paused to look at the actor's office. He wanted to remember the man whom Mous had betrayed. He wanted to remember the words that the actor had said. He wanted to remember the warning precisely.

The pleading voice returned to Popoford. But it didn't come back quickly enough. The sting of smoke stung in his nostrils and brought him back to reality. He spun around quickly and saw smoke rushing under the office door. The hall was on fire. He was trapped

Popoford ran to the door. He clutched the file folders under his arm, pressing them against the pistol that he'd stuffed under his belt. He grabbed the door handle and whipped the door open.

It was a mistake. Instantly Popoford's face was filled with sooty smoke and singeing flames drove him backward.

He spun toward the desk. He had to get out. There was the file room, but the smoke would kill him in there. Then he remembered another door. It led to the interrogation room. Popoford ran to it and saw that no smoke curled up from under it. The door was cool to his touch. He cautiously pulled it open. There was another door across the room that led to the hallway and smoke was filtering through all the cracks, filling the room with smoke.

Popoford looked back into the office. The desk was ablaze and flames were melting the carpet and spreading along the concrete. The floor had been prepared. The slab had been treated with crystallized napalm. Popoford remembered the procedure. He'd used it himself.

Seeing the office erupt, he ran from the wave of fire surging toward him. He ran to the interrogation room and slammed the door just as the heat reached the flashpoint and sucked out all the oxygen. He felt the door bend to the vacuum and felt the draft rushing under the door. He gasped for air, but the fire had taken most of his supply. He dropped to one knee. The smoke was thickening fast. There was nowhere to go.

He dropped to both knees and leaned far forward to get his nose close to the remaining oxygen. He would suffocate in a few seconds. Then he saw a sink.

He ripped his shirt open and crammed the files down his pants. He reached up and turned on the faucet. He grabbed a towel that lay on the white counter and stuffed it into the sink. When it was soaked, he slapped it against his face. The water felt cool, but it didn't revive him. His concentration was slipping. The fire was winning.

Popoford reached up with his other hand and held the cloth to his mouth and nose. He took a slow, deep breath, filling his lungs with the filtered air. He pulled the pistol from his belt, turned, and glanced at the door to the hall, and then rushed to open it and make a desperate run through the heart of the fire. He ran through the heat and down the smoke-choked hall. His breath began to give way. He scrambled to the stairs. He had to make it. Had to.

He found the stairs and stumbled into the stairwell. His lungs shot pain through his chest. He let the dead air out and tried to gasp in the fresh air. It wasn't there for him. There was nothing but smoke to be filtered through cloth and water.

Popoford panicked. His muscles seemed to take a magical strength from his empty blood cells, and he scrambled up the stairs and into Sarah's rooms. He fell on the floor and the spurt of energy left him. He lay there for a minute, choking on the fresh air, stoking his lungs with life. Below him, he could hear an occasional explosion as the fire found a bottle of flammable liquid. Between the explosions, the crackling snapped at his ears; the acrid smoke stank in his nose and made his skin and clothes greasy. He still held the pistol in his hand, and a few of the folders were still under his belt.

He staggered to his feet and ran out to the graveled lot. There already were alarmed people standing around.

"Hey! Someone is coming out of there. My God, Mister. You okay? What the hell happened? You okay.? We called the fire department. They already had the report. Said they'd be right here." Popoford heard no siren.

"You sure you're okay? Why don't you lie down for a minute? Why don't you wait here for the firemen? They'll have oxygen."

Popoford pulled away from the man's grasp.

"Don't panic, mister. It's going to be okay. Just you wait."

Someone else called out from a small crowd that had gathered.

"Hey! Look out! He's got a gun!"

Popoford ran blindly away from the scene. He still didn't hear any sirens.

CHAPTER THIRTY

Castro Street had no sidewalks, and Popoford was forced to run on the drastically sloping asphalt. It was a hard run. He had to fight the slope and the piled flotsam of the earlier rain. Maddened dogs, clamoring to chew through chain-link fencing so they could get at his throat, marked his passing. Their keepers didn't come to their howling calls, and it seemed that only dogs lived in the ramshackle clapboard houses on Castro. The gray walls of the warehouses across the way stood barren. The eroding brick amplified the hollow anger of the dogs. A cold rain began to fall.

He was approaching the main drag, so he jammed the pistol back in his belt. He covered the few manila folders that he'd managed to keep with his jacket, and when he reached the corner, he slowed to a walk and looked back to see who was following. There was no one. He hacked the last of the smoke from his lungs and listened. There was no alarm. There still was no siren, no firemen.

"Of course," Popoford said under his breath. There would be no firemen to save that building. The delay was intentional, planned. All evidence destroyed. All files burned. Only the charred body of a madman would be found. Popoford knew that Home Office would transform Hendricks in death into a madman. The reports would steer all discussion away from Home Office, away from the government. There would be no long-term investigation. But there were more important things to consider. No one was following him. Or so it seemed. Lorain might be thinking that he'd been killed in the fire. He might have bought some time. He needed time.

He stepped into a greasy spoon and walked to the rear of the room. He sat at the counter so that he had a clear view of the street.

"What'll it be? Coffee?"

"Yea."

"Breakfast special's two eggs and hash browns. How's about it?"

"Sure."

"Over easy?"

"Sure."

Popoford hated eggs over easy. His mind wasn't on breakfast.

"Do you have a paper?"

"I sure do. Here ya go."

He looked up at the fat cook and forced a smile.

"Now that's more like it, mister. Don't let the world get you down. It can't last forever."

The cook's unshaven face broke into a toothless grin. Popoford saw eternal optimism in his drooping eyes and looked away. The cook's mushy face seemed to deny too much.

"Isn't that something," the cook continued while turning around to his stove. "That Jason Rosiva is wonderful. Damn! What do you think about that, mister? You ever hear of anything like that? Shot the man right there in the White House. Pulled a gun and shot the bastard."

"Yeah. Wonderful."

"You said it! Saved us all a lot of money, too. And he showed those bastards that he won't stand for this terrorism any longer. Ain't never been a man like him for president. Best thing that could have happened to us. Wonderful!"

Popoford looked at the paper. What he saw didn't surprise him. The whole front section was devoted to Rosiva and his act of heroism. The "Pistol-Packin' Prez" was a national hero. He had gunned down a traitorous industrialist, an assassin, an enemy agent. He had done what all the security agencies couldn't do. The country was enthralled. So was all of Europe. Even Pravda praised the act as a major step in the constant war against worldwide terrorism.

The profiles of P. Y. Mous were extensive and completely inaccurate. No mention was made of Home Office. Not a word about the munitions warehouses in the woods on the other side of the Bay. Nothing was written that could connect Mous to the West Coast. He was portrayed as a reclusive Easterner, a misbegotten patriot, an insane beast. By contrast, Rosiva hadn't withdrawn to obscurity. He had held a press conference. He had made a rousing statement appealing for worldwide unity. He had accepted the praise of members of Congress. He had played it for all it was worth.

"Here ya go." The cook slapped a heavy plate on the counter. "How's about some more coffee?"

He poured it without waiting for an answer.

Popoford looked at the runny mess on the plate and realized that he was very hungry. Even the eggs looked good to him. He was grateful that another customer came into the cafe and took the cook to the other end of the counter. Popoford wolfed the food. By the time he'd finished the second cup of coffee, he had started to dry out. He checked his pockets and was surprised to find his billfold and a few dollars.

"Will you get me some change for the phone?"

"Sure, mister. It's right back there, behind the curtain. Here you go."

Popoford called a cab. He told it to come around to the back of the cafe. It would be there in ten minutes. He went into the bathroom and washed his face in the sink. He looked like a bum. He stared into the mirror at his rheumy eyes. He looked at the stubble that covered his jaw. He saw the wrinkled shirt and jacket. He saw a man that he recognized but didn't know. He forced the panic out of his thoughts. He couldn't think about what had been, not yet. If he survived, he could allow himself that luxury. Now the folders were more important than he was. They had to be secured; hidden away.

He came out of the bathroom and peeked through the curtain. There were no new people in the cafe. He knew what he had to do.

"I called a cab," he said to the cook. "May I have my bill?"

"You bet. Here ya go."

"I wonder if I could have you do something for me?"

"Such as mister?"

Popoford removed twenty extra dollars from his wallet.

"I'm having a little trouble with my wife. I need a place to hide some letters. I thought that this might be just the place."

The cook looked at the twenty. "For how long, mister?"

"Just for about two days. I'll be back for them then."

"And what happens if you don't come back for them?"

Popoford thought fast. He hadn't planned that part. "Here, give me a pen. If I don't come for them in two days, send them to this address. They'll know what to do with them."

Popoford wrote the address on the top folder: Mrs. Gertrude Marshall, Postmaster, Whimsy, California.

"That could cost a bit in postage."

"Here." Popoford tossed another five on the counter. He was left with less than twenty himself. "Will you do it?"

"Sure, mister. What have I got to lose?"

"That's good, that's good. You've taken quite a load off my mind."

"Glad to be of service, Mister. I'll wrap them up and put them in the safe." the cook said as he stuffed the money in his pocket.

"Just be sure to mail them if I don't get back here."

"Sure. I told you I would. I will."

"All right, good. I'm going to wait for the cab. He's coming to the back door."

The cook gave Popoford a knowing look. "Good idea. Just in case the little woman is watching."

"God help me if she finds me before she cools off."

"I sure do know what you mean, mister. I sure do."

Popoford backed through the curtain. He took a final look towards the front door. The rain was pouring, but there was no sign of Lorain. He went to the back door and waited. The cab soon arrived.

The first thing that Popoford did was to direct the cabby to a nearby Sears store and bought himself a raincoat and a box of bullets on Hendrick's dime. He paid the cabby off and walked across the street to a rental yard. It would take days for the transactions to raise a red flag.

By the time he drove away in the new car, he was feeling more confident. He would find a place to park so he could sleep in the car. He wouldn't be going back to Whitnsy yet. The fire meant that he could take a few hours to recuperate, but he had to find Lorain soon. She was the first one he had to stop. There were many more, but she was the most important. She would be coming after him again as soon as she found out he'd survived the fire. She would be at the munitions factory. He would eliminate her first, after dark.

Popoford smiled his first genuine smile since before Mous was killed. As he drove across the San Mateo bridge, he had a strong feeling that he had the better of Lorain. Not only was he acting on his own for the first time, but he thought that if he waited until dark, he could take her. There was all the usual surprise associated with darkness, but, most importantly, he connected it with the time he'd beaten Lorain once before. Along the Missouri River, at night. He thought about it and, as he did, the smile left his face.

"Dammit!" he cried. He slammed his fist into the steering wheel. "That was a setup!"

Anger filled his head. He drove into San Mateo and took the first exit. He parked his car in the lot of the PayLess Drug Store, he checked his pistol and the syringes, and he waited. He didn't sleep.

CHAPTER THIRTY-ONE

Sunset came and the rain slackened. Popoford sat up straight behind the wheel of the rented car. He had spent hours thinking about what he had to do. He'd resisted thoughts of his past. He concentrated on the weapons distribution facility of the late P. Y. Mous. He remembered what he'd seen. The concealed entry road, the rustic stone house placed in the middle of a great clearing in the woods, the Quonsets topped with American flags; he'd seen only those things. Nothing indicated that there was a large munitions operation going on. There had been no employee activity or heavy machinery, and above all, there had been no evidence of trucks, of railroads, or any means to distribute the cargo that Mous claimed was there. Popoford couldn't remember seeing another way out of the complex, and that fact bothered him the most. No operation could be conducted safely with only one exit. And, there was no evidence of a suitable security system. Unless Mous had been lying about the arms shipments, there was more to the complex in the woods than met the eye. It was always possible that Mous had lied about this as he had about everything else, but Popoford remembered his sincere passion when he talked about his business and its moral basis. He had a feeling in his gut that in this the man had told the truth.

He started the car and drove it a few feet to the 7-Eleven that shared the parking lot. He bought a cup of coffee and a map of San Mateo County. He got back into his car and sipped the coffee while studying the map.

He could only guess at the exact location of the complex. No structures were indicated on the map, and only the gross landforms of torn rock that marked the San Andreas fault were noted. No wooded areas were shown, but the complex was on the south side of the road. That was all he knew, but it was enough. After a few minutes with the map, he found a road he had missed. He started the car and headed for the hills.

He didn't go up Highway 92. What he saw on the map had to be checked visually, and to do that, he had to get on Interstate 280 and go south to the first exit. He then turned west and drove on a road that paralleled Highway 92. This was the road he'd seen on the map, and there was a particular curve that came so close to Highway 92 that it almost touched it. Popoford hoped that he had discovered the back door to the complex.

The road was wide and well kept. There were no chuckholes or cracks, only the smooth surface of new concrete. The map had shown the road to be rural access suitable only for light traffic. The wide lanes indicated other uses.

A vehicle approached from the west. It passed Popoford, and he was convinced he was on the right track. It was a set of doubles, and the driver of the semi had his Jake brake on laboring to control his heavy load, even though the downgrade was slight. Two more trucks followed the first, and Popoford continued up the hill. When he came to the bend in the road, he pulled the car into the underbrush and shut it off. He turned off its lights. He checked his pockets, making sure that he had the box of cartridges. He checked the pistol. It was fully loaded. He put it on the seat, then he removed all the syringes and filled each of them with a full load of tranquilizer. He couldn't be sure what he would find around the bend, but he had a good idea that he would soon face Lorain. He would need a lot of luck, all the weapons that he could find, and a bit of the skill that he'd been led to believe he possessed. He may not have been the agent he thought he was, but he had training and maybe even some ability. He would need every bit of it in the next few hours.

He put the plastic tips back on the needles and put the syringes in his right pocket. He picked up the pistol and got out of the car.

Another semi passed going downhill, then two more came up the hill and disappeared around the bend. Popoford saw their brake lights glaring as they made the turn. He could hear the gears whining as the drivers rapidly slowed. He crouched through the underbrush and made his way to the bend. He squatted there and peered through a dense thicket of wild raspberries. He saw what he had hoped to see.

The road did indeed turn sharply in the direction of Highway 92. It swung in a long curve that brought it under a sheer rock cliff. The cliff was crowned with dense woods, but even with the light rain, Popoford could see bare bulbs flickering through. The Mous complex was on top of the cliff.

Popoford saw the two semis parked on the side of the road. From his angle, he couldn't see what was happening, but presently the first truck began to move again. It turned sharply toward the cliff and accelerated. The other truck followed the first, and they both were driven into the cliff through a huge portico cut into the rock. As they passed into the tunnel, a heavy steel fence slid over the hole He'd found the rear exit.

He went back to the car and drove it out of the thicket. Then he drove down the hill about a hundred yards so that he was out of sight of the tunnel. He stopped the car in the middle of the road so that he blocked it in both directions. He got out and ran to the side of the road. In only a minute he saw the lights of another truck coming up the hill. He was getting some of the luck he needed.

The truck stopped. The driver flashed his high beams. Then he blew his air horn. Then he got out of the cab to see how he could get the car out of the way.

Popoford darted out of the underbrush. He pulled one the needles out of his right pocket. He ripped the plastic cap from it, drove it into the driver's neck, and smashed the plunger home. The effect was nearly instantaneous. The driver collapsed without a word, and Popoford dragged his paralyzed body into the brush. He left the wild-eyed man in shock, his head thrashing from side to side, and ran to the semi. No other trucks were coming as he jumped into the cab still wet from the drizzle.

He revved the engine and nudged the truck into gear. He drove it into the rented car and pushed it off the road. Then he rapidly worked his way up to fourth, gaining as much speed as he could in the hundred yards to the bend. He got to the turn and braked the truck. He could feel that the trailers were empty. He pulled it off the road like the other trucks had done and waited.

The seconds of waiting took forever. He didn't know any passwords. He didn't know if he needed any, or if he needed to identify himself. The gate opened, and Popoford sighed. He drove the truck into the tunnel. The gate closed behind him.

Inside, the two-lane road quickly branched, and arrows directed him to stay to the right. A sign indicated that the loading dock was ahead. Popoford drove the rig down the tunnel without seeing other people. He was alone in the white-tiled tube. He wiped the drizzle from his face and shut off the windshield wipers.

The tunnel curved slowly to the left in a great circle, and Popoford judged that the road was following the property line of the clearing above. When he'd driven halfway around the circle, he came upon a white-tiled wall that required him to turn left. He did so and immediately was inside a great, lighted cavern.

The contrast between the cavern and the tunnel wasn't one of lighting. Both structures were brightly lit as if by daylight. It was all the activity that made the cavern spectacular. Activity and the very expanse in which it took place.

It was a wide, open cavern in the rock, lined with white tile and laced with a black, structural-steel frame to support the roof. Only a few columns rose from the floor to help hold up the immense weight that rested overhead: the stone house, the Quonset huts, and the cliff. The effect was astounding. The presence of tons of steel and brick and sod overhead was nearly negated by the lightness of the framework and by the narrowness of the few columns. And within the airy, well-lighted basement, hundreds of men and women, all wearing green jumpsuits, worked feverishly.

Popoford didn't like the green jumpsuits. His sports jacket with pockets filled with drugs and bullets would stand out clearly against them. He decided that he had to have one. He followed the arrows, and soon he saw the loading dock ahead. It was a raised circular platform in the center of the room. It was right below the main house. Several tubes made of clear material and various diameter reached to the ceiling. He could see elevators in two of them. Another held a staircase. Others were narrow and presumably were a means of transmitting messages and invoices to the top. There was a low building in the center of the dock. Yellow forklifts driven by green-uniformed men darted around, occasionally disappearing into the building and returning with a load of crates to be distributed quickly and correctly into one of the many trucks parked at the dock.

Popoford pulled his rig to a stop. He got out of the cab expecting at any moment to be grabbed. He stood out. While keeping an eye on the nearest workers, he unhooked the back trailer. He returned to the cab and backed the remaining trailer up to the dock. He hadn't been questioned. A glance at the other drivers sitting alone in their cabs told Popoford that none of them wore uniforms. Only the workers were dressed in green.

Popoford waited. Presently one of the workers walked up to the cab and knocked on the door. Popoford rolled down his window. The worker climbed up the ladder so that they were face to face.

"Where's your I.D.?"

Popoford froze.

"Your I.D. Now!"

Popoford reached into a nonexistent inside pocket and came up empty-handed. He patted his other pockets, and he came out with the pistol. He jammed it under the man's jaw.

"I forgot my I.D. I hope this will do."

The worker started to yell a warning, but Popoford grabbed him by the throat and strangled him. The man passed out, and Popoford slowly opened the door. With a great effort, he caught the man's waist and pulled him into the cab. He didn't waste another syringe on the worker but instead smashed the pistol into the man's skull. He would be out for several hours.

Behind him, Popoford could hear the forklifts beginning to load his trailer. He had several minutes. He stripped the worker of his green jumpsuit and put it on himself. He loaded its several pockets with the contents from his jacket and then threw his jacket over the man's face. He took the clipboard and the pen from the man's hands, and he stepped down from the cab. The hunt was on.

CHAPTER THIRTY-TWO

The clear shafts were the only way to the top. And the only way to get to them was through the central building. He saw green-clad people rising and falling in them. He would be inconspicuous among them.

Popoford held the clipboard close to his face while making these observations. It was completely improbable that anybody in the complex should recognize him. Except for Lorain, no one would have ever seen him. He lowered the board and walked toward the loading dock. He pretended to be checking the trailer's undercarriage. He kept his eyes open to be sure that he was behaving acceptably. He couldn't make any mistakes. He could sense the girl's presence. She was just above him.

Popoford took on an air of confidence, acting as if he belonged where he was. He climbed the stairs and walked across the dock with a determined yet relaxed stride. He entered the central building.

It too was an open, circular room. Popoford walked briskly to a group of desks located in the middle of the room. There he mingled on the outskirts of a small crowd of green-suited workers. He listened to the instructions that they were receiving from a foreman.

"...and ten class one operators are needed on the main level to distribute the route orders for the next shipment. Do you all understand your assignments? Good. Show your IDs at the gate. Get this job done fast so we can go home. All right men, let's go."

The group shuffled into a single file, and then they split into two lines, one to each of the clear elevator shafts. Each of the men identified themselves employing the card attached to their suits. As they passed in front of a sensing device, each of them turned so that the cards could be read. Once cleared, the men would step into the shafts and onto one of the little platforms that were hung on a continuous belt. One by one they would rise through the tubes and disappear through the ceiling.

Slowly Popoford advanced to take his turn at the sensing device. If the device couldn't match the bar code on the I.D. card with his face, all hell would break loose. He unclipped his I.D. tag.

As the man in front of him approached the device, Popoford stayed close behind. The man turned so that his chest faced the device directly. Just as he turned, just as the man looked up into the camera for confirmation of a match, Popoford slid his I.D. card in front of the man's.

Instantly a klaxon blared. Armed guards leaped from nearby stations and grabbed the man. His protests were silenced with a gag, his kicking seen as proof of his guilt. The punishment was delivered from the silenced barrel of a snub-nosed .32. The dead man was carried out of the building.

Popoford saw the body being carried away as he began to rise in the tube. At the moment of highest confusion, when the troops were busy and the sensing device was locked into reporting the error, Popoford had slipped into the tube where he watched the scene below quickly return to order. Then the elevator took him through the ceiling of the central building, and he rose above the entire underground complex.

As he rose, he marveled at the vast amounts of money that were required for such an operation, and at the huge profits that were undoubtedly generated. Just how dependent was his government upon this particular complex and its presumed corollaries? He wondered how tightly the economy of his country and the economies of the entire world were entwined in this corruption. Surely the whole game had been played for years longer than he'd been led to believe. He feared that the tangle of plot and strategy was too intricate to be unraveled by one man. Was it possible that to actually succeed would be to throw the entire world into economic collapse?

As Popoford passed through the steel-framed ceiling, the tube was momentarily enclosed in darkness. In that short time, he collected his thoughts and fears and concentrated on his immediate prey. One step at a time. He would do what he could.

The tube broke out of the darkness and into the lighted basement of the main house. Popoford saw the men who had gone before him stepping down from the elevator as the little platforms passed an opening in the tube. The opening approached Popoford, but suddenly a man stepped forward from the crowd and slammed a cover over it. He looked at Popoford, a small smile on his face. It was John, Mous's butler. Popoford was trapped in the tube and was being sent even higher. He cursed himself and his overconfidence. He drew the pistol from his pocket as he went through the final ceiling and was forced to step off the elevator at the end of its run.

He found himself in a shaft of pale green lights; his body cast a deep shadow on the floor. The room around him was black. He'd chosen the night to better surprise Lorain, but the surprise was on him.

A flash split the darkness just as Popoford dove into the shadows. A shotgun. It had to be Lorain. He rolled until he hit a heavy object. He grabbed it. A chair. He pulled himself behind it and up into a kneeling position. He held his breath. The flash came again. Buckshot ripped into the stuffing. Some of the pellets penetrated the chair, stinging Popoford's face. He whipped his pistol around the couch and blasted the blinding hole in the darkness. Four rounds. He paused, listening. Holding his movements. A beat of silence, and then a thud -- a body falling dead. Popoford exhaled, relieved.

The next flash came long before the sound, but Popoford could swear that he heard the buckshot whistling at him. Much of it was buried in the chair as before, but some of it passed the chair, whizzing in Popoford's ears as it sliced deep furrows in his face and right shoulder. The pain was sharp; a brilliant light flashed in his eye. His left hand slapped against his shoulder. The wound was bad, but not terminal. The coolness of liquid evaporating on his cheek caused him to gently touch his face. He touched his right eye. It was gone. Shock momentarily locked his thoughts, but his will to survive overcame the shock.

Without regard for silence, Popoford scrambled across the floor. He found a solid piece of furniture. A desk. He slid behind it just as he heard another shotgun blast exploding from a third quarter. Two attackers left. The pain began. His face started a slow burn. His socket seemed a fire pit: a hole for storing red-hot coals. Popoford fought his mind's scream for surrender. He forced his thoughts upon the two gunmen. He made himself reload the pistol. He listened to the quiet room for any sound of their movement. An anguished cry pierced his ears. He recognized his own voice crying out with a will of its own, wailing for relief. Popoford slapped his left hand over his mouth and choked off his plea.

Two quick blasts yanked him back to his purpose. He moved cautiously away from the desk, sliding his body until he found the wall, keeping the desk between him and the shotguns. He rolled over onto his stomach.

The blasts came again. Two flashes in the dark room that was rapidly filling with the rich, pungent odor of gunpowder.

Popoford fired once at the left flash. Once at the right. A final shotgun load was discharged into the ceiling and Popoford jerked off another round at the sound of it. There followed a momentary silence in which even his breathing went unheard. He waited, listening.

Sounds muffled by stone and steel drifted up from the chambers below. The uninterrupted elevator cable rattled and scraped in its guides. There were no other sounds.

Popoford forced himself to move. He crawled back to the desk and pulled himself up. He saw a light under a door. There was no movement outside of the room. The mansion appeared to be empty. This time he wouldn't be overly confident. Lorain might be alive. She could be lurking outside. Waiting for him to think that he was safe. Ready to kill him. Popoford stumbled to the door and closed the bolt. He found the light switch and flicked it on, turning to examine the room.

Three large men lay dead on the floor. Two of them lay face down, big chunks of their backs still clinging to the wall. Chunks of flesh and blood and bone. Their faces were crushed flat to the floor. Their blood startled Popoford, and it surprised him that it did. Assassins like him should be hardened to such sights. He was not.

Popoford didn't bother to turn them over. Identification was unnecessary. They were run-of-the-mill butchers. They might have been Resurrection Runners. They probably were.

The third man was slouched into the corner, his white shirt remaining clean even through his bloody death. Popoford went to the body and ripped at the shirt. He made a compress for his eye and tied it tightly around his head. The pain eased almost immediately.

He reloaded his pistol and checked the syringes. They were still intact. There was a sudden change in the room. The constant racket of the elevator cable thickened subtly.

Popoford ran to the tube. He could see the top of someone's head rising in it. Then he saw the sawed-off shotgun and he bolted for the door.

The hallways were empty as he ran through the great hall toward the front door. Just as he reached the door, the chauffeur emerged from the parlor. Popoford swung hard with his fist and flattened the man on the spot. He ripped the door open and leaped out into the grounds of the complex.

Powerful floodlights poured a unifying blue across the grass field. There was a smell of spring, hard on the rising wind. Rain pelted Popoford's face, soaking the compress. He was a target, alone and vulnerable with no place to hide. Beyond him were the Quonsets scattered near the edge of the woods. If he could reach one of them, he might hide to wait for Lorain. She had to be stopped before he could do anything else. He couldn't walk away from a trained and highly programmed machine like her. To run would be to invite an ambush later. He would have to draw Lorain into his own trap before she could do the same to him - again.

Memories of their past encounters made him run even faster and harder. Anger and fear combined catapulted him toward the Quonset nearest the far end of the open field.

He arrived at the corrugated building and found a small door cut into one of its parabolic ends. He opened it and looked back.

Behind him, jogging across the grass field, without alarm, without panic, was Lorain. She saw him pause and, continuing her chase, lowered her weapon. She fired twice but was too far away and the pellets couldn't reach him. He ducked into the hut.

The instant he closed the door he was overwhelmed by a thick, acrid stench. It was a familiar aroma. It was gunpowder, and even though the walls blocked his view of the entire Quonset, he knew it was packed with explosives.

"What the hell do you think you're doing?"

Popoford turned to see a skinny man whose face reflected each corner of his skull, sharp-edged and deeply hollowed; lifeless, blanched skin stretched directly across raw bone.

"My dear God," the man said stumbling back from Popoford. "What happened?"

Popoford brandished the pistol in the man's face.

"How many people in this building?"

The man only stared at Popoford's lacerated face and shoulder. Blood was dripping from the compress.

"How many? Tell me! Now!"

"Ah...three. In here. Several others are working in the factory."

"How many? Exactly!"

"Ten altogether."

"Sound the fire alarm."

"What?"

"Damn it! Sound it!"

The man opened his mouth wide and turned toward the offices. Popoford couldn't wait.

"Fire! Get out! Fire!" Popoford's voice was filled with rage. The workers mistook it for fear. The ten people only took eight seconds to run from the back and out the small Quonset door. They were well-drilled like all high explosive workers. Popoford hoped the confusion would stall Lorain for a couple of seconds. As soon as the last of the workers went out the door, he escaped down a short hall and into the open space that housed the ammunition manufacturing plant.

What Popoford saw was a marvel to him. The hut was filled with machinery. Robots controlled the manufacture of dynamite, small arms rounds, shells for twelve-inch guns, grenades, and antipersonnel mines. The conveyers were still, a result of the alarm. It was just as well, for Popoford could hear better with the robots in neutral and idling than he could have if the great gears were turning and the crate-packer was hammering.

He ran through the maze of tools and took a defensive position at the far end of the hut. There was a small window there. He crouched beneath it, behind a massive complex of pulleys. He could see the front entrance in the cold, industrial light.

Only a second passed. Lorain appeared in the doorway. She looked around the room once, and then she withdrew a short skinning knife from her belt. She reached over to the wall and snapped off the lights. Popoford was blinded except for a faint light cast from the window above.

He listened closely. He could hear her knees and hands finding the path between the conveyers. She was coming closer, almost silently, her exact position impossible to determine. Popoford knew that he couldn't just wait against the wall, hoping that she would run into him. It was a huge risk, but he had to end the hunt quickly, decisively.

He stood up suddenly, making sure that he was silhouetted against the faintly night-lit window's light. In a fluid motion, he dove through the window, hitting the grass hard and rolling fast away from the hut. Two times. Three times. That was all he could manage before the catastrophe began.

Lorain had panicked. He'd hoped she might. She'd dropped the knife at the first sound of his movement. She'd swung her preferred shotgun into firing position without the slightest regard for the explosive power around her. She'd pulled the trigger twice. Rapidly. Accurately.

The first explosion was a small one. It blew out what was left of the small window. Popoford counted a beat. The shrapnel shot over his head. He leaped to his feet and ran as hard as he could. He ran straight for the trees and the covered arbor that led to the road. Six steps and he heard the next eruption; seven steps and the shock wave slammed against his back. The eighth step came only after he'd been tumbled across the field. He managed to stand up and started running again. He ran and ran, even though the succeeding blasts continued to blow against his back, nearly knocking him to the ground. One after another the blasts came. Sometimes rapidly, one upon another, sometimes erratically, with deathly silences intermittently promising an end to the explosions but never delivering.

With his last few steps, he nearly lost his balance as his feet wobbled with the shifting ground. He dove into a thicket of wild hedges lighted brilliantly by the blaze. He turned on his stomach and beheld the cataclysm.

One by one the Quonset huts were caught in the conflagration. The hut from which Popoford had run was gone, but the explosions had sent blazing projectiles into the next one. It caught fire. Suddenly it exploded, all at once.

Workers running from the other buildings saw the fiery bodies of their compatriots flung through the sky. They were unprepared for the death that was to come.

The sky was illuminated by the golden light. The stink of pyrotechnics filled the clearing. The noise was overpowering.

Popoford watched the huts blow one by one. Even from this distance, the air seemed hot enough to scorch his face. And then the flames themselves rose higher, and the entire clearing was ringed with fire.

Through the flames, Popoford could see the mansion. Racing for the safety of the underground cavity he saw panicked men running from death. But then he saw death find them.

It started with a sickening ripping of steel near the hut where Lorain had died. At first, the thick layers of sod and dirt muffled the noise. Then the tear in the earth opened fully and the grinding screech rose above the cacophony of the flames and explosions. Under the tremendous weight of buildings and compacted earth, the flaw grew. The ground rippled. Then the undulation grew into a great wave. There was a pause. Slowly, inevitably, the reinforced columns and beams gave against the tidal forces of earth and rock, trying all the while to spring back into their proper shape. They failed. The slow-motion accelerated as one edge collapsed. The cave-in then came rapidly.

Popoford jumped to his feet. He couldn't believe what he was seeing. The mansion fell through the ground. The road followed it. All the derelict Quonsets, all the groomed lawn, the driveway, everything in the clearing fell.

Popoford turned away at the sight. No one could have survived. All the workers below were lost. The great, convoluted munitions operation of P. Y. Mous had completely collapsed. Popoford didn't look back. His imagination would be hard enough to live with. He walked away through the trees, letting the immense destruction settle into silence; letting the sirens replace the roar of death; letting the rain beat against his face and the heap of steel, mud, and flesh left in the hole.

Popoford stumbled through the trees. The sirens were close. He could hear them as the rescue vehicles raced up the hill and the police tried to find the nearly hidden entrance.

He tried to think straight. Lorain was dead. Hendricks was dead. Mous was dead. Others, so many others who he didn't even know, were dead. Yet the immediate threat to him was gone. Rosiva and Boscwell would think that he had died in the Home Office interrogation rooms. If they'd been warned that he'd showed up at the munitions complex, still they would have to think him dead now. Popoford had to keep it that way for a while. It was his only advantage. He had to keep it. It wasn't over yet. He still had to stop Rosiva and expose the traitors.

Popoford understood the absurdity of it all. Acting alone, he would be branded a lunatic. No one would listen. Even the Resurrection Files wouldn't be convincing enough. Not in time to make a difference. There wasn't enough time to argue his case, or even to mount his own conspiracy against the traitors.

Then he saw that he - who had been molded into a mechanical patriot and duped into at least one assassination - he was the only one who could excise the cancer that he had unwittingly helped entrench in office. They had made him into an assassin. It was hard to stomach, but he was still a killer.

He would have to kill another president.

Once it was done, the ensuing uproar would allow time for other men, men not involved in the plot, to ascend to office and uncover the truth. Popoford could send the files to these men, and they could quietly move behind the scenes until the treaty was finally abrogated. Home Office could be purged. Boscwell could be removed, and the programmed killers, the Resurrection Runners, could be collected and their threat eliminated. However, to make it work, he would have to come out of hiding. First, he needed rest. He needed treatment. But when these things had been obtained, he would have to make himself known.

He stumbled to the edge of the woods and waited there for an opportunity. He couldn't let the authorities find him. If he were identified as a survivor of the disaster, his face would be plastered everywhere. He would be a dead man. Others like him, like Lorain, would see to it. He had to get down from the hill without being seen.

His chance came when a squad car came to a halt by the roadside. Popoford had made his way to the entrance of the arbored drive. The police had found it and were directing the heavy fire trucks to the complex grounds. There was a great deal of confusion as the trucks rammed their way through the overgrown path. Tree limbs snapped and the patrolmen were called to help clear the way.

Popoford saw his chance. The police car sat unoccupied. He got in and simply drove away. No one seemed to notice the car missing. No one followed him down the hill. His luck wouldn't hold long, so when he got to the bottom of the hill and had asked directions to the hospital, he drove directly to the emergency room and then parked the car on a side street. He did his best to wipe his fingerprints from the wheel and the door, and then he walked to the hospital. His jumpsuit hid his gun and the syringes.

The doctor treated him before asking questions. Popoford's shoulder was bandaged and a fresh compress was wrapped over his eye. The doctor had cleaned the socket and had cauterized the vessels that hadn't clotted. He'd told Popoford to dress in a hospital gown and had left him in the treatment room while a bed was found. The doctor would have him stay overnight for observation.

Popoford wished that he could stay. He needed rest, needed it badly. But he couldn't be caught with his weapons nor be subjected to the interrogation that would come soon. While the doctor was arranging for the hospital bed, Popoford stripped off his green jumpsuit, shifted the contents of his pockets to his pants, and walked out of the hospital. The head nurse was so surprised that she didn't even protest until he was already on the street. He hid in the shadows until he came to the main road, and then he boarded a bus, finding change in his pocket. He sat near the door and watched the sun rising across the bay. He felt its soft warmth on his face. He kept the thought of its warmth with him while he found a motel and checked in. He thought of the sun and then of his retirement home in Whimsy as he locked the door of his room. He lost all his thoughts as his head touched the pillow and he passed out.

CHAPTER THIRTY-THREE

When Steven Popoford finally awoke, the pain in his head and shoulders had returned. His eye was the center of agony, but the pain gripped his whole head and sent fingers down his neck through his entire back. The flesh of his shoulder was tight with scabbed-over wounds. The pain made it impossible to think.

He struggled out of bed and forced his tired and bruised legs to take him to the pants he'd dropped on the floor. He found the little bottle of the pain killer. The doctor had given him enough to get through the night, the lengthy admission procedures, and the interrogations that hadn't happened. Popoford swallowed two pills and then went into the bathroom and slurped some water from the faucet.

He looked at the torn face in the mirror. Beneath the compress, under the beard and the cuts, he recognized a man he'd once seen, who once owned his mind. A mind intact though misled. He recognized himself: Steven Popoford, alias George Mixer, special agent, retired.

In his one eye, he saw a new hardness: cold and resolute. Personal survival was no longer his goal. Fear and uncertainty were gone. He stared at his face for a while and let the drug take effect.

He went back to his bed and slept several more hours.

Popoford awoke again. The pain was bearable, even when he sat up. He was well enough to continue.

He took a long shower, being sure to keep the water away from his bandages. He dressed again, thankful for the money he'd found in the trousers. It would come in very handy in days to come.

He left the room and after paying for another two nights, he asked the man at the desk to have the maid to straighten up. Then he went for a long walk. It was time for him to make his move.

As he walked, he composed a plan. It would be outlandish, but it might work.

He found a payphone and made the first call. The switchboard operator who answered the phone wouldn't take him seriously. Of that he was sure. But he was also sure that those listening in would know what to do.

"Good morning. White House."

"This is a threat," Popoford began. "Make no mistake. I mean what I say. Tell the president that I'm still alive."

"Will you identify yourself?"

Popoford hung up. He waited for a minute. He imagined the procedural activities being performed at the White House. Routine. The pat response to every threatening call. Popoford picked up the receiver again. Soon they'd realize this wasn't routine.

"I told you I mean what I say," Popoford said over the operators greeting. "Tell Rosiva that the first Resurrection Runner has returned from the dead. Tell him to be on the line when I call again."

He hung up, again, and walked away from the booth. It was no longer safe. Any further calls from it would be traced. He took a bus down El Camino for several miles until he was sure he was in another exchange, and then he went into a bar where he bought a beer. He drank it fast. It had been so long since he'd been able to enjoy cold hops.

"How's about another one? You look like you could use it."

"Yeah. That's a good idea," Popoford said to the bartender. "You got a payphone?"

"Sure. Right behind you. On the wall."

He paid for the second beer and went to the phone. He dialed the number.

"This is me," he said quietly. "Is Rosiva there?"

"I'm here."

"Good. How many others are on the line?"

"I'm alone."

"Bullshit! Clean up the line. Be there alone when I call back."

Popoford hung up again.

He returned to the bar and finished the second beer. His head was getting a little light. He had to stop drinking.

"Do you have any sandwiches?"

"Yup. Got some cold turkey left and a corned beef."

"Give me the beef."

"Got some trouble with the little woman?" the bartender asked.

"What do you mean?"

"You got kinda loud on the phone. I couldn't help hearing you. I guess I know what you're going through. My wife used to leave the roost whenever she felt like it. I finally had to put a stop to it. You got to be hard on 'em. Sometimes that's all they understand."

"Yes. I suppose you're right," Popoford replied. It was a conversation he didn't need.

"You can count on it. You got to lay down the law. There's no other way."

"Right."

Popoford went back and dialed the phone. He took a bite of the corned beef while he waited for the answer. Three rings and his call was picked up.

"This is Rosiva. The line is clear."

"Good. Now listen closely. I survived the weapons factory. Do you understand?"

There was a pause.

"Yes. I understand."

"I don't think you do. I have certain files in my possession. Profiles of individuals you would like to see remain undercover. Resurrection Runners."

"What do you want?"

"I want you."

"You're crazy."

"Mr. President, I'm no longer controlled. The injections were terminated. The brainwashing was stopped. I'm clean. I want some explanations. I want them from you."

"I have no explanations. Who is this?"

"Perhaps you remember me, Rosiva. Perhaps you'll be willing to explain a few things to Hendricks' first mistake."

There was a pause.

"That's impossible. You can't be..."

"But it's true. You will talk to me. You'll talk, or the files will go to the press. The operations will be exposed."

Popoford hung up again.

"Thanks for the sandwich and beer. You have a nice place here," Popoford said to the staring bartender. "Surprising what you can hear if you listen hard enough isn't it?"

Popoford left the bar and returned by bus to the motel. He sat around for the rest of the day. He went out once after dark and brought back a bucket of fried chicken. He ate some and he slept. He awoke at four a.m. and went out to a new phone booth. He made the next call.

"You're to meet me alone. Absolutely alone. One mistake and the files will be opened."

"Where?"

"Fly into Oakland Airport. This afternoon."

"There will be press. Secret Service."

"Don't fly a government plane. Take a private flight. Schedule a landing at exactly 2:00 p.m. No secret service. No reporters."

"That's impossible. I have protection that I can't shake."

"Find a way. I'll be watching. Any mistakes and it's over. Believe it."

Popoford hung up. There was no way that Rosiva would fly to Oakland without protection. Even at the moment, security specialists would be surrounding the president. They would all have their plans. Each individual, each agency would have a plan for him. Each one would be desperately trying to prevail. Popoford figured that only Boscwell had a chance. Only H.O. could be trusted to protect the president in this particular situation. No others would need to be involved, and the sphere of knowledge wouldn't need to be expanded. Home Office would be used to destroy the wayward agent and to protect Rosiva and his secrets.

The most viable plan for H.O. would be to send several killers on a commercial flight to arrive early so that the airport could be cordoned off before the president landed. He wouldn't have a chance under those circumstances; he couldn't go to the airport himself. He checked out of the motel, went to a drug store and bought fresh bandages, and a landline telephone. He found a hardware store and picked up several hundred feet of telephone wire. Then he rented a car and drove across the San Mateo Bridge into the East Bay. He drove to the halfway house in the hills above Crow Canyon Road where Lorain had faked Hendricks' death. That was where he would meet the president of the United States and where he would kill him.

When he got to the house, he parked the car and walked onto the grounds. As he had hoped, it was deserted. There was an electrified fence surrounding the property. He went back to his car and grabbed a rubber floor mat. He returned to the fence and draped the mat over the fence wires. Once over the now-insolated electric fence, he was free to prowl around the grounds unchallenged. He walked to the gravel road where Lorain had killed the two bodyguards, and he entered the house through the large window that was still broken from his last visit. The house hadn't been used at all. His plan was on track.

At 2:15 he called the Oakland Airport.

The surprised operator didn't refuse to page the president. She just made it quite clear that he wasn't at the airport, and that she didn't care for practical jokes. "I'm not here to be part of some little game."

"I assure you; this is no game. The president is there."

"I'll page once."

"That will be enough." Popoford was patient. He knew that his request sounded absurd.

"Where are you?" Rosiva said into the receiver.

"I'm glad you took me seriously," Popoford replied.

"You said you'd be here."

"Never. I said you'd better be there. You are. That's good thinking. You're doing fine."

"Where are you?" Rosiva's voice betrayed his impatience.

"Send your friends home," Popoford replied, ignoring the president's question. "I'll call again in an hour. Get rid of the Home Office boys."

"Wait! I can't hang around here for an hour. Someone will recognize me. Too many questions will be asked."

"That's your problem. Get rid of the protection. We talk alone, or the files go public."

Popoford hung up. He didn't expect Rosiva to do as he'd demanded, but he did expect the odds to be improved a bit. Some of the men would be sent away. Only a few, the best, would remain. That was all that was important. The fewer Home Office desperadoes the better. He would kill the bodyguards if he had to, probably Resurrection Runners. But if they survived and killed him, it wouldn't matter as long as he killed Rosiva.

During the hour between 2:00 and 3:00, Popoford searched the house and the grounds. He located the arsenal and secured a .38 snub-nose revolver and a field knife in a sheath. There was a low hill only a hundred feet from the house that gave him a view of the whole stretch of the road from Crow Canyon to the house's front entrance. He would wait there for Rosiva.

At 3:00 he placed the second call to the airport. This time, the operator paged the president at once.

"Yes."

"Mr. President?"

"I'm alone."

"Good. Tell whoever is listening to hang up." There was a pause, and then Popoford heard a click on the line. "That's better. You're not playing fair, Rosiva. Because of that, I have sent the first file to the press. It will arouse curiosity. Further disclosures will have a more serious effect. Start playing by my rules, or you'll be brought to your knees. Understand?"

"Yes."

Popoford knew that his threats weren't as powerful as he wanted them to seem. The president would have ways to block any threatening commentary. That didn't matter. He just wanted Rosiva to come to him. That would be enough.

"Come to the halfway house in the hills. Come alone. Come explain things to me."

"I don't know where that is."

The person still on the extension would come along for the ride.

Popoford hung up, left the house, opened the driveway gate, and then walked to the hill. He looked around the grounds. Everything was peaceful. He returned to the house and tapped the telephone line. Then he strung the telephone wire out of the house, over the grounds, and up to the hill. He attached the telephone he'd bought. He lifted the receiver and got a dial tone. He was ready.

He lay in the grass, thankful that it had been two days since the last rain. The ground was still soft, and he'd left footprints on the hill, but the grass was dry. There was a promising fragrance close to the ground, a slightly sour greenness in the new blades. Spring was upon central California and the long, wet days of the past few months were memories that would fade in time. There would be an end to this madness. Sanity would come as surely as the new grass came. Popoford would just need to give it a helping hand. The sun had killed the winter rains. Popoford would kill the deceit.

The forty-five minutes passed too quickly. The taxi was halfway up the winding driveway before Popoford saw it.

He rapidly scanned the horizon and the grounds about the house. There was no one else about. At least, no one within sight.

He cursed himself under his breath. Rosiva's guards could have spread out in the woods on the east side of the house. They could have been let out down the road. They probably had been. He had made a mistake, but it was too late to worry about that now. Rosiva had paid the driver and had sent him down the road to wait. Popoford would have to deal with any unseen protection as needed.

He watched Rosiva. The president approached the house with caution. Popoford knew that he was probably armed. It wouldn't matter. That wouldn't shake his resolve.

Rosiva opened the front door. He called out and went inside.

Popoford scanned the countryside again. The road was clear; only the taxi sat waiting, its driver casually smoking a cigarette and daydreaming. There was no sign of life any other place. The grounds were clean. The president had come alone. Maybe. There was still the east side, the woods. Popoford had to accept that possibility, but the president's guards would wait until they knew where he was. Then they would show themselves.

The time had come. Popoford lifted the telephone's receiver and dialed the special access number that would ring the other phones on the circuit.

The phone in the house was answered.

"Speaking."

"Rosiva, you found the house. I knew you would."

"Where are you? You said that we would meet here. What are you doing?"

"This is not your time to make demands. Shut up and listen!"

There was silence on the line.

"I presume that you're in the study," Popoford said.

"Yes." Rosiva's voice had gone flat. Popoford glanced around the grounds.

"Take off your jacket."

"What?"

"Do as I say, Rosiva. Now!"

"What's this all about?"

"Information. Arrogance. Intrusion. Walk to the window. Look out. Keep your eyes off the door."

Popoford pressed his face down into the grass. Rosiva appeared at the window. It was him. The president himself had come.

"Very good, Mr. President. You follow instructions well. I wonder if you obeyed my other orders with equal precision. How many men did you bring with you?"

"None. There was no reason to bring any. Boscwell knows who you are. You won't injure me. If you do, you'll die. You've certainly made it clear you're determined to survive."

"You can't count on anything in this wicked world. You should know that. I have you here to kill you. You're my second president. I'm prepared to die with you. 1 owe it to my country."

"What kind of horseshit is that? You don't have to die. There are things you don't understand. Things that we can discuss. You could be valuable to us. It could be worth your while."

Popoford heard an edge of fear.

"Lies! All you can do is lie! There will be no deals, Rosiva. But you're right. I don't have to die today, but I will. I know far too much to live. Hendricks blew it, you must know that. I'm free of your control. We will both die."

"Our country needs us. Both of us."

"Hold that thought," Popoford replied. "Turn around. Walk back to the desk. Now stand still. I want to see you face to face."

Popoford stood up and dropped the phone. He pulled out the .38 and ran down the hill. A glance at the taxi told him that the driver had lit another cigarette. He ran to the eastern corner of the house and checked the woods for intruders. There were none there. Rosiva had come alone. Any help would have timed an attack on the house. They would have consolidated their position by now. Thinking him inside, they would have surrounded the house, would have sprung the trap on him. There was no one. There was no help for the traitor.

Popoford turned back and went to the door. He reached for the knob but only jammed his fingers into the wood. His depth perception was gone, his judgment off. He found the knob and turned it.

He heard the explosion just as the slug smashed into the wall. Popoford dove into the hallway and slammed the door. Three bullets punched through it. They were from a high-powered rifle.

He peeked through the window. The taxi driver was crouched against his cab his head tucked into his scope.

Popoford scrambled along the floor and burst into the study.

"Get away from your jacket. Now!" he yelled at Rosiva. "Put your hands on the table, face up. Freeze!"

Popoford stood up. He closed the study door. Then he cautiously went over to the window and leaned up to the wall. He could see the study door from there. He could see Rosiva and the gravel road. He could see the whole room and the little door that he'd used to escape the last time there was trouble here.

"You lied to me again," Popoford smiled. "You brought friends. But I knew you would."

"There's still time for you to listen. I can call him off. There's still time."

"You talk too much."

So the taxi driver was alone. There was only one killer to call off. Only one.

"Who is he?"

"You don't know?"

"A Resurrection Runner. A programmed killer."

"No. Those individuals have proven to be too unpredictable. This one has more to gain."

"Who is it?" Popoford held the pistol on Rosiva.

"A man named David Konklin."

Popoford knew the name. Somewhere in his fogged memory. David Konklin. Then it came to him.

"The treaty has been implemented that quickly? But of course, it has, and you would have to use Konklin. He's the best agent they have, isn't he? Their best assassin. You couldn't afford to use Resurrection Runners because they might find out too much. It would be too messy having to kill them all. Konklin would be cleaner. Boscwell doesn't even know I'm alive. Doesn't know you're here. I should have guessed."

"There's a lot you should have never known. You would have been much better off."

"I would have been dead! There's no other way for you. There will be no deals. Not ever. You can't afford deals."

There was a creaking sound on the far side of the building.

"Keep your hands still," Popoford demanded. "Relax. We'll wait for him."

The noise came again. This time it was louder.

"Squat down."

"What?"

"Squat down. Keep your hands on the table and squat."

Rosiva obeyed. Popoford saw brilliance in his eyes. Whatever fear the aging man had felt was gone. He thought he knew the score, and he was unafraid.

"You're a dead man, Popoford. He's the best."

"So am I."

"What a fool! You still have some of the remnants in your manipulated brain, don't you? You still think that you're the best damned agent that Home Office ever had. You may have been good under our direction, but you were never the best."

Popoford didn't reply. He was listening for David Konklin.

"Look at you. You missed your chance to kill me. Now you can't afford to do it. Konklin will know just where you are. Now you'll have to wait for him to blow your brains out."

"Shut up!" Popoford hissed. He jammed his pistol under his belt at the small of his back and pulled the knife from his sheath. There was a rage in him that he couldn't control. His eye hurt; the pain drove into his head. He lunged towards Rosiva. The president stood up to ward off the attack. Popoford slashed with the knife, missing Rosiva's chest by an inch, but slicing across the president's right forearm. The wound was deep. To the bone. Rosiva grabbed his arm and squeezed. Shock and pressure constricted the vessels, and the president stared into his arm at raw meat.

Rosiva looked up. He kicked hard into Popoford's stomach and bent him double.

Popoford slashed again as he fell to the floor. He missed and he dropped the knife but spun his pistol out from behind himself and struck at Rosiva's wound. He was accurate. The exposed bone shattered. The blood started to gush. Rosiva staggered back against the table. His face contorted in agony, and he let out a cry. He screamed so loudly that Popoford almost didn't hear the door fly open.

Bullets pounded into the floor around Popoford's body. One struck his left leg and tore a chunk out. Popoford rolled quickly behind the table and Rosiva. The president just stood at the table screaming. He seemed unaware of David Konklin.

Popoford ignored his leg. The bullets were slamming into the table. Konklin was systematically shooting at Popoford, the slugs aimed sequentially, getting closer by the inch. The holes they made seemed to creep along the surface of the wood, leaving a horrible trail on the side of the table. Konklin was playing with him, making him sweat out his coming death. Konklin was so confident. He knew that he would win. Popoford was sure of it too.

He made a wild grab at Rosiva and caught the president's shirt. He pulled Rosiva down behind the table.

"At least I'm good enough to take you with me, you bastard! I only wish you could suffer more than you will."

Popoford screamed into Rosiva's ear, then he pushed his blood-soaked body away.

The bullets skipped from their agonizing crawl and went straight to their mark. The playing was over. Konklin wanted it over quickly.

The next slug killed the wrong man. It took the president's face with it as it killed. Rosiva's final cry was an unearthly wail that had no mouth to transport it.

The bullets stopped. Popoford held his breath. He waited while a long second came and went. He heard the sound of Konklin reloading. Konklin took a step closer to the table. Popoford felt the .38 in his hand. It was squeezed between the floor and Rosiva. Konklin took another step. Popoford was trapped. He pulled at the pistol. It barely moved

Another second ticked away.

Konklin took another step. Popoford yanked hard on the weapon. He had to have it.

It was too late. He saw the feet come around the table. He saw the hair appear overhead. He saw the calm half-smiling face. The rifle swinging into view.

A third second ticked.

Popoford screamed his death cry and wrenched the pistol free. Before the fourth second arrived, he pulled the trigger six times. Six times and then seven and eight, even after the pistol was empty, even after the fifth second when time returned to a normal speed. He finally stopped when he realized that the small explosions had ended.

He stopped and stared at the half-smiling face as it quickly changed, still hovering overhead looking at him but now looking confused. Then Konklin slipped away, and Popoford heard his body crash to the floor.

Popoford forced himself to move. He stood up, dragging his wounded leg behind him. He could walk, but he couldn't run.

He looked at Konklin's face. It was unfamiliar.

He sat in a chair. He'd survived. He hadn't expected to. He'd made no plans for this. He sat and thought for a moment. Then it came to him. He couldn't help the wry smile that came to his face. He'd almost missed the obvious.

He ripped his pant leg to a place above his wound, and then he tied it into a makeshift tourniquet. It would hold until he could get better aid. Then he wiped the pistol clean and put it in Rosiva's hand. He found the gun the president had hidden in his jacket. He took it. Then he went to the phone and unhooked the wires that he'd applied earlier. He wrapped them up and followed them out of the room. He refused to look back at the bloody scene. He would never see this place again.

Popoford traced the wire to the top of the hill and retrieved his telephone. He was pleased to see that the dry grass where he'd lain was no longer bent. His footprints would disappear just as rapidly.

He walked down the driveway to the cab. The keys were in it. He drove away from the house. He hadn't killed the president, but he had won.

CHAPTER THIRTY-FOUR

Spring had been short-lived. The heat of May was already closing in on the seclusion of Whimsy, California. The wild winds of April had slowly subsided. The mockingbirds had grown quieter earlier each day, the flies noisier. Summer hung moist even in the shade.

Steven Popoford didn't mind. For the time being, life held only beauty for him. There was no discomfort that he would complain about. Each irritation or joy confirmed his existence. Every breath was one he once thought would never be. Each day seemed to him a day of resurrection, a day of rebirth. He had won.

Popoford wiped his forehead and took a long sip from his gin and tonic. The dark green lime floated on the liquid. He smiled at its perfect beauty.

He'd just returned from his daily constitutional. They had become longer journeys in recent days. His leg was nearly healed. Very little pain remained when he walked, and the limp had almost disappeared.

He'd visited Mrs. Marshall in her general store. He'd picked up the mail which was becoming more junk-filled each week. The daily papers didn't blast out the news that he wanted to hear, but he found most of the information buried within their pages.

He sipped at the drink and searched for the one item that had been missing over the last several weeks. He smiled when he found it.

AGENCY RESIGNATION

Senator Boscwell, the junior member of the California delegation, has resigned as head of the special intelligence agency, Home Office. President Aston has not indicated his choice for Boscwell's replacement. Senator Boscwell

was unavailable for comment. Reliable sources indicate
that the senator is suffering from ill health.

"Well put," Popoford said out loud. It truly was over now.
Boscwell had been removed.

The files had done their work. He had collected them at the
general store, gratified by the honesty of the cook who had sent
them as promised. He had read them so that he could have a
better understanding of his past, and so that he could recognize
any individuals who might be sent after him. He had them copied
to protect himself, then mailed the copies anonymously to the
Office of the President of the United States. Perhaps the
president had read them. Perhaps not. The results were what
mattered.

From his file, Popoford had finally found the true story about
himself. It was all there from his college days up to the arrival of
the fat man and finally the death of P.Y. Mous. The rest he could
clearly remember. The rest was in a memory he owned.

He'd stowed all of Hendricks' tranquilizing-serum syringes.
He didn't think much about them, just put them away. Waste not,
want not.

He drained the gin and tonic and made himself another. It was
time to celebrate.

When he'd first returned to Whimsy, he'd gone directly to his
old house. He hadn't been sure what he would find there, but he
had to have a place to recover from his wounds.

He'd spent several days in the house. It had been cleaned up,
and then abandoned. A light had been left on. He turned it off.

When he finally came out and took his first trip to the general
store, he was able to walk without a crutch. His eye was covered
with a new bandage. He felt rested and clean. He felt alive.

Mrs. Marshall greeted him that first day as if he hadn't been away.

"Oh my. It certainly is a nice day. Don't you think so, Mr. Popoford? It's so nice that the rains finally stopped. So nice indeed. Now, let's see. I think there's been some mail piling up for you. Yes. Here we are. My, my, but you should get into town more often."

"I'm going to try to do that."

"Goodness, young man, what has happened to your eye? You need a good doctor for that."

Since then Popoford had seen several doctors. The glass eye had been expertly fitted. He'd gotten used to it rapidly. Even the itching in the socket was gone most of the day. His medical bills were high, but it didn't matter. He still had government benefits. The first lot of mail that he collected from Mrs. Marshall was mostly pension checks. Popoford was still on the rolls. He figured no one had survived who would have expunged him.

Boscwell hadn't known that he was alive. As far as the senator knew, Popoford had died in the fire at the interrogation rooms in Hayward. Lorain hadn't told him about the munitions complex. She'd been programmed to kill and nothing more. When Popoford showed up at the complex, she tried to kill him. It was that simple. She hadn't required instructions from Boscwell.

With Rosiva it had been different. But the result had been the same. Boscwell had been kept in the dark. Rosiva had Konklin. He didn't need Boscwell or Home Office. He'd thought so little of Popoford and so highly of Konklin, that the new president hadn't even bothered to seek help from anyone. His arrogance had killed him.

The final judgment on the death of ex-President Rosiva had come in bits from behind the closed doors of several investigations. The conclusions drawn had all been the same: Rosiva had been lured to the farmhouse by an enemy agent and had been killed. The president himself had killed the agent. That was that.

Several weeks passed in which violent accusations flew between the United States and antagonistic world leaders. The new President of the United States, a man named Cleveland Aston, had taken the reins of government and had used the murder to his great political advantage. Presently, the war of hot words settled down to the usual drone of competitive aggression, but not before the treaty had been abrogated out of hand. Several other recent agreements that Aston and, circumstantially, the American people had found unacceptable after such blatant provocation, were dumped as well. No war had broken out. That was unnecessary and would have been unproductive. What really happened was unknown or quietly forgotten, and the losses of the Bjoonic and Rosiva administrations were recouped in spades. The greatest satisfaction to Popoford was that for the moment, the country's secrets were safe. Of course, the voters would undoubtedly be used again. So, perhaps, would Popoford. Still, the new president seemed to have matters of concern other than treason.

Steven Popoford had been forgotten in the shuffle. He was happy for that, and he filled his glass a third time and celebrated his own new life by getting quietly drunk in Whimsy.

THE END

EPILOGUE

A meeting of significance was coming to an end. All thirty lesser members had been dismissed. Only the five principals remained connected through a unique, ultra-high security connection. Each one was known only by a pseudonym. Only their leader, who called himself Vladdruc, knew their real identities. His subordinates had their suspicions, but never dared follow them up. They had each made an oath to Vladdruc which provided them with unsurpassed power and wealth, and they knew that failing in their oath would mean instant retribution: the destruction, of all they loved and horrible death.

Theirs was a balancing act, for Vladdruc insisted that they be forthright and honestly play their roles as advisors. Their minds were respected, and no disagreement with Vladdruc would cause them harm, for their minds were respected. Punishment would come only if one of them tried to discover another's identity, attempted to dislodge Vladdruc, or failed in their objectives.

"We are all agreed," Vladdruc said. "Now that the bad actors have been eliminated and our people are established at the highest level in the American government, we will immediately move forward with our original plans. The Americans and their allies will sigh with relief. They'll congratulate themselves and lower their guard. On to other things for them while we ratchet up our efforts. How predictable and pitiful they are. Now, let's get to work."

If you enjoyed
Resurrection Runner,
please write a review on Amazon.

And please recommend *Resurrection Runner*
as a good read to your friends.

These things will get the word out
and will
make a difference!

Thank you for your help and
support!

Available Soon!

The Supreme Five

Anótato Pénte

A Steven Popoford Thriller Book Two

by Robert Wood Anderson

Made in the USA
San Bernardino, CA
20 July 2020